Minor Miner

Matthew Morgan

A word from the Author

Minor Miner is a work of fiction. Any resemblance to actual events or persons, living or dead, is entirely coincidental. The historical events I mention in this story however, like many through the miner's strikes of the mid-80's, were very real and detrimental to many who lived through them.   Matthew

Should we shout, should we scream "What happened to the post war dream?" Oh, Maggie, Maggie, what did we do?

Roger Waters, The Final Cut, 1983

Chapter 1

Tuesday Morning, 17th April 1984.

Kensington, London, cloudy, windy and 7°C.

Police – St. James's Square Detachment.

There are people everywhere. I can see protesters to the left and right of me. Together they appear as a blurred mass. I cannot see who is who, or even what they're protesting for (or against for that matter). I've been in the police force for three years and this is by far the worst assignment I've been given. Usually we are given clear direction. We are told what to do, where to stand and what time to act. Here it really is a case of reacting to whatever happens. I've already seen a charge on the police by what I can only describe as thugs. They held sticks and rocks and simply ran at us as a group. I know there's a chance it's going to happen again.

We have been stood here outside of the Libyan Embassy for hours now. My shift started three hours early at 6 a.m. and I have been told that I will need to stay here for as long as it takes. That might be all day and all night. When I work with the public, I am reassured by the noises I hear. Kids playing in the streets, cars moving around and the wind blowing through the trees. The noises here are singing and shouting. I take a great deal of comfort from the fact that I can hear people as they move around. The last thing you want in this situation is for someone to sneak up on you. Silence is what would cause a problem.

I look to the left and see a bank of people dressed in an array of colours. They appear to be all as one group, a pattern that marks the start and end of St James Square. There may be more people at the other side of the buildings but for me, this is the view. I can see them swaying backwards and forwards like they are in the crowd at a football match. I have policed many a football match too, but none with the passion that is being displayed here. My home team, Luton Town, could do with supporters as passionate as these. I don't know what makes people go to these lengths. As someone who works for the police force, I suppose I should pay more attention to the news, but I find it depressing. I don't watch to see what is happening. I just hear conversations in the station and let it pass me by. They can have all their chat about events. All I want to do is work my way up through the force. There are TV cameras and journalists snooping around the area, so I guess this event is newsworthy. Just hope that my mum and dad don't see me on camera. They would only worry about my safety.

This is the Libyan Embassy I have been told by a colleague. I don't even know where Libya is or why they would have an embassy in London. Maybe there's a lot of trade between the two countries. I wonder if we have an embassy in Libya somewhere.

There is a lot of noise coming from the right. I can feel it too. As though there's a wall of sound produced by the shouting from these people. I guess they don't agree with the people who are stood to my left. Even though they are around a hundred yards apart, they are pulling angry faces at each other. I can feel the tension in the air. It's like the world has found something to split it. You must be on one side or the other in this place. What at first looked like a mess, a ragtag of people milling around each other has now definitely formed sides. The people look similar and dress similar, but they obviously do not feel the same.

My colleagues don't look as calm as I do. I am trying to portray someone who is in control. I think that this will impress my bosses and put me in a good place for promotion in the future. It's a few years off but I want to make my way up the ranks and be sergeant one day.

I can see movement inside the building. There are people going past the windows every now and again, though they don't stop to look out. It's all happening on the right-hand side of the building as I look at it. They look like they are moving away from the front of the building and to safety. I wonder if they know something that we don't. The protesters hold sticks and stones but haven't thrown them yet. There doesn't appear to be any weapons. This is a civilised protest in a civilised country. There is no reason to hide.

I look across to my colleague to the right. She looks petrified. I've never worked with her before, think she said her name was Yvonne. I'm terrible with names. Even worse when they ship a load of police officers in from different stations for something like this. We have to learn new names, new ways of working on the hoof. It might be easier for the stations to cope if they don't send everyone they have, but it doesn't do us any favours here. I tell Yvonne (I'm certain this is her name now, she looked accepting when I said it last time) that we will be OK. I explain that this looks and feels peaceful, just passionate. She seems reassured by my words and goes back to watching the area. That is mainly our remit. We will have to act if the protests become heavy or one side tries to take on the other, but hopefully we can just stand here, face the odd charge and stand strong. The guy to my left looks like he has seen it all before. In fact, he tells me he has seen it all before. He seems to want to chat more than he wants to do his job. I like him though. His talking lets me focus away from the movement. Noise I can cope with; constant movement does make me feel kind of seasick.

There are moments of calm in all of this, like the protesters needing a few moments to recharge their batteries. It is during one of these moments that I have a feeling that I'm being watched. I can't quite put my finger on it, but it feels like someone is watching me and me specifically. I don't have enough time to process it. The noise starts again, and I have to concentrate on the crowd. The guy to my left is trying to talk to me. I strain to hear what he is saying when a new noise fills the air. There is a whistling sound and then a thud. I look at the two groups of protesters and there is nothing on their faces that suggest they have heard the same noise as me. My colleague is still trying to talk. But all I can focus on is that noise.

I turn to the right to ask Yvonne. Yvonne isn't there. The gap between me and my next colleague has grown wider. As I look *along the line to see where she might have gone to, the next one along makes eye contact with me. Then he looks to the ground between us. His face turns white. It looks like he might faint. I look to the ground as well and see the body of someone in a police uniform with a growing pool of blood around it. Yvonne hasn't gone missing. She's been hurt.*

I immediately call to the colleague who is still trying to talk to me. He hasn't seen what happened either. We gather round Yvonne to see what we can do to help. I check her head to see if she has been hit by a stick or a rock. It's not there, the injury. It must be something else. I look down at my hands and can see that they are red with her blood. The colleague with all the talk asks what he can do. I suggest that we clear the area of protestors and he goes off to find our commanding sergeant.

Yvonne is awake yet she looks like she's in a peaceful place. There doesn't appear to be any sign of pain and she even tells me and the others around to keep calm. There is medical attention on the way, I'm told, and I press with all my might with the jacket from my uniform on the wound that is evidently leaking blood on the pavement. She looks and feels cold, so I ask another colleague to wrap their jacket around her. We make her as comfortable as possible.

I'm covered in the blood of my colleague. I think she is going to die. I can't believe this is happening. I can't believe she was stood there one second and gone the next. I have to call my folks. They have to know that I'm safe and well. I hadn't told them where I was working today, so they probably don't know how I close I was to this. But for my own sake, I want to be home with them now.

*   *   *

Rainer Karg moved as quickly as he could. The way into the embassy had been easy, well as easy as it could be. He was given identification papers by his contact which portrayed him as a plumbing contractor going in to quote on a leaky roof that had been causing a problem. The fact that his contact had also arranged for the roof to leak was beside the point. When you have friends in influential places, these are the kind of things that get you where you need to be. Karg was concerned that his bag would be searched thoroughly but that was allayed when he could see how busy the receptionist was. She looked like she had a million things to do and waved him through. The leak in the roof was close to the room her immediate superior worked in and she wanted to stop hearing him moan about it. She offered to get him an escort but Karg explained that he was an expert in his line of work and would be able to operate without any need for assistance. It was true. He knew exactly what he had to do. The phone call two days earlier confirmed all he needed to know. The instructions were clear. He never let people down.

Karg moved around the embassy looking like a man that was, for all intents and purposes, searching for a leaky roof. The only issue was to anyone who was to have studied him closely was he was far more interested in the windows than the ceilings. He was looking for the best view of the scene unfolding in front of the Libyan Embassy. It was clear where he needed to be, at the front of the building, but there were other considerations too. With an array of TV cameras and people everywhere the last thing he wanted was to be spotted. Even if they couldn't make out exactly who he was, it was still best to do his work in the shadows and leave the same way. That was much more preferential than leaving behind any trace of his presence. This was another advantage of the receptionist being busy. He didn't sign in. Even with a fake name, there would have been another string for the police to pull on if and when they investigated. Karg knew that leaving loose pieces of string would open up the potential, however small, of the investigation gaining traction. He didn't want to run the risk of being implicated in this. It would do his reputation a lot of harm.

He searched the rooms at the front of the embassy for the perfect vantage point. He was also looking for some peace and quiet. The room needed to be secure; someone walking in on him while he was doing his work would mean more than one dead body being left behind. The idea was to work quickly, prepare well and use only one shot. Finally, he found the perfect room. There were high ceilings and massive windows that he could use to get a full view of the scene below. The window ledges were unusually low, so he could get into position and be hidden from the people below. The room itself looked like it hadn't been used in a long time. There was a solid layer of dust on the empty desk. The desk itself had been moved to the corner of the room with a stack of boxes underneath displaying the same level of dust. Karg smiled as he looked around. The door was heavy and made a creaking sound, the ideal warning if someone actually needed what was in these boxes. An unlikely scenario, but one that he had to consider. All things seemed to be in place.

Karg was calm throughout. It was all in the breathing. A single shot from his 9mm Beretta Carbine was all he needed. And immediately he knew that the target wasn't going to survive; even though the people around her were working frantically. Karg watched for around 30 seconds after squeezing the trigger. He loved seeing the effects of his work. It brought it all home to him. He saw blood, fear and anguish. But all of these were a blur, all he could see were the dollar signs. This is what really drove him.

Once he decided it was time to leave, Karg made his way down the small set of stairs at the edge of the Libyan Embassy. There was a main staircase that most people would use. The side staircase was one that contractors went up and down, so they could smoke a sneaky cigarette or take their time while they were on the payroll of a government from somewhere else in the world. It was the kind of job that most contractors desired. You would be paid by the hour and never really have anyone question how long it took. Just bill the rich embassy and wait for the money to roll in. But these jobs still didn't pay anywhere near as much as the one Karg was on. He was on a different pay scale altogether.

The stairs seemed to take an age to climb down. Karg was an impatient man. When he ordered food in a restaurant, he wanted it to arrive straight away. As soon as the last mouthful was finished, he wanted the bill. It was one of the reasons he was so good at his job, he kept telling himself. It was one of the reasons he'd split up with his wife and struggled to see his son. Karg jumped the steps two by two and envisioned in his mind's eye that he would slip and hurt himself. A broken ankle would put him in a tricky situation. With that thought he stopped and forced himself to take one step at a time.

At the bottom of the stairs he saw across through a glass frame in the door that there was an exit open at the back of the building. There were a handful of people leaving that way and making out away from the noise and chaos outside the front doors. Karg made his way slowly along the corridor. He looked left and right into every room. It wasn't that he was fearful of being attached to the shooting, but he didn't want anyone to see him leave. No loose ends. It was just easier that way.

As he approached the last of the rooms on the left, he heard a noise coming from the main corridor which he figured must have led from the staircase in the centre of the building. First one voice, then another. A language he didn't recognise. Voices that sounded full of fear. Karg stepped back into the room and waited for these voices to pass. As they were scurrying to get away, he thought he heard one slip and hit the floor. The heavy wooden boards shook as far as the room he was in. The voices then started again and moved away into the distance. Karg felt that the coast was clear.

He moved across the end of the corridor and looked out into the light of day. There were no movements, so he felt safe enough to stick his head out of the door. All the people who left before him had been whisked off in cars. The car park was empty and there wasn't a soul in sight. Karg knew that this wouldn't be the case in a few minutes time, so gripping his bag he left. There was a small hole in the bushes to the right. Rather than walk out of the embassy compound by the gates, he could leave with a little more obscurity if he went that way. Karg pulled his jacket up to his chin and ducked his head to go through this gap. Within 30 seconds he'd managed to wriggle his way through an ever-decreasing hole and out of the other side near to some houses. It looked like any other residential street he had been down in London or any of the other major global cities he had been to kill someone.

And that was the way he operated. Because he killed from a distance, he was never covered in blood or wearing any other signs that he was a killer. The police would walk straight past him and not distinguish him from anyone else walking down the street. Karg could blend in just about anywhere in the world. Modern cities were filled with people from multiple backgrounds. He didn't look like he was from anywhere in particular. A nomad is what he called himself if anyone ever asked where he was from. 'I'm from everywhere and nowhere.'

He looked at the sun to determine the time of day and route he should travel. He didn't understand people who had no sense of direction. It was something he'd carried with him for as long as he could remember. Karg just knew where North was and would be able to plot a route without the use of a map or compass. It was particularly useful for him in his present role. He travelled light, not wanting to carry things he would later have to dump.

More potential clues. That was why he was in such demand. He worked so hard at what he did. It was no mistake that he was trusted with confidential information and relied upon to carry out sensitive work.

Karg walked slowly as though he didn't have a care in the world. The rest of the world was the same. People just passed him by. He didn't look or feel like anyone who had just killed a member of the police force. He looked like a workman who was taking it easy on a Spring day. Karg smiled again, the second time he had afforded himself that pleasure recently and opened his nostrils to the ever-closer metallic smell of the River Thames. Only a short walk and he would be back at the hotel. Only one more night there and he would be back on a plane. The way out was now clear to him and he was going to enjoy every second of it. Room service had been busy over the last few days. That night he was going to stack up a large bill for his employer to pick up. It was about time he got his money's worth.

Chapter 2

Thursday 9th February 1984.

Doncaster, Yorkshire, 2°C, frosty, with a light wind.

Ellen Minor.

The room was typical for this part of England. Twenty years earlier, the Danum Hotel would have been one of many railway hotels in the town. Each of the rooms identical, drab and each with a constant flow of transient travellers leaving in their wake a filth that none of the hotel workers seemed able or bothered to remove. Today it was much the same, but at least the soft furnishings made an attempt at comfort as well as justification for the *Executive Suite* title it had been given. Ellen pulled the light cord and the neon strip-light flickered on. To her friends, Ellen's job provided excitement that they envied. Travel at a minute's notice, all over the country, as part of a small team supporting a powerful man, a member of parliament. High-powered meetings, press conferences, lunches, dinners, interviews, limelight and of course, hotels. The hotel reality was now staring her back in the face. Not the concierge-welcomed, room-serviced, king-size plushness of her friend's perceptions. But merely the oversized Perspex key-fobbed truth of a small room with an air of stale smoke, a close fibered patterned carpet and a shared bathroom along the corridor.

The phone in the room was already ringing. *No time to enjoy the amenities anyway*, she told herself. Picking up the receiver she recognized the voice immediately.

"Hi Ellen, you've all arrived OK then. I assume I'll be seeing you later at the dinner?" On the other end of the line was Timothy Philpot, one of the younger journalists for The Times. Tim and Ellen had attended the same university. Though they hadn't been friends at the time, the alumni connection had enabled Tim to get some unique insights to the trade policies being developed by Ellen's Boss. Of course, these were insights Ellen's team had wanted shared and consequently nothing had yet garnered Tim much appreciation from his editor. However, as each of them were the younger members of old establishments, they'd become friends at arms-length. For Ellen, good press-relations was a key to success but any kind of deeper relationship with someone from the other-side could be a career-limiting move in politics.

"Hello Tim, yes, I'm just dropping my stuff before going to meet with the others. We'll be there to get ready sometime before seven."

"I've heard that David Hart will be there this evening, any plans for you to meet with him?" Tim asked in his usual off-handed yet rehearsed style.

"It's a Doncaster Chamber of Commerce dinner Tim. I'm sure the organisers have invited many local and notable trade and industry people to the event."

"And you've chosen to attend this dinner over the many other Chamber of Commerce organised dinners you get invited to because you've heard Doncaster's only golf club is so good?" This irked Ellen a little; she preferred straight questions, especially when they came from the press. Though a straight question as to why they were attending tonight would have been met with only one type of straight answer. *No comment.*

"Tim, of course we're up here to get a better handle on union petitions. But I can assure you, tonight as Minister of Trade, Paul is simply here to meet with business leaders, make a speech focused on small business growth, and remind them of the incredible support this government is offering them. Now, let me get ready and I'll see you for a drink later at this golf club."

Ellen took a few moments to settle her things, assuming that by the time she returned to this room, it would be late, and she'd relish being able to climb straight into bed, as simple as it looked. She checked herself in the mirror. She'd always taken great pride in her appearance and it was important she was dressed seriously yet in the current fashion; reflecting the reality of the position she held. Today wearing a well-fitting black skirt that came up just above her knee, a white silk blouse with a dark neck-tie scarf she double checked the collar on her blazer. The blazer itself was teal in colour with wide lapels, shoulder padding and finished off with large round flat black buttons with a gold edging. The shoulder pads were not like those worn in the US TV hit Dallas. They were more conservative but enough to give a girl with a slight frame, like Ellen, a greater presence in a room full of men.

As she got down to the lobby, she could see through the front door her colleague JK talking to a taxi driver. Justin Knight, or JK to most, was a public-school boy typical of a certain set within the Westminster Civil Service. It wasn't that he held his position because he went to the right school, had the right father or was a member of the right club; even though he had all those credentials. And it wasn't that he held the position on his own merits, achieving a first from Imperial College, London, or him being instrumental in helping to negotiate the Bilateral Air Transport Bill that formed the Bermuda II Agreement between the USA and the UK in '77. Nor was it that he'd then become one of the youngest permanent secretaries ever in a British government. It was his swagger that said he knew he'd be in this role with or without all of it, it was his role, without question. Now in his early 40's, with a family he rarely saw, giving people commands, JK felt telling people what to do was what those people required him to do to function at any level.

"Oh hell; here's El!" cried JK as Ellen approached the car.

"Are we ready to go JK? Assume the Boss is going to see us there?" Ellen responded stiffly.

"Yes, I'm just telling the driver here which way I think we need to go to get to this golf club. Get in, it's not too far."

Through the dark and frosted streets of Doncaster the driver picked his way through the evening traffic. On the radio the Pretenders aptly sang the words *gets colder day by day* as the driver ignored the earlier advice from JK on direction. But JK had not even noticed and was in full flight of conversation with Ellen in the back.

"I'm a bit worried about this David Hart fellow. Worryingly he has both money and libertarian beliefs, a shocking combination. Here. Have a look at him, we'll need to keep a close eye tonight." JK passed Ellen a picture of David Hart. He was a good-looking large man with a close-cut moustache and swept back hair.

"I've heard he's a bit of a character," said Ellen. Hart had been declared bankrupt in 1975 in what the tabloids had termed *losing a family fortune in a tornado of extravagance*. He'd owned a grand house in Somerset and came and went in large chauffeur-driven cars. Whatever his financial position now, according to the same tabloids he still kept two mistresses, supported various illegitimate children, smoked vast cigars, and continued to be chauffeured.

"I've heard he's a good fixer for the sort of disagreements that happen between the entitled and the rest of us," added Ellen trying to be positive about such a potentially hazardous figure.

"Rot, you can't run with the hare and hunt with the hounds. I don't think we do ourselves any favours having Paul, or you and I for that matter, seen with him," JK shot back, focusing himself on the night's event ahead.

In under ten minutes they were pulling into the car park of Wheatley Golf Club. Inside the main hall of the grand Edwardian clubhouse was a hive of activity as the caterers set tables and busied themselves for the two hundred or so guests soon to arrive. For Ellen and JK this was situation normal. Check where the minister was to be seated and with whom. Check on the microphone and sound levels for his address and give the speech one final run-through together. Checking there was nothing contentious in it now the news-day had drawn to a close. No doubt that Paul himself would have made changes to it in the car on the way up which he would want to discuss, before inevitably going off-piste when he made the speech itself anyway. Not to matter for now, the effort gave Ellen a short period of single-minded focus.

"OK, we're good for the dinner itself at least," announced JK as he walked up to Ellen who was sat at one of the tables. "Paul's at that table with a couple of directors to the board of the Chamber of Commerce and there are three industrial leaders. Don Kemp, a railways supplier from outside Sheffield, Keith Davis, from Cortonwood Colliery mine and Tom Linney, a brick manufacturer from Peterborough. David Hart is sat all the way over there." JK pointed over to a table nearer the wall, relieved that there was distance between Hart and the Minister. Happy with the setup for the evening Ellen went to find the Club's manager and asked if they could find a small comfortable room for Paul and the team to get ready. With a little bristle of pride, the manager showed her to the Club President's office just off the main entrance. It was a very comfortable room with wood panelled walls, a pair of green leather chesterfield sofas in front of a large desk. Many pictures also charted the successes of the club members through the years. This was another place, like Westminster, where Ellen felt ill-at-ease. Steeped in a masculine tradition, a modern working woman was certainly an unfamiliar sight and at times probably an unwelcome one. As she was reminding herself that she had as much right to be there as anyone else, the door opened and the Club's manager, this time positively bursting with pride, entered showing in Paul Channon, Member of Parliament and the Conservative Minister of Trade.

"Hello Ellen, have you seen the evening paper? They really are giving unfair amounts of coverage to Scargill and his lot." Arthur Scargill was the President of the National Union of Mineworkers, an official union generally referred to as the NUM. Scargill himself was a confident orator and a vocal opponent of the Conservative party, particularly since Margret Thatcher had come to power a few years earlier in 1979. In recent times the press had taken to telling a simple *Them and Us* story with Thatcher and Scargill as the two protagonists.

"Honestly, we couldn't even pay for this sort of coverage," he went on, looking Ellen directly in the eye and giving her a warm smile. It was the mark of a good politician; he made anyone feel that they were the only one he was talking to, and that what they had to say was all he wanted to hear about.

"Is JK here?" he asked before Ellen had a moment to respond to his first question.

"Hello Sir, yes, JK is just doing a final check in the hall. He and I have just been through the speech once more." And with the efficiency she prided herself on, she handed him the beige foolscap folder with the speech in it. "Can I see if I can get someone to fix you a drink?"

"Great. That would be fine," he replied taking the folder and sitting down on one of the sofas. With that Ellen slipped out of the room and headed to the bar to get the Minister a whisky and water. He wasn't particularly fussy about what whisky he drank, though of course he enjoyed a fine one every so often. Nor was he a big drinker, like so many others in the cabinet. A whisky and water were mandatory anytime he was about speak to a crowd. With the drink in-hand, she found JK and the two of them headed back to the makeshift ante room.

On handing Paul the drink, he looked up and focused on them both. To Ellen it was clear that he was feeling greater pressure than normal this evening. It was also clear that he hadn't made the tweaks he would normally make to the evening's speech.

"Everything OK with the speech Sir?" Ellen asked.

"It's fine, thanks," he responded. Ellen had in fact a feeling this was his first read through and his lack of concern for its content made her anxious. Before she could ask and unaware of anything amiss, JK took it as his cue to brief the MP.

"Good, now that's out of the way, I need to talk you through some of the guests here tonight, I'm particularly worried about a chap called David Hart," JK started.

"Yes, thanks JK, we'll talk about that in a minute. And by the way, I'm not worried about Hart, I think he might be able to help. After today's cabinet meeting we've got some bigger things to ready ourselves for."

Paul went on to explain that he was now under the spotlight from the rest of the cabinet and particularly the Prime Minister.

There had been strong direction that a long and protracted argument with unions was to be avoided at all costs. A respectful and private sit down with union leaders and shop stewards needed to happen quickly. Meeting with the NUM's Arthur Scargill was key, and progress was to be reported back to Westminster by Monday morning. Ellen relished the challenge, these were the sort of tasks she knew would help her career flourish, much as JK had done with the Bilateral Air Transport Bill. She was already planning out in her head ways they could organise such a sit down and the things that would need to be covered.

"Right JK, who am I siting with and who do I need to avoid?" Clearly JK was also excited by the prospect of being given another opportunity to showcase his skills. He was already going back through the list of invitees in his head and thinking who might help facilitate such a sit down. But his mind was brought back to his earlier concern.

"Hart Sir, either way, I don't think it'll be good for any of us to be seen talking with him. Other than that, Keith Davis at your table is the Chief Executive of the Cortonwood Colliery mine. There have certainly been some worker tensions there, but he seems fairly well respected all the same, he might be key for us."

"OK, good and JK, don't worry about David Hart. I agree we shouldn't be seen with him, but I'm keen to meet with him. I think he'll be more help than the tabloids might have us believe."

That was Paul's way of saying he knew full well that Hart could be an asset. That surprised Ellen but it was time for them to make their way to the main hall rather than discuss it further.

"Right, given all we've got to do, let's not make it a late night and you two are more than welcome to come and rescue me from anyone you think I shouldn't spend time with. Let's keep a low profile tonight," said Paul closing the foolscap and getting to his feet. As they entered the hall Ellen could see Tim standing near the bar. Unlike almost every other man in the room who was wearing a dark suit, pressed shirt and tie, Tim was wearing a brown corduroy blazer over an open necked shirt. He caught her eye and she made her way over to him. Just as she got within reach of him, a large man quickly turned from the bar and almost knocked into her.

"Terribly sorry," he boomed. To Ellen's terror she had almost been knocked over by David Hart. And in front of a member of the press.

Way to keep a low profile! She told herself.

"Are you OK?" he asked. He was a large and imposing man, he looked dishevelled yet was obviously dressed in the finest tailored black tie. His hair was slicked back in a style from an earlier generation, though it seemed to be right for him.

"I'm fine thank you," Ellen responded looking slightly down and giving a little smile. Why did she do that? She certainly hadn't meant to. As Hart moved away, she felt herself flush as she continued forward toward Tim.

"I'd be careful there Ellen, do you know who that was?" muttered Tim. While Ellen pretended to have no idea who he was, Tim went on to give a potted history of David Hart, seemingly recounting line by line the tabloid press for which Tim did not work. With those gory details out of the way Tim moved on to question Ellen about the Minister's arrival and forthcoming speech.

"Care to give me any details about what the Minister is going to be doing over the coming days? I'm told he's not due back in Westminster until Monday. Perhaps we'll learn a little more out of tonight's speech."

"Tim, I can tell you now that tonight's speech won't reveal much of interest to you. The Minister is here to talk about the concerns from the local industry about union pressure. And I can say that in so much confidence you can buy me a drink afterwards, if you've no story to run as I say. Now let's take our seats. I think we're at the same table."

Ellen and Tim had been sat with some of the Chamber of Commerce members of lesser influence and their wives. All of whom seemed rather excited to be sat with a fashionably dressed young high-flyer from Westminster and a journalist for the famed Times. Next to Ellen was the wife of the founder of a local plumbing supplies manufacturer who seemed intent on trying to set Ellen up with her son. Focused on who was talking to Paul and the speeches being made, Ellen didn't have the capacity to explain her personal life and simply said thanks for the flattery.

As Paul got up to make his address, Ellen could see a trace of anxiety on his face, though she was sure it was slight enough that most wouldn't see it. There was a stillness in the room as he approached the lectern. The discussion at her table had made it evident that the assembled room all feared the unions being successful in their campaigns for picketing and that the Minister somehow held the key to stopping it from happening. In reality, Paul and his team were yet to really grapple with the issue. Until now, a policy of *ignore them and they'll go away* had been in place. But sitting down with them and negotiating terms was what was required to move forward.

Ever the consummate politician, Paul managed to deliver a pithy and enjoyable address while making a serious point on the Conservative government's commitment to manufacturing businesses like theirs. While statements like, "I can promise you that this government won't bow to union pressure as this would be the undoing of the economic growth to come," seemed a little overstated given the task they had been set, the audience was clearly buoyed by it all and gave a very encouraging round of applause as Paul made his way back to his table.

While the coffees were being poured, Ellen and Tim said goodnight to the rest of their table and made their way over to the bar. JK approached them both on route. "Looks like the Minister is done too, he's one last person to speak with, then I'm going to take the car with him back to the hotel. You OK to make your own way?" he asked, clearly the better for a few glasses of wine over the dinner.

"I'll be fine thanks, see you in the morning," replied Ellen, not wanting to have any deeper discussion with her colleague in front of Tim. As JK headed off, she picked up the conversation from before.

"Tim, I'm not telling you officially, but you may want to extend your time away from the office too, we've got a lot to do over the coming days up here. Wouldn't want you to miss anything." While she'd not cleared this with Paul or JK, she was sure that having Tim close at hand would help in the weeks ahead. "I think this drink is on you, right?" she added.

Chapter 3

Wednesday 15th February 1984.

Brampton Bierlow, South Yorkshire, 0°C, frosty and windy.

The Miners.

Even for February it was a particularly chilly 4 a.m. as Harry approached Dale's house on Rother Street. The street was lit by a couple of dim orange streetlights. Neither was near Dale's. The house, as with every other at this time of day, was in total darkness. Yet before Harry had even arrived at the gate, the front door opened and out slipped Dale in his thick wool overcoat and heavy steel toe-capped boots. In his left hand he was holding his flask and lunch tin. In the six years since dropping out of school this had been their ritual almost every morning on their way to work the Cortonwood Colliery mine. As Dale reached the gate down the short and unkempt path, Harry pulled two No.6 cigarettes from his packet and handed one to his friend.

"Morning Cock," said Harry in an upbeat manner. "What's the day in store for us today, eh?"

Despite rarely having to actually knock on the door in the morning, Dale was not really a morning person and a grunt in response was the best Harry could expect. As they turned on to Knollbeck Lane an electric milk-float whispered past them. Full milk bottles clinking quietly on the back tray, its' driver setting out to make his rounds of the morning. Through the open cabin-door the driver called out "morning lads," and continued on his way.

"Why the fuck are you all so cheerful this morning?" spat Dale.

"Shh, calm down lad," said Harry. "What's going on mate? What's got into you, hey, too many down The Plough last night, eh? I'm surprised your Mam would put up with your boozing during the week."

"It's not a hangover."

"Alright then, what is it?"

"D'you see Betteshanger on the news last night? I mean, it's just—" he paused. "What are we going to do after this? Not today, but after they shut the mine; and they're going to shut it well before we retire mate. What are guys like you and I going to do next?"

"Well, they aren't going to shut it today mate and we pay our Dues to make sure the big man doesn't screw us, so I think we've got it alright for now."

Dale huffed and kicked at a stone on the path, scowling at the ground. Clearly not placating his friend, Harry decided to leave it there and they walked on in silence.

By now, while still pitch black, Harry could make out a small hoard of other figures, like he and Dale, walking their way to the pithead. Since the mid-nineteenth century the landowners of coal rich areas of the country had capitalised on the nation's growing need for coal.

"Hey Dale, watch the news last night?" Asked a large bearded miner everyone referred to simply as Bin on account of his eating habits.

"Alright Bin, of course, seems our brothers in Kent are getting the press again."

Betteshanger Colliery in the Kent Coalfields had been one of the most vocal unions three years earlier in calling for official NUM strikes against the government's proposed closure of twenty-three pits. Betteshanger Union had actually held unofficial strikes at the time and were a significant player in forcing the government to back down. Since then, the Prime Minister, Margret Thatcher, had appointed ex-steel chief and anti-union hard-man, Ian MacGregor, to head the National Coal Board. As a result, yet again the spectre of pit closures was looming. Having been a key player before, media attention was now on Betteshanger and the last night's evening news had featured forthright Betteshanger miners talking of "imminent action," as they finished their day's work.

"They were the first to strike in '81 and they reminded Thatcher then who we are. Seems like it's time for another reminder before MacGregor gets too carried away," said Bin.

"If they strike again, we'll need to strike too within the day. Official or unofficial, we must fight back. Right now, no-one is listening," replied Dale and there was a murmur of ascension as the second of the two lift gates were closed behind them and the lift started to descend.

"Dale, wind it in mate, there will be no action of any kind that isn't sanctioned by the Union." Just behind Harry stood Fred Stokes, one of the Union representatives. Fred was in his 40's, with no particular reputation. He'd simply been appointed a Union rep on account of his time at the mine and his age compared to the others. There had been some stories floating about that Fred's eldest daughter had been seen going around with the mine Boss's son, Ben Davis, yet this hadn't affected Fred's standing. After-all, no man could control his 19-year-old daughter and no 21-year-old man could influence his girlfriend's father.

"I know Fred, of course, but I think if our brothers elsewhere start to strike it's necessary for all Union members to move as quickly as possible to make it official, so we can support them." As the lift slowed to the bottom there was another murmur of ascension from the occupants. The air was thick now, but the warmth of it and the talk of action seemed to have lifted everyone's spirits. As the gates opened the men set-off to their workstations in a lighter mood that had lacked only moments before while up on the surface. As they cleared out Fred spoke quietly to Dale.

"Seriously Dale, we need to be careful, we won't gain any sympathy by starting anarchy. That's what MacGregor wants, then he'll have the excuse he needs to shut us down."

Dale grunted in response. In his heart he felt any kind of organized bureaucratic approach would only ever work in the favour of the bureaucrats. Real and swift action would result in real and swift change.

"Dale," Fred continued, "listen to me, some of the Union reps from the other collieries are meeting tonight to talk about what's going on. Why not come and join us? You're a good talker and we're going to need more leaders. We're meeting at The Plough around four." And with that Fred headed off.

"Careful Cock, they'll be putting you forward for Union rep next and that's a whole load of agro you don't need, I'd stick with the ale if I were you," said Harry as the two of them headed to their pit area. But Dale was excited. This could be his opportunity to do more than lift a pick and grumble about it, maybe something for the future too. The mention of *leaders* by Fred had both given him hope that real action was being planned as well as playing to his own ego that he could be more than he was today.

The hard and monotonous work did little to speed the day, but around 2 p.m. through the gloom the men were aware of others downing their tools and readying themselves for the lift back to the surface. For the last hour or so Harry had been separated from Dale and he was keen to see if his friend's earlier mood had lifted. "You up for coming to The Plough with me to talk with the Union guys later?" asked Dale, his mood clearly lifted, if not directed where Harry might have preferred.

"You're going to go along then are ya?"

"Sure, why not? I've got nothing to lose and we need to be pushing for change. Come, we can have a couple of drinks. Let's just see what people have got to say."

"Of course, I'm coming with you Cock. I just don't want to see you putting yourself in the firing line," replied Harry. With that the lift cage door closed behind them and they began their ascent.

It was mentally hard at this time of year. Dark and below zero in the morning when they went in, then starting to get dark and barely above zero when they came out. Today was no different, even at just gone two thirty it was cold and grey going on black.

"See you a little later on then Dale," said Fred Stokes as he headed off in the other direction.

"Dale," said Harry as he pulled a much-needed cigarette from its packet "I've gotta say it to ya, I'm all for action mate, but you don't want to be tagged as a trouble-maker." But he could already see in his friend's face that Dale's mind was made up.

Despite the cold and grey, the streets themselves were now in stark contrast to how they had been earlier on their way to the mine. People were out and about, talking with one another, doing the daily shop and mothers waiting for school to break for the day. On their way back to Rother Street, in the closely-knit community in which they'd grown-up, they said hello to many of the people they passed before seeing Dale's mother, Fiona. She was a small woman who lived a hard yet simple life raising Dale and his two younger sisters single-handedly. Dale's father had died during the hot summer of 1976. Like Dale, he had been a miner at Cortonwood. He'd been a heavy drinker and smoker and while ultimately it was silicosis contracted from years down the pit that had killed him, his vices hadn't helped in any way. Fiona was talking to a neighbour over the front fence six doors down from her own house.

"Hi Mam, hello Mrs Pennard."

"Hello Dale, Harry, you boys had a good day at pit?"

"All good thanks Mrs Edwards, I'm off home to clean up as we're heading to The Plough later," replied Harry.

"OK, well once you're done cleaning up come back by ours and I'll fix you boys up some dinner before you go," returned Fiona. Over the years she'd frequently looked after Harry. Fiona had known but struggled to understand the poor relationship between Harry and his own mother. She felt it her duty to keep an eye on him. She also knew that her own Dale could get himself into trouble and that he always fared better when Harry's cooler head was about.

"Thanks mate," said Dale to Harry. Union rabblerousing was one thing, but he had a greater fear of his mother's distain of the pub and knew she was more comfortable when he and Harry were together.

The Plough was a one of four pubs in Brampton Bierlow. It was probably the oldest of the four, certainly the biggest and while rather shabby, it was well frequented by the men of Cortonwood and busy every night. Its size and proximity to the pithead had meant it had always been a place for the workers to congregate and discuss the working conditions. It was the un-official Mineworker's Union Lodge for the Cortonwood Colliery. Strikes by the workers even in the prior century had been orchestrated from here. Today was no different.

The publican was a stereo-typical heavy, pot-bellied man called Ian Henderson. He was not unaccustomed to and certainly capable of pulling apart rowdy and brawling miners. He didn't care much for the discussion or the politics of the miners who chose to unwind in his establishment. He did however find it easy to relieve them of their hard-earned cash; either through ale or by running a book on the horses, or preferably both.

"A'up 'Enderson, two pints please," said Harry, and Henderson proceeded to pull the beer into handled beer mugs.

"Alright lads, good to see some younger guys here for this. What's your take on last night's news?" The tall man standing behind them was John Armstrong or Lanks to his friends. Lanks was short for lanky on account of his height and though this was not a great attribute for a miner, Lanks had been at Cortonwood over 20 years and, like Fred Stokes, was now a Union Rep.

"Alright Lanks, I think we need to help ourselves, no one else is going to. It looks like our brothers down in Kent have got the right idea again. Reckon it's time we show them our support," responded Dale.

"Well come and take a seat, I think we're about ready to get going, some big-wig from Peterborough is here to talk to us."

Harry picked up the pints and he, Dale and Lanks headed through to the Plough's saloon bar. There was already hearty discussion happening between the thirty or so men in the room. While there were a few familiar faces, neither Dale nor Harry knew most of the attendees. Harry and Dale found a place to sit and looked at one another, neither quite sure of the etiquette of such a gathering.

"Brothers, I'm calling this meeting to open. I think it's time we collectively decide that if over the coming weeks we are to take action, we do so in a coordinated manner across the south Yorkshire coalfields." David Oley was a Union rep at the Barnburgh Colliery in Doncaster. He continued, "There is clearly attention on us as Minister Channon is in the area and I now understand that he intends to stay up here and meet with many of the bosses." With both the words *Minister* and *bosses* the assembled crowd let out a deep and boisterous chorus of boos and jeering. "For Channon to show no sign of leaving Yorkshire even after last night's news report on our Brothers in Kent shows we're the focus for Westminster." Many of the men had now taken their seats and on finishing his sentence David Oley also took his. As if choreographed and well-rehearsed, Oley sat and another rose to continue the discussion.

Paul Wardle from Grimethorpe Colliery in Barnsley stood and in almost a whisper thanked David for opening. Wardle's voice was strained after years of pit work and even more on the Benson and Hedges cigarettes he smoked. His rough whisper made him sound like a Bond villain, but this had the effect of bringing the room to total silence. The assembled crowd clung to his every forced word. "I'm comfortable that the men of Grimethorpe will stand in solidarity of any official and coordinated effort in Yorkshire." He paused, clearly having difficulty in making even the limited volume he was achieving. "But I tell you now Brothers, we have a growing dissent in Barnsley that a more radical approach be taken. Last night's news reports from Kent are giving many of us inspiration." As Wardle took his seat the saloon bar erupted again in strong and vocal agreement. As the crowd settled, another Doncaster man stood. Peter Dodd was from the Hatfield Colliery.

"Brothers, the night before last I attended a dinner in Doncaster where Minster Channon gave a speech with no reference to us workers, only to the profits to be made by the bosses and his government." Dale watched on as Harry rose to his feet, shouting with the others, before Dodd continued. "This shouldn't surprise us; they've done it before."

"Yeah, and they're trying their luck again," spat Lanks.

Dodd went on, "Even though I was witness to this blatant disregard for us, I also had the fortune to meet a good man. I want to introduce him here now and for us to hear what he has to say. Tom, tell them what Arthur has up his sleeve." Peter Dodd turned slightly and gestured to a man sitting over to one side. While he was heavy-set, he was clearly not a miner. He was well-dressed in comparison to the rest of the room; his hair was clean and tidy and his face cleanly shaven.

"My name is Tom Linney. I have a small brick manufacturing company in Peterborough that employs a good fifty Union men. I'm a friend of both Arthur Scargill and Roger Windsor and have worked alongside the NUM for the last 20 years." The room fell quiet again as it had when Paul Wardle had wheezed his opinion earlier.

Tom continued, "In the coming days, Scargill will be sitting down with Minister Channon to explain that the NUM will be coordinating walk-outs across the coalfields of England. This will be unlike any other strike seen before. It will be orderly, while at the same time causing mass-disruption." He paused to build anticipation of the plan. "In the first week of March our intention is to cease all coal mining in Yorkshire and put massive pressure on the coal supply to the country's power stations. A country with limited power will limit the power of the government."

There was another momentary pause as the idea sank in. Then Steve Conyers of Hickleton mine in Barnsley piped up. "So, we have to hold off our members from picketing by almost two weeks before strike action can begin?"

"Yes," replied Tom immediately. "But this needs to be the worst kept secret. We need to put the fear of god into Channon and MacGregor from the Coal Board that we, the Union members, have organised ourselves. They won't stand a chance against a united us." And with that the room erupted in a chorus of excited agreement and plans for the action started to be drawn.

Chapter 4

Wednesday 15th February 1984.

Barnsley, South Yorkshire, 0°C, frosty and windy.

Ellen.

Number Two, Huddersfield Road was a grand Victorian townhouse built of York stone that featured a curved front, pillared entrance, decorative steel balustrades around the roof and a four-story tower at its centre. The streets surrounding it were filled with grand townhouses and terraces, but Number Two was the grandest of them all. It had also been home to the National Union of Mineworkers, the NUM, since 1912. Today, as Ellen approached it, she was filled with excitement, not the fear she had expected. Paul Channon had decided to send her to the "hornet's nest," as he had put it, to do the pre-meet with Arthur Scargill's team ahead of tomorrow's meeting between the two men.

At first, JK had been opposed to the idea of sending Ellen. Typically, it would be he who attended such pre-meets. But on discussion, they decided sending a young woman would signal less serious intent to the meeting itself.

"We don't want to get their backs-up by sending in the big guns for the pre-meet, do we now?" JK had declared, as if consoling himself, while at the same time demeaning Ellen. Ellen couldn't care less for JK's comments, this was her chance to prove to Paul her abilities and it filled her with excitement.

Today she wore a black dress, a blue blazer over a tight black roll-neck sweater and her large grey woollen overcoat to fend off the cold. Still based at the Danum Hotel in Doncaster, Ellen had taken two trains to get to Barnsley for the afternoon. Changing at Wakefield and subject to some delay, she'd completed two sides of a geographical triangle. The trip taking two hours was in reality less than 15 miles as the crow flies. She however had factored in National Rail's reputation; so wasn't late for the pre-meet and the additional time had allowed her to prepare for it thoroughly anyway. The uphill walk and her layers of clothes were now making her sweat and as she entered the reception, she felt decidedly hot.

"May I help you?" said a rather stern looking woman sat behind the reception desk as Ellen closed the front door behind herself and removed her coat.

"I'm here to meet with Mark Turnbull. Ellen Minor, he is expecting me." With that the receptionist prickled further, lifted the handset and dialled.

"Mr Turnbull, a Miss Minor is here to meet with you," she said emphasising the *Miss* and returned the handset without saying another word.

Crikey, this might be a lot tougher than I first assumed, Ellen thought to herself and without invitation she took a seat to wait for Mark.

A few moments later Mark Turnbull entered the room. In his mid-thirties, he was tall, good looking, smartly dressed and not what Ellen had expected at all. "Hello, Mark Turnbull, seems like we've a few things to get organised you and I, good to meet you," he said, extending his hand to shake.

He showed her through the building to a well-appointed office on the ground floor. Tea was brought in along with a typical selection of simple biscuits. "So, the first question is, your place or mine," said Mark. Not to be won over so easily or predictably, Ellen kept her head and got down to the point.

"Thank you for extending the offer to have the meeting here. Our feeling is that the NUM headquarters is too high-profile a venue, the choice of which will be miss-construed by the media from your genuinely hospitable offer. We'd prefer to find a venue with some common ground. Perhaps a hotel?" Ellen was pleased with her own directness and authority in the response she gave. Clearly it had some effect on Mark too who seemed to sit up a little more, intrigued by his attractive opponent. "We thought the Danum Hotel in Doncaster, might be a good option for all. We've been staying there a few days now. It has all we need."

"Yes, the Danum is fine and Doncaster is better for us anyway tomorrow. There will be five of us. How many on your side?"

"Five? This should be a one on one meeting Mark." Five! Ellen couldn't believe it. Did the NUM think this would be a general meeting, a petitioning, a brainstorm?

"I feel Scargill would prefer to have at the very least Roger Windsor our Chief Exec with him, together with Tom Linney.

Surely Mr Channon can accommodate the three of them," replied Mark, though clearly not happy not to have the whole team, including himself, there.

"Who is Tom Linney? I don't think I know his name," asked Ellen too quickly. She was instantly cross with herself for showing she didn't know something and that clearly all her preparation still wasn't enough.

"Tom is a friend of ours. He has a small brick manufacturing plant in Peterborough. He understands first-hand the issues this government will create for small businesses like his who rely on big local industry for workforce, materials and many support services."

Tom Linney. Of course, he was sat on the table with Paul at the Chamber of Commerce dinner the other night. JK had mentioned him, why hadn't Ellen remembered this? Ellen made a mental note to ask Paul if he'd spoken with Mr Linney at the dinner, he'd certainly not mentioned it. She thought carefully before replying, "If Paul elects to have anyone else with him in the room it would be Justin Knight, his Permanent Secretary. I believe both Mr Scargill and Mr Windsor have met Justin many times before."

"Ah, the overly-privileged JK, yes. I'm a little surprised he didn't come to this meeting himself; to dictate to me what he wanted us to do." The ridicule in his tone reminded Ellen of the division between the NUM and the Government. The last thing any successful meeting needed was either Roger Windsor or JK throwing their weight about in a verbal sparring match with one another. Or for that matter the unknown quantity that was Tom Linney.

"You know," Ellen went on, "I really think the meeting needs to be just the two of them, the Minister and Mr Scargill. All of Paul's other meetings have been one on one, we don't want to be seen to be giving favour just because you are the NUM. Perhaps you, Roger, Tom, JK and I can meet separately to discuss the related issues? We'd be keen to understand Tom's point of view in detail before introducing him to the Minister, of course." She was a little off the agreed plan now but felt Paul and JK would be agreeable if Paul could have a meeting with Scargill without the usual entourage or unknown characters.

"Very good Miss Minor, I think I can agree to that. Now, we need to decide on what needs to be discussed and what is off the table, shall we say?"

They proceeded to establish the format of the thirty-minute meeting, together with a list of items not to be discussed by either party. By four o'clock they were all agreed, and the meeting was set for two the following afternoon at the Danum Hotel.

"Taking the train back to Doncaster now?" Mark asked as Ellen collected her things.

"No, it took forever to get over here and I don't fancy an extended stay in Wakefield again this time. The Party can cover my expenses for a taxi I think."

"Well, just a suggestion, how about joining me for a drink and I'll introduce you to Tom Linney?" offered Mark.

Ellen was immediately wary. *Could this be a trick? How might it look to others if I'm seen drinking with the enemy*? she asked herself. She then realised; this was a golden opportunity. JK spent much of his life at lunch, dinner or drinks with the opposition. It was how he was able to see the bigger picture, understand the inner-workings and facilitate the right introductions. Politics could at times be counter-intuitive but in recognising this she felt a rush of excitement of the offer Mark was making. "Sounds like fun," she replied as coolly as she could manage.

"Fine, I'll drive us, and you can take your Party taxi when we're done. The Plough at Brampton Bierlow is on your way home anyway. It'll be good for you to see some of the real people we're all talking about too, the news reels don't do the miners much justice."

Once in the car, Ellen was surprised by how many things in common she and Mark shared. On reflection, she'd assumed that someone working for an organisation like the NUM would be different in every way. Not so. Mark had grown up in the South of England, in a middle-class family, and had been to a good university before practicing law for a very reputable London firm for many years. The law firm had then been taken on by the NUM and this was where Mark had met Arthur Scargill. Mark spoke of being wooed not by Scargill's ideology or political views, but by what he saw as a genuine desire to help the regular working-class man, the common man. Scargill organised this help by bringing together the right people with the right skills, no matter their backgrounds. And Mark was one of them. A valued member of a team doing good things. Ellen could only find admiration for Mark's choice for and subsequent role within the NUM.

While Ellen had been expecting a simple establishment, The Plough was not what she'd had in mind at all. As they pulled into the car park, Ellen could see heavy set men, roughly dressed and clearly intoxicated, stumbling back and forward to the outside lavatory block. The pub itself looked as if it was ready to be condemned. Failing guttering, rotted window frames and walls blackened by years of weather so close to heavy industry. Mark sensed her feeling.

"Well, I'm not sure they've seen a girl like you in here before, but don't worry, the working men will be too busy drinking away the day and betting on the horses to pay much attention. They look like a rough sort, but they're generally a well-behaved lot. Come on, I'll buy you a drink."

Ellen knew not to embarrass herself or the landlord by asking, as she would in a London bar, for a gin and tonic, and so opted instead for a half of cider. On getting their drinks they made their way to a small round table. Ellen realised, true to Mark's words, no one was really paying her attention and she began to feel a little more at ease.

"Ellen Minor, let me introduce you to Tom Linney." Not particularly tall, Tom was still a large heavy-set man who looked the part of a brick manufacturer very much. He extended a hand, a little surprised that his friend Mark had such good-looking company with him. "Ellen here works for the other side and she and I have been discussing the ins and outs of tomorrow's key meeting."

"I'd keep that down if I were you, I just met with the reps and the stewards through in the Saloon Bar there. I told them that the *key meeting* was going to be happening. Not sure they'd take too kindly to having the other side here, no matter how attractive. Could be seen as spying," explained Tom, lowering his voice slightly.

"Quite Mr Linney, but I assure you, I'm just here for a drink with Mark. He tells me you're a friend of the NUM; can I ask what your involvement is?"

"The closing of pits doesn't just affect miners Miss."

"Please, call me Ellen. OK, who else does it affect?" she asked.

"It affects the whole of the country. I need coal to fire my kilns and cheap, local coal is the only way I can compete with product coming in from Europe. I have fifty men who work for me at my brick manufacture in Peterborough. Most of them came from the mines originally and I can't afford to find them elsewhere or train up a load of apprentices. I need other services too. Electricians for example, truck drivers, the railways. Without the mines as their main employ, they won't last to service a small company like mine. Even if they do, I won't be able to pay them what the mine pays to keep them in business or me competitive. Everyone loses."

"It seems you two have a bit to cover; excuse me for a minute. I want to say hello to the Cortonwood Union man Fred Stokes," interrupted Mark, and with that, he headed to the bar. On looking up to see Mark move away Ellen became aware of a very good-looking younger man at the bar looking directly at her. He was sat with another man of a similar age and they appeared close. As Ellen's eyes met his he quickly looked away to his friend.

"And what did the men you met with just now have to say?" Ellen asked, returning her gaze to Tom.

"Good try Ellen. They all share my concern. Miners know they're the smallest cogs in the wider machine, but are no-less critical. They want to know that they'll be able to continue to provide the simple life they currently afford their families. It's not much to ask as anyone from Westminster should be able to see for themselves," said Tom, casting his hand towards the rest of the pub. "I'm keen to ask your point of view Ellen. What are the justifications from Westminster that closing pits is actually a good idea? Is it simply that the numbers look good on paper? I'd suggest that you've not factored in the cost of re-training these men or helping businesses like mine."

"I'm afraid Tom, I'm not here as a representative of Westminster, I'm a Civil Servant, here to help provide context to my Boss. What I will say is that the government's, in fact any government's, priority is ensuring that anyone who wants to work and provide for their family and society can do so."

"Let's hope tomorrow's meeting has the right people in it and that they are well informed with the context as you say," responded Tom "Before we go on, can I buy you a drink? Doesn't seem right me sitting here asking you questions without a drink in your hand."

"A half of cider would be great, thanks Tom," Ellen replied and Tom headed to the bar.

"Well, hello, this is a turn up for The Plough and to think I wasn't going to come today," said a new voice with a thick and distinctive Yorkshire accent from behind Ellen. On looking up, standing in front of her was the younger man she had locked eyes with only minutes earlier. She couldn't believe how attractive she found him. His face was dark and chiselled and he had a very well put together physique. He instantly reminded her of Tom Cruise's character Joel Goodsen in the movie Risky Business, which she'd seen at the cinema with her girlfriends. The man in front of her now certainly wasn't as polished as Joel Goodsen, he was wearing a faded Clash t-shirt and dirty jeans and was holding a near empty pint glass and lit cigarette in one hand. "I'm Dale," he continued. "You're not a local, are you?"

"I've actually come from Barnsley today and am on my way to Doncaster," Ellen replied hoping her Home Counties accent didn't sound too haughty.

"Well, can I buy you a drink before you're on your way?"

"That's kind of you, but someone is already getting one for me," she replied.

"Ah, yes, with the big man from Peterborough," and as Dale looked, he could see Tom Linney on his way back to the table. "Maybe some other time then," he closed off.

"Maybe," she replied, surprising herself on being a little flirtatious and with that Dale turned away.

Tom and Ellen were joined again by Mark and they talked for a little while longer about the news coming from Kent. Between both of Tom and Mark at least, there was a strong opinion against non-organised picketing, which was a relief to Ellen. Anarchy was one thing she knew the Minister would not want on his record. Even if the likes of Ian MacGregor saw disruption as an opportunity to strong-arm the unions.

"Right, time for me to head off, Tom can I give you a lift anywhere?" asked Mark.

"Thanks Mark, I'm actually heading back to Peterborough and I better get going too. Ellen, very nice to meet someone from the other side. You're clearly not all bad."

"Thanks Tom, the feelings mutual," Ellen shot back.

"I'll see you tomorrow then. Are you OK getting to Doncaster from here?" Mark asked.

"I'm good thank you, I'll finish up and get the landlord to order me a taxi. Thank you both for your time." With that the two men left The Plough together. Ellen sat for a moment, looking around the pub packed with miners. She was pleased with her effort and couldn't wait to report back to Paul and JK. She knew that both would be impressed and find value in what she'd learnt first-hand. She'd also proved to herself that she could survive on her wits in random, tough and complex situations.

"Alone again Love, how about that drink before you disappear to Doncaster forever," said Dale who hadn't let his eye off Ellen since first seeing her. She was amazing to him. Like something he'd never seen in real life. His good looks had always ensured he'd had the pick of the bunch and paired with his best mate Harry's cheeky charm, the two were very popular. However, there were few women Dale wasn't related to in Brampton Berliew. Of the potential partners, there were a couple of girls who worked in the mine office he found attractive, yet their eyes were always set for more than *just a miner*. Perhaps Fred Stokes' daughter, Jane, if a little young, would be a great catch but nothing like what sat in front of Dale now.

"Excuse me?" said Ellen, put off by being called *love* and this time certainly sounding haughty.

"Look, you're not likely to ever come into this shithole ever again and I want to be the one who at the very least is able to say *I bought her a drink*."

"Well, Dale, wasn't it? I'm Ellen and I need to order myself a taxi from the bar, so I guess I have time for a drink while I wait."

The move was lost on most of the patrons who continued about their drinking, talking and gambling. However, Harry and a couple of the other single miners watched on in wonder as their friend Dale, predictably, headed to the bar with the mysterious girl.

After ordering himself a pint of beer and a half of cider for Ellen they moved to one end of the bar and remained standing. "Come on then, why are you here at The Plough with a rough load of miners, lovely as we are?"

"I've had some meetings today in Barnsley and was heading back to Doncaster when I was invited to meet with Tom Linney, who it seems you know," said Ellen trying to deflect the conversation back onto Dale.

"Oh, I don't know Tom. He just came to talk to some of the lads from the Union tonight. I'm only here with my friend over there, we just came to listen."

"So, union action isn't really your thing then?"

"No, it's important and we can't lose the fight. My mate Harry says they're going to shut pits and we need to be thinking about what we do next. They should have bloody told us at school there was more that we could do with ourselves." Dale's frankness and obvious comprehension of the situation made Ellen warm to him further.

"So, what would you like to be then if not Dale the miner? Dale the bus driver? Dale the schoolteacher?"

"Ha, fat chance of that, I never liked the teachers I had, and I couldn't face being the focus of that much hatred. I'm a miner, I can't do anything else. That's why I need to fight to keep the pit open. And why I want to help the Union help me."

"I'd suggest that it's never too late to do anything, how old are you?"

"Twenty-eight, and I…" but before he could continue Ellen interrupted.

"Well that's not too late. Two years to train in any profession, you could have your own business by thirty. And there are some great programs open to you for free nowadays. All you have to do is apply." Ellen thought she might have overstepped the mark.

"No one ever told me that, do you work for one of these programs or summat? You should talk to Harry; he seems ready to throw in the towel and do something different."

"I need to call a taxi or I'm never getting home, one for the road?" Ellen asked feeling their conversation had moved forward too quickly. In the background a new band called the Smiths was playing on the jukebox. They sang the words *I'm not sure what happiness means, but I look in your eyes and I know that it isn't there*, and Ellen thought of her mother who would have been horrified that her little girl was in such a place being so direct with a man. And a working miner at that. But it was no longer her mother's era and anyway, Ellen could see a response of happiness in Dale's eyes. Momentarily contemplating all of this she turned to the landlord and felt a small rush of excitement to what might be as she ordered. "A pint of Best, a half of cider and can you call me a taxi to run me back to Doncaster please?"

Dale worried that he really wouldn't understand who Ellen was or why she was at The Plough and now, starting her fourth drink, why she was still talking with him. He certainly didn't want the conversation to end, so while still in the dark as to her world, Dale started to talk about his. He focused on the ideology of his colleagues from Cortonwood; sensing this was her interest. He talked a little on how some saw direct action as the only way to secure an income in their future while sacrificing it in the present. He saw that many just couldn't care less about a changing world and that no amount of incentives for *retraining* would stop them picketing.

"Easier for them to make a noise than make a change, huh," said Dale. Ellen's head was starting to race, the discussion with Mark Turnbull and Tom Linney, insight from Dale and the atmosphere of The Plough itself, the air in which was now thick with smoke and stale air. The cider was making her feel tipsy and she started to fear that she would forget the important detail of the night needed for the morning. As she finished her drink, she looked Dale straight in his dark brown eyes. She drew breath.

"Time for me to get some air and see if my taxi is here." And Ellen made for her overcoat.

"Well I'll see you out then Love." This time Dale noticed her slightly wince at being called Love.

It was barely above zero outside and the fresh air hit them both harshly, particularly Dale who was still in just his old t-shirt. With no immediate sign of a taxi Dale instinctively put an arm around Ellen to shelter her from the cold. Ellen turned slightly to Dale and put an arm around him in response. Even through her coat, blazer and roll-neck jumper she could feel his rough hands and muscular arms gripping her. Looking slightly upward toward him they held each other's gaze for a moment. A second later a car pulled up near them and Ellen turned to see the taxi. Escaping Dale's grip she made for the car's door.

"Well, come on, can I at least get your number?" asked Dale, sounding like a child whose new toy had just been taken off him.

"Give me yours," said Ellen trying to maintain the upper hand.

"You're joking, right? I don't have a phone, I'm a miner. You can try calling me here at The Plough, though. Bugger it, I'm here often enough."

"Well, I'm staying at the Danum Hotel in Doncaster for the next couple of nights, you can try me there."

"I know the Danum, me Mam used to clean there", but before Ellen's good manners let here comment on this statement, something deeper forced her to keep an air of mystery and she got into the waiting taxi and disappeared into the cold February night.

Chapter 5

Thursday 16th February 1984.

Doncaster, Yorkshire, -1°C, frosty and windy.

Ellen.

Ellen enjoyed staying in places like the Danum Hotel because she could be anonymous. The bubble in and around Westminster meant that nobody there was anonymous. Every character in Westminster was analysed for what they could bring to the table. If you were someone enough to help their career, then people were nice to you. If they felt like you were of no use to them then they had little or no time for you at all. This level of scrutiny just didn't exist in Doncaster.

Ellen raised her neck a few inches from the pillow and then back down again. It was part of her normal morning routine to do a few stretches. The fact that she had consumed a few halves of cider the night before made this particular stretch less comfortable than usual, but she continued anyway. Long days, always on the move, made her feel like she was tired more often than not. She looked forward to a time when things were a little quieter and she could slow down; but at the same time, she didn't think that quiet would suit her. After the stretches, she showered, towelled down and got dressed. Ellen applied the smallest amount of makeup she could get away with. Some of her friends from school would plaster their face in the stuff, but she wanted to look as natural as possible. The fact that her Boss, Paul Channon didn't want her to wear it made it seem more acceptable. She just didn't see the point.

As the sun crept through the cheap curtains of the hotel, Ellen noticed that there was no sign of rain. This had been a rare occurrence over the previous few days she had spent in the area. Looking across the street, she noticed that the rain gathered in swelling gutters had frozen solid in the building opposite. Pausing momentarily, Ellen could see the building needed some attention. She was no builder but knew that the gutters were supposed to clear rain, not store it.

After a short time, she was ready for the meeting that was due to happen before long. Ellen was just one of those people who was early for everything. Having a mother who ran late all the time had a profound effect on the way she lived her life. Being on the receiving end of lateness could have had one of two effects; either to make Ellen late or have her rail against that behaviour. She chose the latter. Walking down the stairs to the reception, she looked to the right to see the last of the breakfast being served. Although dressed for the meeting, her hunger took over. Until she'd seen and smelled the food being taken across in front of her, she didn't have any connection to her appetite. Now she was ready to eat.

Returning to the reception area, she took a seat and waited for the rest of the party to arrive. Ellen had already arranged the room with reception the night before but double-checked in the way she always did before breakfast. That way she could relax and not be brought to task by JK, Paul or anyone else for that matter. Being a woman in a world dominated by men was hard enough. Making a mistake as a woman in a world dominated by men could end her career.

As the grandfather clock in the hall ticked, Ellen grew increasingly aware of time passing by. The night before had been interesting for her. She wanted to see and hear more about Tom and was intrigued to see Dale again. As her thoughts slipped back in time, she didn't notice the others enter the hotel and make their way towards her. Looking to the floor, she missed them enter to her right and it took a loud cough from JK to stir her back into the present.

With her bag under her arm, and her tail between her legs, she took the lead and showed the rest of them to the two rooms they would be using for the meeting. The first room they entered was the one where she and the rest of the entourages would sit. Through large double doors was the second room, the inner sanctum. This was where Scargill and Channon would meet.

"Here is your room, gentlemen," Ellen said with a trickle of uncertainty in her voice. She wasn't ready to be disturbed from her thoughts. "I'll get them to bring up teas and coffees. Any special requests?"

Although Ellen had stayed in the hotel for a few days, she had no idea whether there were any specialties available. It just seemed like something she should say.

"Just as it comes for me," Arthur Scargill said, looking her up and down. He nodded towards Mark Turnbull and the two of them shared a smile. Ellen knew she was being watched. She didn't know how much the NUM leader knew about her movements the day before. She had a feeling he knew a great deal.

The hotel staff arrived with drinks and the doors were shut. The people sat in the outer room had little to say to each other. There was small talk, but each was itching to be invited to the room where the big boys were talking. None were going to make it that far, Ellen guessed.

"So, Ellen, how was your visit to the pub?" asked Tom with a sense of mischief. Ellen flushed red and before she was able to answer JK butted in.

"What's this all about, El? Weren't you supposed to keep a low profile? I'm sure Paul knows all about this?"

JK wanted to control everything. From the way he straightened his shirt with his hands so that every button was in an exact line to the way he spoke to others that worked for the minister, JK was a control freak.

"Something that you don't know about, JK? You'd be surprised at how often that happens!" said Mark. He'd always wanted to get one over on JK and was relishing the confrontation. JK, on the other hand, was not.

"Who exactly are you in all of this?" he demanded with a raised voice.

"Why don't we discuss this outside? El, you can stay here and have a think about how you might explain whatever this is to Paul." JK gave direction and Ellen knew this was a small battle she couldn't win. The rest of the room emptied, and she looked across through the window for some solace. Just at that point, something caught her eye in the window opposite. It looked like a bird had got stuck in the window and was frantically trying to break free. She stepped across the room in a hurried state and realised at that point there were also raised voices coming from the room where Paul Channon and Arthur Scargill were meeting. She lost thought of the bird and slid her feet across the carpeted floor towards the doors. The voices of the chiselled Channon and the working-class hero Scargill were distinct enough that she could make out who was who in an instant.

Scargill spoke. "The strikes are going ahead. They're planned, organised and will happen no matter what you do in the meantime. This government needs to be reminded of who is in charge. It was the people who elected them. Not you."

Ellen's heart rose from her chest and felt like it occupied a place at the top of her throat. She froze on the spot, waiting for the ground to swallow her up and deliver her back to her bed, as this must be a dream. She was alone in the room, close enough to the door to hear every word that was being said in a private meeting between a minister and a union leader. Surely this wasn't happening.

Instead of moving away from the doors, Ellen shuffled a little closer to ensure she wasn't imagining the voices from the other side. She wasn't. The voice she heard clearly was that of Arthur Scargill. He continued to tell Paul Channon what was going to happen, come what may. This didn't feel right at all to her. The meeting was set up so the two of them could negotiate, not so her Boss could be told there was nothing he could do.

Before anyone else re-entered the room, Ellen decided that she had better look like she wasn't eavesdropping. Although the voices behind the door were not making much of an effort to hide themselves, she would face disciplinary action, probably leading to the sack, if she was caught listening in. As she moved back to the chair farthest away from the double doors, she heard voices from the other end of the room getting louder. The rest of the entourage were making their way back into the room. Ellen had sat down just in time as the door swung open with a red-faced JK immediately on the other side of it.

"...And that is the way it is going to be. It will never change," she caught the end of what JK was saying to the rest of the people following behind him. *Typical JK*, she thought, *putting the world to rights no matter what the situation.*

"What's going on here?" bellowed Tom Linney as he followed last into the room. Ellen's head shot round to see what he was talking about. Was it obvious that she'd been listening? Did she leave something near the doors? Her head raced with what she would say if Tom knew she'd overheard what the NUM leader was saying.

Her fears evaporated as she saw Tom looking out of the window at the bird trapped in the building opposite. He released a deep laugh that filled the room and possibly the whole hotel.

"When something is trapped, the best thing to do is put it out of its misery, isn't that right Love?" he said looking at Ellen. She didn't answer. Her thoughts were already on leaving the room, the meeting, the hotel, the town. The hangover was over, in its place was the desire to be home.

*   *   *

Back in London, Ellen quickly got back into the groove she felt was missing somewhat in Doncaster. The encounter with the handsome miner was an exciting distraction but in order to process this in her own brain she labelled it as just that, a distraction. The main reason she had to train her mind to be this way was her boyfriend, Rhys. He would be heartbroken at the brief encounter between her and Dale. She would push it to the back of her mind and carry on as though everything was normal. But Ellen knew after overhearing Arthur Scargill the day before that nothing was quite normal in the world she occupied.

Catching up with Rhys over breakfast at a café near their flat in St John's Wood, Ellen spoke quietly as she always did around him. Even as her career grew, her confidence around men in her private life didn't make the same journey. She came across as timid and subservient.

"How was your trip? Any juicy gossip?" Rhys asked.

"You know I can't tell you about what goes on in my job. It's the same as yours," Ellen replied. Rhys already knew what the answer would be to his questions but asked anyway. In his role as a bank manager he understood confidentiality just as well as her but liked to tease a little. And maybe one day she would forget and let something really interesting slip.

"How has your week been, Rhys?".

"More of the same. People bringing money in, others taking money out." Rhys saw his job as something mundane and boring in comparison to the potentially exciting world of politics his intended was linked to. As she didn't say a great deal about it, Rhys wondered if it was actually as exciting as he pictured but he was sure it was better than sitting behind a desk all day listening to mortgage applications and the like.

The conversation petered out into nothing as the two of them ate. Ellen had one eye on the clock on the wall behind Rhys. She'd chosen the seat carefully for more than one reason. Firstly, it gave her an uninterrupted view of the clock. She had time on her hands but would never forgive herself if she was late. Secondly the café wasn't the cleanest place, but convenience had won out over standards. It was a typical greasy spoon with most of the grease still occupying the gingham design tablecloths, the lino flooring and, most importantly to Ellen, the bright red plastic seats that were pulled tight to the tables in order to get the most amount of tables in the room while leaving people at least some space to walk to and from the counter to order their food. The seat she had spotted looked like it had a dishcloth run over it more recently than the others. The time clicked towards nine o'clock and Ellen gave Rhys a quick peck on the cheek to say goodbye. The next half hour would consist of a short walk home and a quick change. And then she would be back on her way to the office to convene with the rest of the team for the official debrief following the meeting the day before. There had been talk on the train on the way home yesterday between them but with it being a public place it hadn't led to much at all.

Walking into her office just under an hour later, Ellen held her head high. The last few days had dented her confidence in the political system and her place in it, but she was dammed if she was going to show it. The offices of the Trade Minister Paul Channon were a short walk from the entrance to the House of Commons and Ellen thought she could travel it with her eyes closed, she had done it that many times. So, she tried it. Walking up the stairs, Ellen elevated her sense of hearing to make sure she didn't bump into anyone who might have thought her mad at trying this.

As Ellen got to the top of the stairs it was a left turn and a walk of around fifty yards to the office door she would need. Without peeking, she steadied herself in the old corridors of the magnificent parliament building and walked in a line she was sure was straight. *A yard is about one large step*, Ellen decided and proceeded to count her steps one by one. If anyone saw her walking with eyes closed and a huge smile on her face, then she would be the subject of some ridicule in the department but at that precise moment Ellen didn't care. The corridors were silent with most people already in and at their desks. The fact that her team had all travelled back to London the day before and got back late and with today being Friday she knew that she would be alone when she got to their office.

As she reached the door Ellen heard voices as if she had been transported back 24 hours. Unlike the heavy doors and formal setting of the hotel in Doncaster, this was obviously from the more hushed tones an ad hoc meeting. One voice she could make out clearly. Her Boss, Paul Channon. Although she hadn't been working for him for long, she had listened intently to him for days on end, so knew instinctively the way he held his breath before an important sentence or clipped the end of his words if short of time or angry.

The other voice wasn't one she was familiar with. Ellen wasn't great at accents but knew that it wasn't from the local area. It could even have been foreign for all she knew. Feeling a huge sense of déjà vu from the day before Ellen froze and took in all she heard from the unknown voice.

"Libya and the miners are friends. We will stand together in the face of the Tory onslaught. We will rise up and make the changes this society needs. Don't ever underestimate the corners of your society that we can be found in. We have placed our men in powerful positions. You already know this in more than one case, Mr Channon. You did nothing to stop it."

Ellen walked away from the door without bending her knees, thinking that the lack of movement would allow her to escape as quickly as possible without attracting the attention of the two people who were discussing something very out of the ordinary behind the office door. She walked back down the stairs, this time with her eyes open in more ways than one. She knew that there were always conversations that went on behind closed doors but had no idea the depths they could reach, until now. Ellen decided that a walk around the grounds of the Commons was in order. Even in the cold of Winter this was a place to think clearly. Ellen consoled herself that this building must have seen conversations like this happen thousands of times over hundreds of years and democracy still stood. A sharp cold wind pricked at her face, but she didn't care. There were bigger problems she was now facing.

Chapter 6

Thursday 1st March 1984.

Westminster, London, cloudy, windy with a high of 11°C.

Ellen.

The last few days had been a whirr of activity for Ellen and the rest of the team supporting Paul Channon in his work. It was only the highest-level meetings such as those with the cabinet and one-to-one with the Prime Minister that Channon discarded his full team and went alone, or occasionally with the assistance of JK. So, Ellen got her head down and worked. It was the best way to keep her from thinking about the two conversations she had overheard. All the time she was working, the memories of these conversations kept replaying in her mind. She suppressed them as best she could but the times when she took a small interlude from work, a cup of tea or a visit to the loo, then they were writ large at the front of her mind.

She wondered if the two conversations were linked. She also wondered if she was meant to hear them. Thinking back over the events of the last few days, it seemed as though things were stage managed to get her in the perfect situations to hear what was being said. The visit to the working-class pub, the argument between JK and Mark and being the only one early to work all came together to mean she was placed on the outskirts of all these conversations. Close enough to hear, far enough away to not be detected. How else could this have happened?

But she was busy enough for her time to be taken up and her attention be drawn away from these thoughts. The added bonus of a heavy workload and long hours was that she fell asleep as soon as her head hit the pillow. The thoughts wouldn't invade this private time if she exhausted herself enough during the day. That was her plan, at least.

Working for the Trade Minister at such a crucial time in the miner's strike meant that a trip away from London to the coalfields further North was always on the cards. When she signed up for the Department of Trade, Ellen pictured exotic locations and a life of boarding airplanes. She'd soon swapped those dreams for a reality of ministerial cars and the dreaded British Rail transportation. Ellen wasn't totally dissatisfied with the job she had taken on but thought when the coal situation was resolved that she would be far more likely to see foreign climes. That was if the coal situation was ever resolved. That afternoon she was heading to Grimethorpe with the rest of the minister's team. In the morning she'd packed her bags for the North again. Not that much colder than London but enough for a second pair of bed socks in case the hotel didn't keep their heating on through the night.

Arriving in Grimethorpe, JK decided to take the lead and spent the first hour talking to the reception and hotel manager about what they were to provide for the minister and his team. Although room bookings were made and accepted days before the trip, the rooms allocated were not together and JK didn't like this. He wanted everyone to be close.

While JK read the riot act to the poor hotel manager, Ellen and Paul spoke to each other in general terms about what they were there for. Ellen listened intently to the instructions given by the minister, as though he were the one that had come up with them. She knew well enough that all of this came from the mouth of JK. She could even hear his voice speaking the words as though Paul Channon was a ventriloquist's dummy just having his mouth moved up and down by a superior force. He was a strange mix of privilege and meekness in her eyes. She knew that he knew his stuff but wasn't sure where the knowledge had come from. Ellen watched his tie bob up and down as the Adam's apple underneath pushed backwards and forwards against it with his voice. An old school tie, no doubt. One that might have impressed others but was totally wasted on Ellen.

She had heard enough of JK's instructions being relayed by someone else and decided that this was her opportunity to explore what she had heard. Maybe letting her Boss know that she had heard both secret conversations was tantamount to confessing she was a spy, so she went with the one that sounded more plausible. It was perfectly normal for her to be stood outside the door of the office she worked in at the House of Commons. And it was perfectly normal for people to overhear conversations against the backdrop of echoing corridors and thin partitions that had been built hundreds of years earlier.

"Paul, what did that man mean when he said you did nothing to stop Libya putting people in powerful positions?" Ellen asked.

"I beg your pardon. Were you listening to me?" Paul demanded in a hushed tone. She decided that silence was the best retort.

"I guess that you didn't hear the whole conversation, and you may have missed the part when I said I had no idea what he was talking about," Paul Channon replied with as much confidence as a small child lying to his parents for the first time.

"He seemed pretty sure about what he was saying," Ellen shot back. In her time as a Press Secretary she had become pretty good at spotting the difference between the truth and a lie. It was par for the course. Channon choked on the words as they came out. He wasn't convincing at all. Ellen had noticed that some politicians were comfortable in telling lies. Paul Channon hadn't developed that habit.

"As someone who is in the know with the higher workings of government there are many things I know that you will never be informed of. You are my Press Secretary and will organise my dealings with the press. It doesn't mean that you get to know every little detail about my past, present or future," he replied as he backed away into the darkness of the corridor opposite the reception area. It was as though he didn't want to be seen. Ellen saw this as an admission of guilt. She wasn't sure of the details but was sure from that moment that the voice behind the closed door, the one she couldn't put a fix on, was right. Paul Channon was involved in some dealings way beyond the depths she thought possible.

"As your Press Secretary, I need to be able to handle any negative press that comes your way. If people can come and visit you in your office to discuss this, then they can also speak to the tabloids about it. Fancy being on the front page of The Sun?" she responded, spurting out the words as quickly as she could to stop from holding herself back.

"I... I... Well..." Paul didn't quite know what to say. "You and I need to chat. But not here. I have a lot of information that you won't be given, but in case certain things come out in the press, I'm willing to paint some of the picture for you. This is solely to help you fight off any accusations if they arise, mind you. For no other reason."

Ellen saw the first flush of sincerity since she had asked the question about his clandestine conversation and backed off her words a little. She wasn't sure whether he was playing for time or genuinely wanted to speak to her, but this was a truce in the conversation. He was right; they couldn't talk in the corridor of a hotel for a long period of time without someone walking past or JK returning from the sergeant major style instructions he was giving the hotel manager and his team.

"Let's set something up in the next couple of days. And I'll choose the location. I don't want someone overhearing our conversation, now, do I?" Ellen was planning ahead. She wanted to take control, or at least make it appear that she was. Paul nodded and the two of them turned on the sound of JK's Blakied brogue heels chinking on the tiled floor of the hotel reception.

JK was walking along with the kind of smile that he could only wear after giving someone a dressing down. The kind of smile that showed he was enjoying himself too much.

"Did you get a kick out of that?" asked Ellen.

JK waved her away and beckoned the minister toward him. Ellen knew this was her cue to leave. She didn't need to be asked once, let alone twice.

The room in the hotel was cold. Ellen took her bed socks out of her case and placed them under the pillow with her pyjamas. She had started her life on the road as a Press Secretary with a nightie as the bed wear of choice but soon got used to hotels where the heating was stifling during the day and non-existent at night. The room was decorated in a series of brown shades which made it look like it was decaying from the floor up. The ceilings were not painted white like many of the other hotels she had stayed in but were a shade of brown. Maybe it was all they could do to hide the tar stains from constant cigarettes smoked. Maybe they got a job lot of brown paint cheap and didn't want to spend again on white. Whatever it was made the room feel claustrophobic and Ellen felt the need to get away from there. Stepping into the bathroom where there was no natural light from a window just made things even worse. She just had to do something different.

What are the options? she mulled. And there weren't many. Go down to the bar and listen to some drunk men spout whatever wisdom alcohol gave them. Ask JK or Paul if they'd like to talk. Go out of the hotel and find a cinema. None of those felt anything like the kind of activity that would take her mind off the depression in the room or the conversation she had explored with her Boss.

Ellen picked up the phone and asked reception to make a call for her and to put her through. She didn't know the number but was sure that the reception staff would be able to sort that part out for her. As she was put through the rings came and went before a voice answered, "Hello. The Plough. How can I help?"

What was she doing? Was this a huge mistake? She had said goodbye to her boyfriend only a few hours earlier and here she was phoning a man she had met after a couple drinks in the pub.

"Hello. Can I speak to Dale, please?" Ellen murmured, unsure if the voice on the other end of the phone could hear her. They could alright.

"Dale? There's no Dale here," the voice stated in a matter of fact way. It was off the cuff, but she didn't expect anything else from the landlord. He'd been pleasant to her when she was there last, but Ellen knew he was suspicious of someone new entering his world.

"Oh, I'm sorry to have wasted your time, good day," Ellen replied with as much humour as she could drag into her voice.

"His friend Harry is here though," the voice sounded almost before Ellen had finished her sentence. Before she could say another thing, she heard the receiver at the other end being placed on the bar and the landlord shouting for Harry. Though muffled she could hear him say it was a lady calling and this was followed by a crowd of laughter. The muffled noises got louder and then a voice entered her ear.

"Hi, it's Harry. Who is this?"

"It's Ellen. You probably don't remember me but..."

"Oh, I remember you perfectly well. Dale stole my thunder that night. Story of my life, that is. I can't believe you're calling The Plough. If you're coming back here, then it's my turn to buy you a drink."

"Well I was calling for Dale."

"Dale isn't here this evening, he's helping one of his sisters out, so I'm at a loose end and it sounds like you are too. What do ya'say? Have a drink with me. I'll come to you, where are you?"

Ellen's mind started to spin. It started to dawn on her that her relationship with Rhys had a serious flaw, it seemed that anyone with a humble and direct manner would pique her interest, against all her rational reasoning. Ellen relented. As she told Harry where to find her, the conversation ended, and they hung up. *I'm not sure I meant that to happen* Ellen thought to herself. Within a couple of minutes, Harry was on the bus and on his way to the hotel. Ellen gave him half an hour before going downstairs to wait in reception. She was nervous, meeting a man she'd only glanced at once before. But his voice on the phone had been a comfortable assurance. A feeling of safety that she couldn't quite put a finger on. Ellen quickly went to the bar and ordered a gin and tonic. She wasn't sat in a working-class pub now, so could order whatever she wanted. She drank it quickly and sat back in reception. The world looked a little happier than when she last spent time there. She felt more in tune with the world, realising a new confidence in herself. She enjoyed the feeling.

Four men walked into the hotel before Harry did. With each one she would sit forward hoping it was him before having her hopes dashed slightly. The fact that she was sure he was on the way made the disappointment only last a few seconds. Her excitement of doing something spontaneous, even a little naughty meant by the time he walked through the door her heart was beating fast in her chest.

Harry was still wearing what he had been dressed in when she'd seen him at The Plough. It was a brown bomber jacket and dirty jeans along with work boots and a jumper that looked like it had been washed far too many times. The original colour was a dark green but by now only Harry knew that. His smile caught her attention straight away. She knew smiles having worked in politics for some time and this one was as honest as the day was long. He was more than glad to see her. Ellen's heart settled into a more normal beat and she felt protected.

"Well, where shall we go, local boy?" she asked, hoping Harry would know the area well. He didn't.

"I only ever go to The Plough, and I'm not taking you back there. Some of the older guys are playing dominoes and that always ends up with bad language. No place for a lady tonight, I'm afraid," he responded with a natural charm. "Let's go for a walk and see what the world shows us. Have you eaten?"

Ellen was starving. The gin and tonic had brought this home to her. They decided that somewhere to eat was in order and turned right as they left the hotel. They stopped outside of a café that looked like it was closing for the evening. Harry wanted something simple and homecooked, so told Ellen he would stick his head in and see if they had room for two diners. She laughed at his use of language; it didn't seem natural.

When they sat in the café, it was clear that they were going to be the last two diners of the evening. Nobody else was present, the owner was ready to cook for them and go home. Ellen preferred this.

"So, what exactly do you do? I know you work somewhere in the government but nothing about that means a great deal to me," Harry asked.

"I'm a Press Secretary. I make sure that the truth gets out there," Ellen replied.

"I haven't associated the press with the truth that much recently. Tell me how you do that?" he pressed with a strong sense of mischief in his voice. Ellen knew she was being teased.

"There are two sides to every story, Harry," she said while sipping from a glass of water, "anyway, what is your interest in it all?"

"I'm concerned for the pits. They aren't the greatest place to work but they're all we've got. I need to work. My kids will need to work too."

It was Ellen's turn to have a bit of fun "And how many children do you have, if you don't mind me asking?"

"When I have kids, I mean," Harry replied in a deadpan voice that made Ellen wonder if he had realised she was playing with him. "This is important stuff. It might be a game to you, but as Dale would tell us this is the life of thousands of people that your government is messing with." She detected some frustration in his voice.

"I know. I think that there's a lot of messy communication going on. But there's something I can tell you if you promise to keep it a secret."

"I promise," Harry replied, having a weird feeling that they had already developed a deep trust. He wouldn't let her down. His word was about all he had. She felt like they had known each other a lifetime. A strange feeling, one she had never experienced with anyone else.

"They're going to close more pits. They're going to close them soon. Paul Channon will make the announcement really soon, I can't say when, and the pits will be closed almost immediately. It's part of the government's plan to push this forward without protest," Ellen spoke while looking around the room. The information she was imparting could cost her the career. But she just knew the information was safe with Harry.

"I can't quite believe what I'm hearing, surely there are other options for all of us to look at," Harry responded. But he looked as though he had been shaken to the core.

"Time to clear out," the café owner shouted from the kitchen behind the counter.

Harry was starting to think exactly the same thing.

Chapter 7

Monday 5th March 1984.

Westminster, London, 10°C, wind and rain.

Ellen.

Westminster always looked grey and drab in the cold. And the early days of March were still cold enough for Ellen to dislike them. It was supposed to be her day off after accumulating a lot of time in lieu over the recent weeks, but her Boss had requested a meeting that afternoon. She'd been in the office late the night before, weekend working not uncommon for her, so had cherished a lie-in, getting up around eleven. Despite the day off, turning down a request from Paul wasn't an option. Whether from a professional point of view or simply to satisfy her curiosity.

The rain hadn't started at that time, but she was sure it would open and cover her as soon as she stepped out of the door. The wind and rain were the only usual things for Ellen on this day in March. It would not follow the usual pattern of briefings, meetings and debriefings. As much as Westminster looked exciting and varied from the outside, the reality for Ellen was that she did a lot of the same things, day after day. Once you had sat in one Westminster meeting, it felt like you had sat in them all.

The walls of the rooms were painted calm and muted colours, presumably to ensure that tempers didn't fray but all it did for Ellen was take the life out of the conversation. Etiquette and procedure always got in the way of good debate and lively interaction. The most common outcome from a meeting was to set up another meeting. Ellen didn't like this side of government life.

After eating a lunch that consisted mainly of eggs, Ellen got ready. She had certain suits for certain occasions and today felt like it might be important and potentially confrontational. That called for the brown trouser suit and a plain white blouse. Nothing said, 'I mean business' more than this combination as far as Ellen was concerned.

Walking through the gloomy streets, Ellen looked forward to the day. She was due to sit with her Boss for a one on one meeting. She knew it could only be about one thing. Libya. As much as she distrusted him on this subject, Ellen couldn't bring herself to press him more on the issue. She trusted him in every other aspect. A rare occurrence in Westminster Ellen knew. Every time she did strike up enough courage to start to question him on Libya, something else got in the way. The phone would ring, or someone would enter his chambers and she would lose her nerve. Not this time. She and Paul had a meeting, it was in his diary and nobody would disturb. Even the phone would be switched off, so they could have the quality time she craved. She was sure he felt the same way too, as it was he who'd arranged the meeting. If it was anywhere but his parliamentary chambers, she would have worried that it was far enough off the record that she couldn't push him. But the fact was he had set an official meeting to talk to one of his team. She had a duty to discuss with him all that mattered.

Ellen arrived at the chambers around fifteen minutes before the meeting was due to start. Passing row upon row of level-arch files she walked serenely to her desk. She wanted to acclimatise and let her hair calm down from the dampness of the rainy journey to work. She didn't like the way her hair would frizz when damp, but this would reverse with time and heat. On reflection, fifteen minutes probably wasn't going to be long enough for that, but that's all she had. Ellen ramped up the heating in the office she shared with JK and hoped this would do the trick. Hair problems wouldn't stop her from being professional during the meeting, but it wasn't the way she wanted to look when pressing a member of her majesty's government on his dealings with another country. As she looked up at the clock, there were creaking footsteps from the corridor outside. They could have been from anyone that worked in the entire building, but Ellen guessed that they belonged to Paul Channon. She was right.

"Afternoon Ellen. Be ready for you in ten minutes," he said as he walked into the room and back out of the adjoining door to his private chambers.

"OK, Paul. I'll be ready. Just let me know when I can come in," she replied. Then she cursed herself. Straight away she had handed the initiative to him. Immediately she had let him have the upper hand. That was the last time she would do that, Ellen told herself. She resolved to lead the conversation when the door opened, and she was beckoned inside.

Those ten minutes disappeared in a flash. Ellen took the time to go through the conversation the two of them had before regarding the thorny issue of Libya. She recalled the hotel corridor, the feeling that she was being ignored and the way that Paul looked when she pressed him. But more importantly, she recalled the details they had discussed. There was no way that she was ever going to forget those. And he knew that. This made her feel safe and vulnerable at the same time. She thought that the fact she was talking from a position of knowledge and information made her safe. She was invaluable to Paul's team. But she was also aware that Paul Channon could deal in some of the darker arts of politics and this made her feel vulnerable. He hadn't got to the top of his particular part of government by being soft. Maybe if he saw her as a threat, Ellen could be out of the door, or even worse.

As she composed herself, looking up at the clock, Ellen could again hear the unmistakable footsteps of Paul Channon in the room next to her. The door swung open slowly like in some horror movie. But this was reality. Ellen checked herself in the small hand mirror she always kept in her bag. Her hair was starting to return to its normal state. It would have to do.

"Come in," Paul said without appearing around the corner of the door. She wondered from his voice whether it was a call of a happy man, or one with an agenda.

Ellen slowly walked over to the door, entered the room and closed it behind her. It was time to talk.

Paul wasn't quite so convinced. He started with all the small talk of a man that really didn't want to get down to business.

"...the weather isn't glorious today..."

"...how was your weekend...?"

"... where are you living these days?"

Ellen answered all of these with the patience of a small child that had been told to be good or there would be no sweets after dinner. But inside she was desperate to get down to business. She told herself that patience was a virtue. She persuaded herself to play the long game. But that patience didn't last for long.

She zoned in and out of what he was saying. It was pointless tuning into the whole piece when she could get the gist and nod her head in the right places by picking up the odd sentence in an ongoing monologue. When you've worked with someone for such a long time, you have a pretty good grip of their views on most matters.

"...and I told the minister that it wasn't his department. He wasn't happy, but he had to..."

"There is something I have been meaning to talk to you about." Typical Ellen. Just threw it out there. Now there was no going back. "And I think you already know what it is."

"If you're referring to our last private conversation, then all I can say is that I hope you have kept it private," Paul said whilst maintaining eye contact. It was a technique he had learned from the Prime Minister herself. Although he didn't have the same mastery of it, he found it to be quite effective. He didn't reason on Ellen having seen him employ it far too many times in the past.

"I've worked for you long enough for you to know I am discrete. I want to talk to YOU about it, nobody else. What exactly do you have in your closet that I need to be worried about? I think I have the right to know. It's not just *your* political reputation on the line," Ellen explained as she noticed Paul's attention wasn't totally on her. It was the first time she'd noticed that there was a television playing in the corner of the room.

"I trust you, but this isn't a matter of trust. It's a matter of belief. I can assure you that there is nothing at all to worry about. I don't have a skeleton in my closet regarding Libya or anything else for that matter," Paul responded with his attention drifting more heavily to the television in the corner. "Turn that up, please. I have a feeling we need to hear this."

'And now for the One O'clock News from the BBC. The government has just announced plans to close 20 coal mines with immediate effect and a further 70 over the coming months. As part of the plans to close these outdated and unproductive pits, sources are telling us…"

"Shit. That was fast, even for the Beeb. OK, what's our next play?" he asked, turning to her.

Ellen had no answer.

The rest day had been one of little rest for Ellen and now it looked like it was going to be both a busy and a late one. She had worked after the meeting to write up some notes and get her head straight. The diary for her Boss showed he was marked out for the rest of the day following their meeting, but without a great deal of detail of what he was doing. That wasn't an unusual occurrence, but the things she had heard over the recent days made Ellen think differently about the movements of Paul Channon. For all she knew, it could have been totally innocent, but she now felt a sinister overtone to his every move.

As she finally headed home, she found herself wondering what he was up to. Ellen thought that he could have been meeting shady characters in any part of the country; or the world for that matter. But she also felt that there were enough shady characters in Westminster that he didn't have to travel far in order to conduct these deals. She'd looked forward to this day off for such a long time that it had taken over in her mind. The reality of it however was very different and as she climbed into bed her mind was swimming in all the possibilities of what she knew and what she didn't.

It was very different for Paul Channon. He left their meeting and walked straight into his ministerial car. He worked as he was driven. There was little he missed in his role, reading reports and newspapers on his own rather than relying on the team to do all of this for him. He felt it was part of his job to devour all the relevant information himself, not to receive it second hand in a redacted form from someone else. Today's announcement on the news was an unusual miss for him, but his guess was that it had come from the top direct to the BBC to avoid any kind of leak. This impressed even him.

The driver said nothing for the whole journey. He had driven him around enough times before to know there was little point in making any conversation. As he neared the destination, the driver slowed before coming to a complete stop and letting his passenger out. His next task was to wait until he was needed again. The job of a driver could be an easy one or a tough one depending on the minister they were assigned to or the day of the week. Mondays always seemed to be the worst.

"Wait there," the instruction came from Paul Channon. The driver wondered what else he was expected to do. He looked around the area and wondered what a member of parliament was doing in a place like this. And while they were still in Westminster, this wasn't a typical hangout for a politician.

He searched the street for an obvious venue for a member of the cabinet to visit at this time but could see none. There was a pub, a few cafes and nothing much else that was still open. He watched intently as the politician walked in a zig zag line as though this would stop anyone from tracing his whereabouts. Indeed, if anyone was watching this tactic would draw even more attention to him. The driver laughed to himself. He saw so many things that tickled him that it had just become part of his everyday existence.

Paul walked along the front of the two cafes before entering the pub. The driver looked up at the sign, *The Red Lion*. Why did pubs have so little variety in their names? he thought before disappearing back to thoughts of football, with his team Watford going well in the FA Cup. He wondered if he might be able to get cup final tickets if they made it that far. He closed his eyes and got some rest. It might be a long night.

Paul Channon walked into the bar and ordered a pint with a whisky chaser. He thought that he might need a little settling. Meeting this close to Westminster was somewhat of a risk, but he needed to talk. The only others in the bar all looked as though they had been there all night. There was a group of men playing dominoes and a couple of women who were chatting about anything and everything.

The door had a large glass pane in the middle, so he could see anyone approaching, lit by the streetlight handily positioned just outside. Paul felt safe with this set up. There was even access to the rear of the pub via a door at the end of the bar, so a quick escape was possible if he needed it. As he settled, there was a movement in the street outside. Paul held his breath as he saw a large figure approaching. It had to be male from the size of the character and he was sure it would be his contact. Paul had chosen a darker corner of the pub for a reason, it made him feel less conspicuous. But looking intently at the door every time someone walked past would take a lot of this secrecy away. The door opened, and a large figure walked in.

"Yes! I'm here!" he shouted. The whole pub turned to look at the man at the door. Paul's cheeks reddened. He hadn't taken his eyes off the door but was in a state of confusion. The man walked to the group of domino players and sat down with them. It was a false alarm. Anyway, his contact wasn't so silly as to walk into a crowded pub and shout his arrival.

Paul relaxed. He decided to look into his pint and nowhere else, as he saw many single men do when in pubs. It was a tactic that he hoped would keep his anonymity. The door opened a few times, but he didn't raise his stare from the drink in front of him. Then he felt a presence sit beside him. Paul looked up to see David Miller, or Dusty to those who knew him, only a few inches from his face. It took Paul by surprise as did Dusty's next action, to get back up and walk over to the bar. Paul wondered why he didn't order a drink before sitting down. A few seconds later he was sat back with Paul again.

"How's things? Been here long?" Dusty fired quickly and momentarily, Paul struggled to work out which one to answer.

"You know why we are here. It's late. Shall we cut to the chase?" he replied in the softest voice he felt he could muster.

"There could be a thousand reasons someone from the government and someone from the MOD meet. How would you explain this to the papers? What would your press secretary think?" Dusty had an air of mischief. He didn't have nearly as much to lose as his companion.

"What is going on with our mutual friend?"

"That could be anyone. Why don't you be more specific? Don't you think you should spell it out to me?"

"I could have this conversation with a number of people in the MOD. You need me more than I need you. It's about your career as much as mine," Paul replied smoothly, calling his bluff.

"OK. Shall we start again? You want to ask me the first question one more time?" Dusty had his fun and knew it was time to retreat gracefully.

"What is going on with our mutual friend? What's going on with the Libyan connection?" Paul Channon felt the need to give a little ground. He was prepared to meet halfway. After all, what harm could it do? There was nobody in the bar that was even vaguely interested in what they were talking about.

"That's all over and done with. There will be no more action on that front. You'll need to forget about that," Dusty replied with a confidence that betrayed his true thoughts. He finished his pint in silence before leaving the minister sitting in the same corner of the pub where he found him.

Dusty walked on the darker side of the street deep in thought. He had to tell the minister to cool off and walk away. But he really thought the exact opposite of what he had said. He felt that there needed to be an escalation relating to Libya. With all that was going on in the UK, he felt that there needed to be some external influence to bring things into proper order. He was skating on thin ice, but was prepared to fall in. He smiled as he walked past the ministerial car and wondered why the member of her majesty's cabinet was so brazen as to sit in a pub with such a car outside. Maybe he actually did feel he was doing nothing wrong. Dusty walked off into the night, while Paul was haunted by action and inaction in his life. For all the power he had, there were still so many people he relied upon to get his work done. He finished his pint then downed the whisky in one. Paul knew he wouldn't get much sleep that night.

Chapter 8

Tuesday 6th March 1984.

Cortonwood Colliery Mine, South Yorkshire, 9°C, cloudy and windy.

Harry and Dale.

"They're really doing it!" Harry said to Dale.

The events of the last few hours had seemed surreal to him. They'd been sat at the pub the night before, as most nights, drinking and talking. Harry had been his usual self, chatting to different people around the room, gauging the mood and trying to lighten it wherever needed. He spoke to several of his fellow pit workers who felt that the world was weighing down on their shoulders. Harry always had the knack of lightening that load and providing everyone he met with a reason to be cheerful, in fact he was often that very reason.

Dale had spent much of the evening playing cards. The barman turned a blind eye to these kind of games on the understanding that people played them out of view of the bar. This meant only one table. It was in the corner of the pub and wasn't very well lit. The dark wasn't the reason people played there, it was almost parallel with the bar and, as such, couldn't be seen by the staff. They would have to crane their necks to see, and nobody wanted that. On the slight chance that the police came in and questioned, there was enough deniability to get away with it. Dale wasn't very good at cards. No matter what game they played, he walked away with far less cash at the end of the night than he walked in with. It wasn't so much of a problem that he lost all his wages but was enough of one that he missed out on the last couple of pints of the night on occasion. He could handle that. Dale had fun when playing cards, even if he didn't win.

"They're actually doing it!" Dale replied.

While rumours swirled about closures the night had been light-hearted for all until nine o'clock. Harry was passing happiness around like he owned it while Dale was losing money like he didn't need it. Then nine o'clock struck. The pub had an old black and white television set precariously balanced on a wooden plinth above the heads of the people sat opposite the card table. The plinth had seen better days. Harry thought it leaned farther out from the wall, and closer to the floor, every time he walked through the door of the pub. It was the only place he wasn't willing to spend much time. His happiness and joy spreading only went so far when seated under the television. The TV had a strange place in The Plough. It hadn't received much airtime until the political climate changed. The landlord had bought it cheap when the local branch of Radio Rentals closed. He thought it might come in useful one day. It was now switched on just a few minutes before nine each night, when the events of the day would be relayed to the nation by the BBC.

The clock struck nine.

"And now for the nine o'clock news. The government has announced today the plans to close 20 coal mines with immediate effect and a further 70 over the coming months. As part of the plans to close these outdated and unproductive pits. Sources are telling us…"

All hell broke loose. Cards and happiness were soon discarded. Bitterness mixed with more alcohol took their place. Harry needed help if he was to turn this mood from one of despair into anything close to what he could call happy. Dale picked up his remaining cash and inspected it. There were only a few pounds left but he had probably been saved from more losses by the news on the television. He left the card table, got another pint from the bar and joined in the nearest conversation.

"This has been coming for a while. We've just sat here and waited for it to happen. Well, the time for waiting is over. It's time for action," a voice slurred. Dale had heard threats like this before. All talk from the drink, he thought.

Another voice piped up, "We haven't been organised. We aren't ready for action. What is it you think we should do? What is it you think we could do?" Dale thought this voice was correct. All the talk in the world wouldn't change anything. They'd been talking for months, probably even years if his memory was correct. He smiled and looked for Harry. Maybe he had a different angle on things.

"Harry, what's going on?" asked Dale.

"You heard the news? They're closing the mines. People have now got to stand up and be counted," Harry replied as if Dale had just arrived from another planet.

"But what does that look like?" Dale enquired. He was aware that the more he acted dumb, the more he would be treated like he was. So, he reworded his question before Harry could answer. "What are people organising?"

"Nowt," Harry responded, "just a load of drunken ramble so far. Nothing constructive. Let's see what the morning brings."

Dale wasn't satisfied with this approach. He spoke to anyone and everyone who would listen to him. He wanted people to rise up. He wanted people to feel differently in the morning, not at night when they had some Dutch courage inside them. He found a few allies and planted the seeds of action with them. He hoped his talk would inspire people to do something that would change their world.

"Let's see what the morning brings, indeed," Dale said to himself on the last few steps of his way home.

And the morning brought action.

It was 4 a.m. At this time of morning there was usually a flurry of activity as people made their way to work. In the still-cold mornings of March, there would be a sea of overcoats making their way through the streets to the Cortonwood Colliery. As you got closer to the pit, the sea became an ocean with bodies filling up the pavements and spilling onto the roads. It was a silent march to work for many, considering the day ahead and wondering how they would feel physically on their return. But that day, there was a noise to this ocean. There was a rumble of voices as people turned the drunken ideas of the night before into action.

There was a walk-out. The unions had gotten off their backsides and organised the miners into an efficient unit for protest. Dale was filled with glee as they heard the people around them talk of making a difference and standing up to the government. Dale left Harry behind in his haste to be a part of the protest. Harry had similar feelings to Dale in many ways, but wanted to be part of the group, not leading it. By the time Harry turned the last corner to join the picket line, Dale was already standing with the leaders, shouting direction and encouraging his fellow miners to stay strong.

The scene was one of mixed emotion for Harry. He was glad to see his friend taking an active role and being part of the movement. Dale had always wanted people to fight for what he felt was right. The night before hadn't felt any different for him. He wanted to see sober action, not drunken words. Dale was excited, Harry could see that. For every hundred men who were there on the picket line to do their duty, there was one who revelled in the occasion. Dale was that one in a hundred. He'd always had a strong sense of right and wrong from his upbringing. His mother had taught him to do the right thing every day of his life. Fiona was a god-fearing woman who took him to church every Sunday and followed the gospel without exception. Maybe being part of a strike wasn't the way his mother would have gone about her business, but Dale took lead from her sense of justice. When he was stood tall at the front of the group, he hoped his mum would be proud.

Harry watched from the side-lines. He thought that this mass walk-out might bring a heavy police presence, so he kept a watchful eye on what was going on. He wanted to protect the people around him, especially Dale. Wherever Dale went, Harry was no more than fifty feet from him. Dale had been really pleased for his friend when Harry had explained the meeting with Ellen. Though he hadn't said so, Dale could see how taken with her Harry already was and he couldn't begrudge his friend that. Besides, Dale's desire burned for something else, the Union. Harry was careful not to get caught up in the furore, but he was close enough that he could get there to help if Dale needed. His friend was going to go places, Harry was sure. The fact that he could encourage others to act and then become a leader in the action was something Harry was proud of. Not that he could have managed anything quite so vocal himself, he thought.

Dale was smiling and shouting, Harry was watching. Little did they know that the world was watching too. There were television crews in the centre of the action. Now they were stood among the protesters, taking interviews and filming the events. Harry wondered why anyone else was interested. Yet someone he knew was watching intently.

* * *

"These people don't really think they can make a difference, do they?" asked Paul Channon. It wasn't a question that needed to be answered. It was obvious from the action and the faces of the people on the television in front of them that 'these people' very much did think they were making a difference. The others in this particular room had their own thoughts.

JK was looking at the screen thinking that he was in the wrong department. He always wanted to be at the heart of the action and felt he was missing out on things if he wasn't front and centre. This time he would have to take a back seat. He straightened his tie for the seventh time since they had all sat down. Each time, he moved it only half an inch in one direction or the other. It made no difference to the naked eye but made him feel a hundred times better. JK wanted to look the part. He spent huge sums of money on clothing and having his hair styled. He felt that it made him feel more respectable. Respect wasn't a common commodity in Westminster at the time. All wanted to get ahead, and many felt that this was best achieved by putting others down. JK could play that game as well as anyone, but he liked to be smartly dressed, all the same.

Ellen wasn't listening either. She was scanning the screen for a familiar face, concerned that Harry was caught up in all of this. She knew for a fact that this was his place of work and was told by the television that nobody actually got through to work, whether they wanted to or not. That left Harry outside of the pit and in the crowds that were forming in front of her eyes on the television set that she, Paul, and JK were huddled around. He was nowhere to be seen.

"This needs to be dealt with as soon as possible. There is very little that can be achieved by protest, they should sit down and talk. That is the only future," the minister explained like he was talking to primary school children. He had a way with words that could come off as pompous when trying to calm a situation. He spoke like he had all the knowledge and there wasn't a single person who could teach him anything at all. JK and Ellen were about as close to him as anyone could be, and it was usually water off a duck's back when listening to him. But Ellen found herself concerned about the two good looking and honest men she had met in The Plough.

"Don't they have the right to let their feelings be known?" she asked with a degree of abandon. Going against the wishes and thoughts of the minister could lead to being shown the door. He didn't want to be undermined and felt like he needed confidence in the team around him. Ellen had already shaken this confidence with her repeated questions on Libya. Here was another reason for him to doubt her.

"Grow up El. I don't think that I need to explain the basics of law to you, now do I?" JK stepped in and spoke on behalf of his Boss. Paul smiled across the two of them, making clear his pleasure in what had been said. Ellen turned her attention back to the screen. And there it was, a familiar face getting a lot of media attention. But it wasn't the one she hoped to have seen. Dale was there, taking a most vocal and leading role. She sat forward on her chair to take a closer look. Maybe Harry was there with him. She might see him if she looked more closely.

"The question now is what do we do about this, guys?" Paul Channon asked. He was right. There needed to be a response. None of them had yet put any thought into what that might be. They'd been too engrossed with the scene unfolding on the TV screen in front of them. JK thought it was a television event like an episode of Dallas. He had a warped opinion on just about everything in life and this was no exception. All events were analysed to see if they could be exploited for the good of his career. This one didn't feel like it fit into that mould, so he just derived a sick pleasure from it instead.

JK grinned from ear to ear. "This plays into our hands Minister. These people will make our case for us. The fact that they're stopping work when so many of the rest of us are sat at work for eight hours a day will sway public opinion to us. The government can't lose from this action."

Ellen wasn't so sure. She pointed out what JK had missed. "Those people who are hard at work for eight hours today might see this as their fellow worker being deprived of the right to do exactly the same thing. Don't forget, JK, that many people come to work to feed their family, to put food on the table. You might understand if you ever thought about settling down."

The air turned cold. The room was silent. Paul Channon had got up from the seat to the right of JK and was now pacing up and down behind the other two occupants of the room. Ellen and JK glared at each other like two children who had been told to be quiet by their father.

"There's a lot to think about. And I want to do this on my own. You've got two minutes to pack your stuff up and leave me to it," he explained. JK slowly grabbed the things he'd brought with him. He wanted to be first out of the room to prepare for whatever conversation he and Ellen might continue. Ellen was thankful that she had brought nothing with her. Those last two minutes were spent scanning the television, looking for Harry. But all she saw was Dale. He was still at the forefront of what was going on. Why wasn't Harry with him? She wanted to know he was safe.

Ellen and JK sat in complete silence at their desks, ruminating on what to do next. Ellen had a mound of paperwork to read through and correspondence to answer. She worked better when she was angry and JK had seen to that. But all the time, her mind kept wandering back to the scenes at Cortonwood Colliery. She realised that she desperately wanted to know if Harry was OK.

The day ended for Ellen. She didn't have a set schedule and her Boss trusted her to keep time effectively, but she wanted to stay on his good side today. This, along with the fact that she didn't want to disturb him, meant she worked through until normal time and disappeared.

She trudged home through the rush hour London flow of people and opened her door. The last of the daylight had long gone in the close terraced streets she walked on the last leg of her journey. She felt the cold of the wind on her neck and wished she had worn a scarf when leaving the house that morning.

"You OK Love?" asked Rhys. He had no idea she was worried about a handsome stranger from the North of England. He also missed the wince Ellen gave him, as she had so many times before, as he called her *Love*. The more she grew in her own self-confidence in the male-dominated world of Westminster the more that term grated on her.

"Yes, it's just been a long day. I'm going to run a bath and then probably go to bed," Ellen answered. She just wanted to be alone.

Chapter 9

Thursday 29th March 1984.

Westminster, London, wind and rain with a high of 7°C.

Dusty Miller.

"We can't keep going like this. Something has to give."

The room reverberated with the voice. Nobody inside wanted to listen, but they all knew he was right. Leon Brittan was a large man. As the *Level 42* song went, he barely fit his circumstances. As Secretary of State for the Home Department, he was vying for the position of the most senior person in the room in political terms. The only other candidate for that role in his eyes was Ian MacGregor, Margaret Thatcher's Chairman of the Coal Board. He wasn't a significant player in the government until the start of the tensions surrounding the National Union of Miners and the current stalemate being played out across the nation. Leon Brittan looked across the room with his hands laid across his large belly. He always wore a suit, no matter the occasion. This location was a Ministry of Defence room, deep inside the dark and dusty corridors of the MOD. Not many people had access to rooms this far into the building. One who had was proud to organise and shape the events that day. Dusty Miller.

Miller was part of the old boy's network and loved that tag with all his heart. His scraggy green jumper and stonewashed jeans were at odds with the more formal attire of the rest of the room, but he didn't care one jot. He was on his home ground. They would have to dance to his tune. Miller was one of the people who could just come and go as he pleased in most corners of the MOD. His status meant he didn't have to stop or bow to anyone. And whenever he got the chance, he rubbed this in the faces of the politicians that made his life hell most of the year. Like a cockroach, no matter what happened in the world, he would survive. They say that roaches would survive a nuclear war and still thrive. Miller was built from the same stuff and, if the MOD estimates were right, he could survive the nuclear winter that followed an atomic bomb for some time inside the Ministry's bunker. Top secret, of course.

"There is too much publicity relating to this. The people smell a rat. They're firmly on the side of the miners and we're losing popularity every day. The longer we let this go on, the worse it will get for us. I know I'm in a fairly safe seat, but many of my colleagues will lose theirs. Being out of power is too much of a pain to bear," Brittan continued, knowing he had the ears of the rest of the room. He wondered how much of this was being recorded and monitored. In the Ministry of Defence at the heart of one of the most invasive governments in the world, he knew that there would be some way of bugging the room if anyone wanted or needed to. That might run all the way to the top as far as he was concerned. Even if some of the words that came out of his mouth were not his true feelings, he felt he should toe the party line as much as he could.

"I'm not sure how much I care about your colleagues. Or your desperate cling to power, Minister. There are more pressing needs. And better ways to deal with this than words from a politician," Miller responded.

Ian MacGregor looked across the other faces and saw a lack of life, a lack of energy. If anyone was to stand up to the two other voices, he figured it had to be him. He wasn't the tallest or strongest specimen of a human being, nor a career politician. Having made his name in industry, MacGregor decided he needed to give something back. The fact that he was now caught up in a department that was causing his Boss a great degree of pain meant he had to act quickly. The truth at that moment in time was that he (and his team) had run out of ideas. The miners had gained a lot of momentum and developed sympathy in the public eye. MacGregor didn't know what to do to counter that. He spoke with a soft voice but was determined to be heard.

"There's jobs on the line here either way. The miners are fighting for their livelihood. We are too, Miller. Don't forget that." He was pleased with his opening salvo. It was the kind of speech that laid down a marker. He took a deep breath, ready to continue as Brittan caught his eye. He was mouthing 'well done,' but MacGregor was a hopeless lip-reader and had no idea what message his government colleague was passing on. He swallowed and spoke again. "Don't think that we won't fight as hard as these miners. And we have enough power to take the fight a lot further.

They've captured the hearts and minds of the public. We need to wrestle that away from them. There must be something we can do."

"As it happens, there is," replied Dusty Miller with a grin etching its way across his face, starting at the eyes and moving South until it reached his mouth. Miller knew a smile would speak a thousand words where he didn't want to. Let them read between the lines, he thought, let them fill in the blanks.

The eyes of the rest of the room joined him in a smile. They were all smiling together when Miller next spoke. He wasn't quite sure of the words but was prepared to see where it all took him.

"Remember the Falklands War? Quite a handy little escapade for your government, don't you think? The positivity towards your dear Maggie was immense after the war. It got the press onside, made the voters feel like they were protected and kept you in power. Not bad for the loss of a few lives. There are other wars to be had. Maybe not so public, maybe not so costly for our armed forces but something that could take the wind out of the miner's sails, if you know what I mean," Miller spoke in the clearest language he would allow himself. Anything more direct and he could cause a huge amount of trouble for his bosses; anything less and the dumb politicians might not understand what he was talking about. One clearly did.

From the back of the room, a voice piped up. It was male, they were all male, and shrouded in the darkness of the far reaches of the room. "Do you mean Libya?"

That was all Miller needed. He'd sown the idea in the heads of the room without actually saying it himself. This wasn't something they taught in the MOD, but it was a skill he had picked up during his time there. Nobody could trace it back to him, nobody could point the finger. But the seed was definitely sown. Now to water it.

"What do you mean?" he asked in his most sarcastic voice, one that he'd been practicing all day.

"We could use the escalating tensions in Libya to divert the attention away from the miners. The press will go for it, the TV will go for it and the public will have no choice but to follow. What's the other option? Wait for this to blow over? I'm not so sure that will happen."

The voice was right. Something active had to be done. The faces of the senior politicians were a picture. They wanted to get out of there as soon as possible. It was one thing hearing all of this but being implicated at a point in the future was going to be politically harmful. MacGregor and Brittan looked at each other as if to say, 'let's go,' and Miller spotted this reaction. It was one he had been waiting for.

"Gentlemen, we're all in a safe place here. This isn't an official meeting; this isn't an official room. You won't see it on any plans or hear of it in any descriptions of the place. It doesn't exist. And nor do any conversations that are had in here. Let's all settle down and get to work. This could keep all of you and your paymasters happy," Dusty Miller spoke. He had an air of calm and authority that washed over the rest of the room.

As the night grew from young to old, Miller and the others laid out the details of how they would wrestle the initiative from the miners. It wasn't fair play, but they had the power and tools at their disposal to make things work the way they wanted. The night passed overhead but none of the men realised. The security of the room meant no windows and the only door itself was at the end of a corridor no one would be walking down. They even got used to the fact that there were no refreshments. Leon Brittan undid his tie slightly at one stage, there was so much pressure. The only one not feeling it was Dusty Miller. He was planning for a busy few weeks. He had work to do.

* * *

A couple of weeks later Ellen was finally able to take a day off and enjoy the beginning of Spring. She liked to rise as early on her days away from the office as she did when going to work. Ellen told herself that she would be thankful in later life when all of this became a habit. For all her modernity she still felt that as a mother and wife, which she believed would eventually happen, it was good practice to be the first one up in the morning and the last to bed at night.

The streets were starting to fill with people heading off to work in the various parts of London. The Tube was by far the most popular method of transport in the city, but people needed to get from their front door to the underground station, and then from the station to their place of work so there were always bodies in the streets of London at rush hour and beyond. As one of the busiest capital cities in the world, and one of the global financial centres, it was a city that felt like it was full of bustle. The fact that this Spring day had started wet and grey kept the pace of the people up as they rushed to find cover.

As the morning showers cleared Ellen spent a few minutes looking in the window of each shop she passed as though it would prepare her better for when the doors opened, and she was finally allowed to enter. Shop assistants looked in her direction and offered a vague smile while they waited for someone inside to let them in to get ready for their shift. But none offered any words. Save all the talk until they were on the clock and being paid for their time. Ellen felt the same. The time before she started work was her own and she protected it with all her might.

Looking in shop windows always made Ellen eager to buy. The displays told of a lifestyle that she had always wanted. Not too ostentatious, but elegant enough to aspire to. Images of a home where she served food on fancy crockery with stainless steel cutlery on a solid wood table appealed to the host in her. Ellen was picturing a future where she was the reigning queen of her own country estate when a voice disturbed her fantasy and brought her back to the real world.

"Is that you? It can't be you? Ellen Minor?" the voice asked these three questions in fewer than three seconds. Ellen turned around and found in front of her a man that she didn't recognise at first. Maybe it was the fact that she still had one foot in the country manor, but something stopped her from putting a name to that face, or a location to it either. She looked into the eyes; for Ellen it was always the eyes that told a story. She paused, waiting for her brain to click into gear. Timothy Philpot, of course, but something was different.

"Hello Tim, how are you?" Ellen looked him up and down as they spoke, searching for whatever it was that had stopped her from recalling him instantly. Was it his hair? No, that was a little longer than she remembered but not different enough for him to be incognito. Was it his shoes? No, they were as shiny as ever. Tim was known for the cleanliness of his shoes and also for the way he judged others on their shoeshine. Ellen thanked herself that she took the extra minute or so that morning to give them an extra polish. She was sure Tim had already noticed but pushed her toes forward anyway so there could be no doubt. How about the beard? She hadn't seen him with one before, but there wasn't a great deal of it and the only thing it made him look was a few years older. The glasses! That was it! Ellen had never seen Tim in glasses before. These were horn-rimmed glasses with a thick frame that seemed to cover half of his face. Tim was a man with a small face and the last thing he needed was a large pair of glasses. Ellen chuckled inside before continuing the conversation.

"What's up with you? How's work? What's your latest scoop?" She decided that his technique of firing multiple questions to others was also the way he wanted to receive questions. It was part of her training. Mirror the conversation techniques of the other person to make them feel at home. It had stood her in good stead so far.

"Do you know what? I was just about to ask you the same thing." Tim paused as though it was Ellen's turn to talk. She held fast and waited for him to realise that she had asked first. It took around 20 seconds, but he twigged that she wasn't going to give up any information until he did.

"There's a lot of talk about Libya," he said while looking around to ensure there weren't any ears pointed in his direction. Tim felt bold enough to continue. "It's as though the government's trying to drum up as much noise as possible about Libya, so people's attention is diverted there instead of somewhere else. There's definitely something in the works."

As a journalist for The Times, Tim saw the inside of what happened inside the worlds of business and politics. When he first joined the newspaper, he thought that business was separated from the political world by a wall of money and power. How wrong he was. The two were intertwined and he was one of the people Ellen could rely upon to share and guide on what he knew. She now had to imprint on her mind the image of Tim with large glasses instead of a face free from obstruction. She was sure she would be able to do this in future.

"What do you mean?" she replied with an air of innocence that they both knew wasn't real.

"Just that. There's so much noise and it all seems to be coming from one place. Westminster. I can usually tell when a story is global, national or local. This one is very local. All the talk about Libya emanates from the government and the corridors of power. It has a lot of people spooked," he explained in no uncertain terms to Ellen. She got the message loud and clear.

"I'm not sure that I've been kept in the loop with all of this," Ellen blurted out without thinking. She wished she'd engaged her brain before opening her mouth. She needn't have worried. Tim didn't bat an eyelid and smiled as he said his goodbye.

Walking along the street, Ellen felt the need to sit down and take it all in. She stopped at the first café, a new styled French coffee shop, on the corner of a busy junction. It was a little closer to the country estate daydream at least. As she sat, Ellen thought long and hard about recent events.

Paul is playing me for a fool. As his press secretary, I should know the way he is operating. I know he likes to work based on plausible deniability, but I don't. There is a lot that a clued-up press secretary can do. But one that operates in the dark isn't a great deal of use to anyone at all.

There might be a lot of noise going on about Libya, while at the same time I had overheard Paul twice in conversations about the place, but I can't just put two and two together. Four is the obvious answer but it could be five, six or seven for all I know. Would he have lied to me? Would he have deliberately misled me over this? I have to assume not. Otherwise there isn't a lot of point in me turning up for work tomorrow.

Ellen sat and looked across the busy junction as car after car waited at the give way sign before proceeding when the coast was clear. Every now and again a car jumped too early and caused another on the main road to brake sharply. Horns were sounded, tempers flared but all of this was lost on Ellen. She looked out of the window in the direction of the movement but took none of it in. Her mind was on a country that she knew was far away but had little other understanding of. Ellen was wondering how deep her Boss was mired in Libya. She wondered if she was being dragged down with him.

Chapter 10

Thursday 8th April 1984.

St. John's Wood, London, wind and rain, with a high of 7°C.

Ellen.

Rhys wanted answers. He and Ellen hadn't been getting on as well lately, he felt things were going to slide further and he was unsure on what the problem was. He had known Ellen for several years and worked things in exactly the right way. At first, they dated, often with other people and always in a public place. He didn't want anyone to get the wrong idea. He was an honourable man and wanted the world to know this at all times. Later, as he got to know her better, he made sure she was treated with respect and felt like her place was with him. The little gestures like flowers every now and again, not just on her birthday, and writing her the odd letter were what Rhys used to keep Ellen happy and involved in the relationship. Both of them worked long hours at times, so it wasn't always easy to make the time that many couples enjoyed naturally. It was only after they had courted for a full six months that he asked her to move in with him, making a call to also ask her father to ensure everything had been done properly.

Rhys waited at home for Ellen to arrive. She had started the workday late, so he thought it only natural she would end it late too. She worked a full eight-hour day most of the time, so he calculated that she would arrive back around half past seven. He made sure the dinner was ready for her return, a bath run with only hot water and a bottle of wine open. This would get her in a relaxed mood and open up the conversation that he had been sitting on for a few weeks now. The atmosphere between them wasn't what it should be, and he was desperate to know why.

As the front door opened, Ellen could smell the casserole in the oven, fortunately this was overpowering the enduring cigarette smell that was clearly there too. But Ellen immediately felt at home. The day, like her week, had been long and monotonous and filled her with little joy. Only thoughts of Libya and what it might mean for her had been any kind of distraction and not a positive one. The walk home felt pretty much the same. The smell from the kitchen was enough to wash most of that away. She spotted the opened bottle of red wine and the two empty glasses next to it and smiled for the first time. Rhys was a good man, she had no doubt about that, and he obviously adored her. Yet she wondered if that was enough.

"I've run you a bath. All hot, so you may have to add a bit of cold in," Rhys shouted from the living room, fighting with the television for volume control. He just about made himself heard.

"Thanks Rhys. See you in a little while. Mind if I take a glass of wine up with me?"

"Of course not. Enjoy!"

If only every evening could be like this, Rhys thought. *If only I could see the best of Ellen every day. If I'm not getting the best of her then I wonder who is. I bet it's that boss of hers, working her into the ground. I don't know why she puts up with it.*

The next twenty minutes or so felt like they took several hours for Rhys. When he wanted to get on with something, every second spent waiting dragged. He was thankful for the fact that Ellen didn't mess around when getting ready. Some of his ex-girlfriends took over an hour to wash, dry their hair and get ready when coming in from work. Ellen looked beautiful without all of that pampering and Rhys hoped it would stay that way. She bumbled down the stairs, Rhys frequently likened her to a baby elephant in this respect, before arriving at the dining table in time for him to bring through two plates of dinner that smelled divine. Ellen set her empty glass down on the table and nodded towards him for a refill. He obliged and the two of them tucked into their casserole dinner without as much as a word.

"Thanks Rhys. This is really nice," Ellen said in between mouthfuls.

"No problem. You know how I enjoy cooking when I get the chance. You know me better than anyone," he replied. Ellen blushed. She didn't like people pointing out things about her, no matter how complementary.

"You're a good cook. I'm a lucky girl," she responded hoping to keep the conversation on a positive keel. She could always sense when there was some tension in Rhys. This was one of those occasions. The way he fumbled with his knife as though it was the first time he had used one. The way he wiped sweat from his brow with his napkin. The way he strained his words as though each one needed to be checked for accuracy before being delivered. She looked across the table, hoping to see a smile on his face, a calm that belied the signals she was picking up. She saw nothing but a frown.

"Then why don't you act like one?" he snapped. Rhys didn't look in her direction. It was another strong sign that he wasn't happy. "We've been living together for far too long now. I've been wanting to propose to you, but I get the feeling you don't even want to be here. Every time I bring up the future you change the conversation. That doesn't sound like the actions of a lucky girl, now does it?"

Rhys was almost shouting by this point. Ellen looked around the room for escape routes. It was her own home, but she needed to familiarise herself with all available exits, as though she was on an airplane and listening to the safety instructions before the flight.

"Marriage?" her heart sank, and for the first time she really knew that Rhys wasn't the man for her. "There's so much going on right now for me. You know the pressures of my job better than just about anyone. I promise it will change," Ellen lied. She wanted to buy time. All she could think about most days was Harry. Rhys never really crossed her mind at all.

"At this rate it will never happen, Ellen. I just want you to commit to me. It feels like I'm playing second fiddle to someone. Who might that be?" he demanded.

"For God's sake Ree. You need to grow up a bit. Between my job and you there's no time left to do anything but sleep. Who do you think it might be? Margaret Thatcher?"

"Don't call me Ree. You need to be straight with me. I'm sitting here waiting for you. I have put my life on hold for you, waiting for the day you will be my bride. I want you, but if you don't want me then you should set me free. At least then I could get on with my life," Rhys replied with all the intent in the world. He knew that if he pushed her far enough, he would get an answer one way or another.

"Rhys don't push me!" Ellen shouted at the top of her voice. She felt like she had nothing to lose.

"I want to know what's going on. I demand to know. Tell me what on earth is happening to us. You're more and more distant every time we speak."

"How about this for distant!" Ellen screamed before storming out of their home. She grabbed her coat on the way out and splashed into a puddle with her first stride. The heavens had opened since she had returned from work and now she stood outside in sandals and a coat with no hood. She didn't care. Again, her mind went back to Harry and the way he had treated her. She felt safe when she was close to him, safe in a way that Rhys had never made her feel. She had a decision to make, but it didn't feel like there was any option but to be with Harry. She hardly knew him and he lived a long distance away and came from a totally different world, but Ellen felt like she had known him all her life. She was as clear about this as anything she had been in her whole life. Harry was the man she wanted to be with. As Ellen walked aimlessly along the street away from her home and the argument with Rhys, all she could imagine was being close to Harry. She wanted to spend time with him and get to know him. Ellen set her course for a new chapter in her life. She was excited and terrified all at once and barely registered the cold seeping into her.

*   *   *

Bzzzz, bzzzz, bzzzz.

As the phone rang, the occupant of suite 126 looked across from the bathroom. He was sure the noise would go away. Emptying the minibar in the hotel last night suddenly felt like a bad idea when his head was ringing louder than the phone. It was one of the ways in which he switched off from his job, one of the ways he forgot about the work he did. He was a professional. He was someone that his employer could rely on one hundred percent.

The phone didn't stop. He would have to answer it. He knew the ring would go on all morning if he let it. There were so few people in the world that knew he was there. If they were contacting him then this was the chance to earn some more money. His gambling debts had taken over his life for the past few months. Every job he took would put him on the road to paying them off and keeping the nasty people he bet with from finishing him off. He controlled so much in his life that it was always a source of disappointment when he thought about the way he frittered hard-earned cash on the horses. So, he stopped thinking about it... with the help of alcohol, of course.

Rainer Karg was a strong man who might have fitted the Aryan ideal of the German army in the 1940's had he been around in those days. Tall, with cropped blonde hair and blue eyes, the kind that pierced anyone he set them on. And you didn't want Karg to set his eyes on you. He was a hitman, a gun for hire if you had the right contact and enough money. In terms of international hitmen, he was considered the best by the very few in the know. One of those in the know was at the other end of the phone waiting for him to pick up. Karg walked naked across the room, still drying himself from the shower with a towel that was far too small for a man of his size. He couldn't even wrap it around his waist to cover himself if needed. Good job there was nobody else present.

"Suite 126," he answered the phone.

"The wind blows cold across London tonight," the voice at the other end of the phone spoke in a clipped accent that could have only been a native English voice. Karg already knew who it was. He didn't have a lot of contacts in London. This one always played first contact by the rules. First the code, then the reply. Answering in one way told the voice at the other end of the phone that he was alone, could talk and was available for work. Answering in another way told any caller to try again later. You never know, Karg might have struck lucky and been in the presence of a girl. No risks, complete professionalism. That's what kept him in demand.

"And it looks like rain," Karg answered. He was sure the man at the other end of the line could hear the smile in his speech. This contact paid well. He had his sights set on a return to his homeland of Austria, but the lure of the cash was too much to turn down. He wanted to see his son, who was living with his ex-wife. It was painful being away from the six-year-old for months at a time, but this life was all Karg knew. The prospect of a nine to five job filled him with more fear than killing another man.

"My friend, how are you?" Karg asked. It was protocol to never mention names when making or receiving these calls. Dusty Miller at the other end of the line was following the same rules.

"I've never been better," Miller retorted while suppressing a cough that was growing in his throat. He reached into the left pocket of his coat and pulled out a pack of Benson & Hedges cigarettes. It wasn't the best cure for a tickly throat, but it was all Miller used. "And you, how's things for you?"

"I'm fine," Karg replied, "just finishing up here and looking forward to going home for a few weeks." He spoke directly to flush out the intentions of his caller. Karg didn't have time for small talk, even with a friend. His conversations with other human beings were rare. In his line of work, he didn't have a secretary or colleagues to discuss matters with. His clients were shadows and his customers were corpses not long after they met.

"Home. Where is that for you now? The world is your home, no?" Dusty Miller tried to divert Karg from his intention of flying home. He wanted him to stay around for a few days. He didn't have an exact target in mind at that time but knew that he would need the service of a reliable hitman in the very near future.

"Home is Austria. Always has been and always will be. I might travel the world, but my family is back in Vienna," Karg responded with some irritation, even though his ex-wife and son lived in Innsbruck, "let's cut the small talk. There's only one reason you're calling me. Do I need to cancel my flight home?"

"That would be a good idea," Miller told him with a degree of certainty that Karg wasn't expecting. Usually Miller danced around the subject until Karg stepped in and made the decision for him. Karg had always thought this was a tactic employed by Miller in the early days. But the more he worked for the guy, the more he became used to the way he worked. He got to the point where he just let the man get on with it. This was different. This time Miller was taking the initiative.

"I'm ready when you are. All I need is for you to pick up the bill for the hotel while I'm waiting around. You know the routine, all my food and drink, room service, the lot. And then the rest is at the usual rate," Karg explained to his contact in the MOD. He'd thought about putting up his price for a job. After all, they couldn't advertise in the local newspaper for someone to kill people. He was a rare find for the MOD, CIA or any other organisation that called him. They would have to pay the rate he demanded. Even with money problems, he didn't want to get greedy. Being bold when sitting, thinking about his money was one thing. In actual conversations with others he wasn't quite so confident. But his normal rate was more money than most of the people walking to work on the streets of London below his suite would earn in a couple of years.

"That's fine. I'll call through to the hotel reception when I've finished speaking to you. We'll make all the arrangements and then I'll call when I have the full details. I'm sure you'll like this one. It's right up your street," Miller replied. It was as casual as you like, not the kind of conversation you would expect from two men discussing the end of life for another human being.

Almost at once, Karg rang off. He had all the information he needed and was thinking about when someone from the cleaning service would arrive to sort out his bed and, more importantly, to refill the minibar. The banging head from his drinking the night before was showing no sign of receding, so he decided that topping up his alcohol level was the best course of action.

Miller smiled. He loved being involved in the shadows, plotting the course of the world while others sat back and watched it all unfold around them. He never felt like he was going to be a passenger in life. At school he was the one that organised others to challenge authority but never got his hands dirty. The petition to get one of the teachers sacked was instigated by him but his name never appeared on anything related to it whatever he had started. He operated in the background and was never linked to it. The fact that those with their name at the very top of the paper found the rest of their school life an absolute misery wasn't his problem. He had a teacher he didn't like fired and he was happy about it. That was Miller's first taste of working from the shadows and he loved it. He had carried on in the shadows ever since. Just like the night a few weeks before inside the MOD, the motivations and greed of others allowed him to play with incredible power without any personal recourse.

Karg dressed in his usual black jeans, t-shirt with military-style lace-up boots. He liked to be ready at a moment's notice, but all that came this time was a porter to restock his minibar. He switched the radio on to Paul McCartney's Pipes of Peace and set about the whisky first. Straight from the bottle, without any mixer. He didn't like the taste but needed that hit. He wanted to forget. Karg fell back into a deep sleep. He dreamt of his son, going back to Austria and tasting the pastries from his parent's bakery again. But the phone call he had a few hours earlier had made this dream distant in the real world. At the same time, it kept his illegal bookmakers at bay. Karg would have another wedge of money to give them in the coming days or weeks. He would be closer to staying on the right side of them. He slept like a baby.

Chapter 11

Monday 16th April 1984.

North London, cloudy, windy with a high of 10°C.

Ellen.

Ellen had longed to go back to Yorkshire ever since the row with Rhys. The juxtaposed proposal mixed with the harsh words of her boyfriend rang in her ears whenever she let it. Shutting out noise was something she had learned to deal with over her years as a press secretary. Working with the press meant she was exposed to all manner of rumours and hearsay. She just had to learn to blank it out. But when it was this personal, that was so much more difficult to do. She filled her days with work, stayed late and got in early the next morning. The only time in between was the hours where she got ready for bed, slept or prepared for the following day's work. She was living with her brother in his small Bayswater flat, sleeping on the sofa. It was far from ideal, but the change was good for her. She felt fresher and freer not being beholden to Rhys and his constant conscious and sub-conscious questions. He was a good man, but he wasn't the right one for her and this realisation made her feel like a caged bird that had been let free to fly. And Yorkshire was where she wanted to fly too. A sensible girl, Ellen had told herself that it was the way people were there. She persuaded herself that she wanted to be around people who spoke their mind rather than deliver her riddles. But deep down she knew that it was Harry drawing her North.

"Are we all set for the day?" asked Paul as he looked out of the window of the British Rail InterCity125 as it sped out of London. From Ellen's perspective it didn't appear that Paul Channon had a care in the world. He sat looking at the scenery like it was the most pressing engagement he could possibly have in his life. Maybe it was his way of switching off. Ellen couldn't explain it in any other manner.

JK, on the other hand, was a flurry of activity. Never one to sit still and rest on his laurels, he was making notes at a pace that Ellen could never match. She wondered if the result was legible. She didn't wonder for long. JK handed over a sheet of paper with a series of ideas to work on as a department. He wanted Ellen's input, he said. What that really meant was that he wanted Ellen to make things happen. A manipulator at the best of times, JK was on overdrive with his machinations. The Department of Trade's Permanent Secretary knew that his Boss would see a lot of action over the coming months with the miners looking like they would cause a headache at the very least for the government. JK felt this was his chance to continue to build his reputation. He had seen other permanent secretaries become in high demand when they handled a crisis with grace and style. He wanted Paul Channon to cop some flak, so that he in turn could help the minister out.

Ellen scanned the page. It wasn't really sinking in, but she would have to provide answers, that much was clear. She went back to the top of the page and looked at the items one by one. JK wanted her to use up a lot of favours that she'd built up over the previous year. She would be all out of credit for a while if she carried out all his instructions to the letter, that was obvious. Maybe there was a different way of doing this. But JK didn't deal in maybes.

Apparently neither did Rhys. The promise of a future together wasn't enough for him. The lure of a beautiful girl with a career was fine to begin with but soon faded into the background when he wanted to trade an unspoken promise to the definite. The pressure made Ellen sure that there was not going to be a wedding, a honeymoon, a life together and whatever else Rhys had in mind. Harry was different. He didn't expect anything of her, he just liked her for who she was.

"Well?" Ellen heard a male voice ask. Her Boss Paul Channon had broken his own fixation with the countryside and expected an answer.

"Are we all set for the day?" he asked.

She had forgotten that he had spoken.

"Yes, I'm just going through these notes from JK, but we have everything lined up as expected." It was a straightforward series of meetings and handshakes. The day was over in a flash with little to stir the memory. Ellen was thankful for that. The evening promised something different, and maybe a little more memorable.

She had arranged to meet with Harry. This time it felt more like a date than a random meeting. They arranged to meet at a restaurant near to the hotel she was staying in with Paul and JK. The two of whom had invited Ellen to eat and talk through the day in Paul's room, with room service providing all the food and drink they needed. Ellen had declined to join them. Paul seemed nonplussed and JK was happy to get rid of her. He felt that the *boys* worked better together. JK was always resentful of Ellen's place in the team. He felt it should have gone to his friend, Dan Winton. But when Ellen got the role, he conceded defeat. As influential as he was, even JK couldn't overturn a decision like that once it was made. If he made Ellen's life a little uncomfortable at times it was only because he still felt Dan should have been given that role.

Ellen hadn't told JK or Paul that she had split from Rhys. On one hand it was none of their business. On the other she didn't want them to know. JK thought himself a bit of a lady's man, while Paul was at that age where men looked for that last fling before they got too old. She didn't want to fend off advances from either of them, let alone both.

Ellen set off on foot to the restaurant to find Harry standing outside smoking one of his No.6 cigarettes. In contrast to Ellen's morning, it was a pleasant Spring evening and Harry's bus journey over from his hometown had taken far less time than he had initially expected.

"Good evening," Harry said, expelling the smoke via a smile that lit up his face. Ellen blushed slightly. "Shall we go inside?" he continued.

"Yes," Ellen replied as she got close. They embraced in a way that belied the way they felt. Barely touching anything but arms and shoulders. Ellen hoped the hug at the end of the night would feel very different.

Once inside the restaurant, Harry was bowled over by the range of options on the menu. "At The Plough we have the choice of pie and chips or sausage and chips. And that's on a good day!"

Ellen was reminded that they were from very different worlds. They felt at one when she was with him but had to acknowledge that there would be some new experiences for both of them if they were to get together. Harry settled quickly, and the conversation flowed.

"What was the picket like? I saw the scenes on TV and couldn't pick you out from the crowd. I was worried," Ellen admitted with the concern that was in her heart.

"It was actually quite calm," Harry joked, "just like a normal night out for us Northerners!"

Ellen loved the way he took everything with equal measure. He made her feel calm and at one. She looked across the restaurant and wondered if anyone else there felt that same sense of protection from whomever they were with. She doubted it. But something ate away at the back of her mind while they spoke. The talk of the picket line amazed her. She was both excited and concerned for Harry being involved in such a potentially dangerous situation. He told of Dale's increasing involvement in the movement. He joked about the militant blood in Dale's veins and wondered where it had come from. Ellen was reminded of that first encounter and how Dale had held her attention. Her interest in Harry suddenly wobbled. Perhaps this attraction was less about interest in Harry, or even Dale for that matter, and more about her deeper issues with Rhys.

She shook the feeling quickly and focused on something else she needed to address.

"Harry, I need to speak to you. I've got something to get off my chest."

Harry sat forward at the very edge of his chair.

"I've recently overheard some discussions that were not meant for me," she began as she realised the irony in having this conversation in a public place where others could hear something *they* were not meant to hear. "It's about Libya." Harry knew that Libya was a place and had overheard the name on the evening news while eating his dinner but nothing more than that came to mind when he heard the odd word, obviously not English.

"I think that my Boss is involved in something illegal there. I think that he has some shady contacts there and that there is a financial element to this. I can't quite put my finger on it, but there's something not quite right," she continued, looking for support from Harry.

"What does that mean?" Harry asked. "Why would a member of the government need any more money than the huge sum he is being paid?"

Ellen looked on his face for the sign that he was telling a joke, but no sign followed. She smiled at Harry's naivety.

"Because they are all greedy. Because they can. Because money buys influence. There are a thousand reasons that they would do this for," she reeled off the first few ideas that came to her mind. Harry's face didn't change.

"And this makes their life better?" he asked with a large scoop of confusion. He had no idea why someone would risk their happiness for more money. Not the world he was involved in. As the night deepened, Ellen took the time to explain further the dealings that she had to endure in Westminster. Harry was captivated, by her and her world.

*   *   *

Back in London, Dusty Miller was pulling one of those faces. The one where he hoped a furrowed brow would stop anyone else from talking to him. Sitting in the canteen at the Ministry of Defence wasn't his idea of a good time but every now and again, usually when the weather was awful, he would sit and have something to eat and drink there. On this occasion it wasn't the weather outside that was keeping him close to his office, but the storm brewing inside his head. There was always a lot going on, but this felt different to Dusty. It felt like some of the elements were out of his control. He had to fight to get them back to where he wanted them.

Other occupants of the room took heed from the way he looked and gave him a wide berth. Part of that could have been down to his camouflaged outfit of choice. The brown suit, brown shirt and brown tie he wore distinguished him from most of the other people in the Ministry. While they wanted to be seen for the next promotion or recognition, Dusty wanted to fade into the background. In a room full of dark suits, white shirts and bright ties, this made Dusty stand out from the crowd. In a dusty, dark basement cafeteria however it had the opposite effect. It was as if the suit designer and the decorator had got together to match colours. Dusty might as well have been invisible from the neck down. That suited his mood.

The last few days hadn't gone to plan. He liked working from the shadows and making things happen in his own way. But the events of the world didn't always follow the plans of Dusty Miller. Sometimes he just had to accept that he couldn't turn things around. His employers didn't expect that he could work miracles. But they did expect that he was successful more often than not. It was this success rate that kept him in demand. The government liked to control the lives of the people in the country. It wasn't like a dictatorship where the army and police cracked down on behaviour. This was something far subtler than that. Events that unfolded on the television screens and across the front pages of the newspapers weren't always what they seemed. And in order to affect control it was the likes of Dusty Miller that guided things to happen at the time they happened and often in a certain way.

The time in the staff canteen was a painful one for Dusty. His left knee had been playing up for the last few years and this was exacerbated by the ongoing damp weather. The physical pain was matched by the temper he was developing over his work. It was easy to meddle in the fortunes of another country. There was always someone in power to bribe or persuade in some other way. It felt more difficult when doing it in his own back yard.

Dusty stood up, first putting his weight on the good knee before applying pressure to the other. It started when he'd played sports in his younger days. A hefty tackle from a prop forward was the first time it buckled. His knee was never the same again. He never played rugby after that, preferring to concentrate on his work rather than pleasure. He had mulled over it enough. There were a thousand things he could do to wrestle control back and make the situation work to the advantage of the people who were paying him. Dusty marched to his office to abate his temper and take action. Sometimes he needed a moment of clarity. Somewhere in the cold tea he must have found that.

Dusty returned to his desk. The most spartan of places to work, he didn't like all the family photos, memorabilia and tat that others managed to collect throughout their life and bring to work. If it wasn't a tool of the trade, Dusty didn't think it should have any place in the office. As such, his desk comprised of a pen, notebook and a telephone. Even the pen and notebook aroused suspicion. He didn't want anyone rifling through his bin and finding anything incriminating. On the rare occasion he did write anything down, the note would come home with him and end up on the fire. He limited his risks, no matter how small.

He stared at the phone. It was time to make a call. He dialled a series of numbers. Dusty had always had a photographic memory for numbers. Names and faces he could forget. Numbers stayed with him for life. The dialling tone started, and he waited for the other end to pick up. A nondescript voice answered.

"Hello, who do you need?" A gatekeeper. Dusty hated these guys. They talked in code and did whatever they pleased. If this man didn't want him to make contact, then it wouldn't happen. He might have to play this carefully.

"The Eagle, please, if I may?" Dusty replied. He was picking up more of an accent from the gatekeeper, a well-educated English accent from the Home Counties if he wasn't mistaken. It wasn't the voice he expected. When someone found a safe place in England, they would hide and tell nobody. When they found a safe place anywhere else in the world, they told as many of their allies as they could. Only people they could trust implicitly, but it was their role to extend this protection. It was obvious that the man Dusty wanted to speak too had opened up his sanctuary to the people around him. They were probably all in the same line of work.

"Hmmm," the Eagle came to the phone but didn't want to give too much away.

"Eagle, it's DM. I need your help," Dusty spoke. He didn't feel the need for the same level of anonymity as the voice at the other end of the line. He was protected. Dusty continued, "there's a rally tomorrow. Some anti-Gaddafi people are planning to spend some time making noise outside of the Libyan embassy. I understand that some of your friends may be attending to provide opposition to this."

"Hmmm," came the response again.

"I wondered if some money might help make their opposition felt a little more deeply. I know this is your field of expertise."

"That's something we can do. I'm aware of the rally too. Shall we arrange a price now or later?" Tarek asked, already knowing what the answer was. He liked working with Dusty. He always paid well.

"The usual," Dusty replied after a few seconds thought. He scanned his brain for the figure the two of them agreed the last time he needed a crowd to make a counter noise. It was acceptable. "How many people can you muster? I need quite a distraction. We don't want those anti-Gaddafi protestors to have it all their own way, now do we?"

"I'll get what you need. I have ears to the ground. I'll find out what the other side is doing, and I'll match them. This way we get our point across without scaring them or the news crews off."

"Sounds perfect."

Dusty returned the phone to the receiver and grinned, satisfied with the plan. He hadn't much practice in smiling over the years and this one came out awkwardly but with nobody there to see he didn't much care. He was back on track, shaping the world the way he wanted it to look. Dusty knew that he wouldn't be in this career for life. It took the toll on his health, and he coped with the stress with other habits that were hardly conducive to health. Once the call had ended, he pulled a packet of Rothmans from his pocket and proceeded to light one with an old lighter that looked like it too was on its last legs.

The cigarette tasted bitter but the action he had taken provided the sweetness he savoured. He was a man of simple pleasures. A drink, a cigarette and the ability to change world events for the benefit of his paymasters. What else could a man want?

The next few days would be a test of his ability to get things done. If the countercoup was to be a success in London, then it would prime another action that had started in the brain of Dusty Miller. Rainer Karg had been waiting in his hotel for the call. Dusty had made that call. He had work to do. Dusty looked at the pieces of his masterpiece and felt the need to write them down. He knew that the pieces of paper would end up on the fire soon after, but he couldn't help getting these words down in his shaky handwriting just the once. He started to write –

Tarek and his crew will provide the backdrop. They will make enough noise that we will be able to enact part 2.

Karg will use this to...

There was a knock at the door. Miller grabbed the paper and shoved it into the inside pocket of his suit. The note would remain unfinished. It was destined for the fire. The interruption didn't last long but it was enough to distract Miller and remind him that he was playing with fire again. He loved being in this position. He now longed for the next 48 hours.

Chapter 12

Ellen wanted to see Harry. Sitting back in the London chambers of her Boss, Paul did nothing for her soul. She was happy that there was a lot going on in Westminster to distract her from her feelings, but this wasn't always enough. If only she could work 24 hours a day and be totally distracted from the person she truly wanted to be with. But life wasn't like that. Even the disturbance of working with JK had become boring. In the past she had always been able to rely on him being a pain to stop her from over-thinking. He would come up with the most ridiculous ideas and the arguments could go on for hours if left unchecked. But now she dismissed him pretty quickly and moved on. She sat with JK and talked about what was going on in their own small world, though others considered it large. The bubble of government. The machinations of politics meant that there was always something (or someone) to talk about. Though never the end user, Joe Public. Ellen didn't get too involved but wasn't frightened to admit she liked to listen to the gossip. Never one to pass it on, but often one to absorb it in case she needed it at some stage in the future. The role of a press secretary was one where knowledge was vital. Knowing what others didn't, was, well, always going to be an added bonus.

The day's news was awful, and they knew a late night was ahead of them when the minister arrived. By way of avoiding the elephant in the room, JK was telling a story verging on gossip. Worse still, Ellen found herself engaged and listening when Paul Channon walked in. He overheard the end of one conversation and the start of another. But nothing he could put together –

"... and he has always said the same things. He would never sell his soul for a promotion," said JK. "And there is the woman he was dating a while back. I can't remember her name. Is it the one who now works with...?"

JK stopped dead. It wasn't something that Paul Channon hadn't been guilty of himself at times in the past but none of them wanted to be caught in the middle of that type of conversation. JK wasn't as reticent as Ellen, and it was him that had done all the talking, but Ellen flushed a shade of reddish pink. She didn't want Paul to think she was snooping more than usual. There was still the air of tension between she and Paul regarding the Libya question.

"Are you guys coming through? The news will be starting in a few minutes and I'd like to have chat before it starts," he said with an air of authority that belied the fact he was asking a question.

"Yep," JK and Ellen replied in unison. She didn't want him to speak for them both, as JK tended to do. In fact, Ellen tried to get her 'yep' in first but wasn't quite quick enough. She looked JK up and down like it was the first time they had met. He didn't even notice the look. He was too preoccupied with jumping out of his seat and being the first of the pair into the room.

What a child, thought Ellen with a small shake of her head. She let him play his games. It might cause a longer discussion and provide her with something to do that wasn't thinking about Harry at any rate. She slowly followed him into the room. JK had a favourite chair and was already sitting in it. JK had a favourite everything in life. She just had to ask him and within half a second he would reply.

Favourite colour? Blue.

Favourite book? Catcher in the Rye.

Favourite footballer? Kevin Keegan.

Favourite breakfast? Quakers Muesli of course.

No matter what she asked, JK had an answer. Even for some of the most obscure things in life he had a favourite. She knew that she could wind him up with this at times. Dropping in a quote here and there from a nameless source who wore a red tie (JK would never wear one and was obviously the source in every other way) meant he would have to bite at her the next day. She chuckled at the prospect of the next wind up.

"Now, we need to talk about what the next steps are in all of this," Paul interrupted Ellen's thought process and brought her crashing back into the room.

"What do we already know?" Channon followed this up with an open question. He had received some level of training in this and remained a good speaker most of the time. Ellen noticed the confidence reappear in Paul's voice when the two of them sat up and took notice. He didn't have total authority in the room as he faced two strong characters who knew how and were paid to push back on him, yet he certainly had the floor.

"We're facing the unknown at the moment. We can't control an uncontrollable situation," Ellen explained. She wanted Channon to be loose and reactive with the recent events. But JK couldn't let that happen.

"I totally disagree, Ellen. There's always a way of controlling what people think and do. We're in a position of power. It's why we're sat here in this office and the average Joe isn't. We can set the scene," JK snapped. He didn't like any thought of helplessness in his life. He wanted to take the initiative and needed his Boss to think the same. Although JK wasn't afraid to go out on a limb at times, directly disobeying an instruction from the minister wasn't going to do his career ambitions any good.

"It's time. We'll talk about this later," Paul Channon said while looking at his watch. Ellen turned up the television set. She didn't want the conversation to go any further at that point. The Nine O'clock news was about to a start and the three of them didn't miss it when they were in the office. The miners' strikes, and the surrounding press interest meant that they often worked late into the evening. Ellen was happy for the late night. All she had to do was go home and crash. Thoughts of Harry would have to compete with the tiredness.

"Murder outside the Libyan Embassy. 25-year-old WPC Yvonne Fletcher gunned down in cold blood. Shots reportedly came from inside the embassy..."

Ellen turned down the TV set immediately, but not quite off. They had heard enough to know that there was a lot of work to be done. There might be something else that followed and needed their attention.

"This throws a spanner in the works," exclaimed JK while Ellen and Paul shot daggers at each other from across the room. "How does this affect the miners' strike?" he asked.

"I don't really know what the effect will be, but the media's focus is clear. We need to know and quickly. I can guarantee that we'll be meeting with the Prime Minister about this tomorrow. That poor girl. Her parents," said Channon, momentarily looking crestfallen. The moment passed immediately. "What do we have to say, team?" He wanted to bring them together. He rarely used the word 'team' but felt he would need heads together and not apart for the next few hours at least.

"I think that there is little or no connection, is there?" Ellen asked with a sense of mischief. She had asked Paul on more than one occasion about his connections with Libya and he had denied that there were any. She could feel now that he was nervous. And it was more than general nerves about the cabinet meeting the next day. It was as though he had a vested interest in the event that was relayed by the television newsreader. His shirt was starting to show signs of sweat under the armpits and across the collar at where his shoulders met. She could feel a difference to the timbre of his voice too.

"It's how this pushes buttons. There's too much going on for things to be unrelated. Every event has a knock on for the next. I need your head in the game, Ellen," Paul motioned towards the door as though that was where she could leave if she wasn't going to be constructive.

"But the Libya question keeps on rearing its head. What has Libya got to do with miners and the government?" Ellen replied.

"We need to focus. This is a major world event and we are close to it. We have the ability to set the scene and force the narrative," JK spoke for the first time since the news headline had been turned down.

"Right. JK is in the game!" Channon exclaimed. He wanted the focus firmly away from his links to Libya, that much was obvious.

The conversation carried on and Ellen was prepared to react rather than set the agenda. Her role as the press secretary was to absorb the information and work out the best way to present it. She knew her time would come.

As the chat petered out and moved towards the end. Ellen saw this as her chance to talk. She didn't care that JK was still present.

"And the links between Libya, this, the miners and you? As your press secretary I have a right to know if I'm going to be asked some sticky questions tomorrow. Might that be a possibility?"

JK looked stunned. He hadn't heard this from Ellen in front of Paul before.

"There's nothing in it. Silly rumours from silly people," Paul replied. He might have convinced himself, but Ellen wasn't anywhere near as sure. She reserved all judgement. There was a journey home and a night of sleep to be had. Even Ellen had run out of battery for the day.

The next day Ellen awoke with a bit of a start. She hadn't slept particularly well because of the events of the night before. The fact that Paul was so adamant that there were no connections at all between him and Libya struck Ellen as odd. She knew that as the trade minister he would have made all manner of contacts in all manner of countries across the world. There would have been meetings in faceless hotels after long flights countless times. Regardless, Paul solidly stated that he hadn't had any dealings with Libya. It felt like a man who was trying to cover his tracks.

The other main reason for her lack of sleep was that she was using her brother's sofa as a temporary bed while she sorted herself out. The breakup from Rhys was clearly more painful for him than it had been for her. He called every now and again, at work or at her brother's house, and this unnerved Ellen. She wanted a clean break but wasn't fully able to have one.

The sun crept through the gap at the top of the curtains. Ellen had tried to cover it with her cardigan, pull them together more closely or Sellotape the seams. Nothing worked. The early morning light was seeping into the room and hit her in the face long before she was ready to get up and go. Her brother didn't work long hours in his role as an advertising executive. It was something he managed to get away with every day. The art of being late but never being in trouble. His bosses were lenient because he produced results. And he had a list of bluffs as long as his arms if they ever caught him turning in late and asked questions. Excuses like:

'I was out checking the billboards had been put up for the Heinz campaign.'

'There were missing adverts on the Tube train I was on so asked who was in charge of them.'

'I went for breakfast with a rival to see what they were doing.'

And these were just the mundane ones. There were more outlandish ones up his sleeve if he ever needed them. This meant Ellen was always the first up. She needed a hot drink to keep her going in the morning, so the first task was always to clear up the mess her brother had left from the night before. He wasn't one for cleanliness and seeing as he had shown the good heart to give her a place to stay, she felt it was the least she could do to add a little order to his life. He would accept no money from her for the use of the sofa. She felt that he rather enjoyed being close to his sister once again having inevitably grown apart since growing up.

Ellen made a cup of whatever she could find in the cupboard. Sometimes it was tea, sometimes coffee, sometimes hot chocolate. The cupboards had no discernible order, so when she opened it up there was often something completely different staring her in the face. She just went with the flow and grabbed whatever was easiest. It was early, and she needed a pick me up.

Ellen got washed and went back downstairs with her towel on. The light seeping through the curtains was stronger than when she had walked up the stairs, but the gap wasn't wide enough for anyone to see in. This was her bedroom, living room, dressing room and everything else while she was staying with her brother. It would have to do. But it didn't have to do for very long that morning. Ellen was soon on the train with Paul and JK back to Yorkshire and a meeting with Mark Turnbull.

Mark intrigued Ellen, but it wasn't him that made her stride out of the door with a spring in her step. She hadn't heard from Harry for a couple of days and didn't know if he was around. She couldn't call him directly and didn't like leaving messages at The Plough, so had to rely on him calling her when she was at her brother's place, which wasn't very often. But all this aside, the thought of being close to him in Yorkshire made her heart flutter. She would see how the meeting with Mark went and then maybe try to track Harry down, even if it was for a few fleeting minutes.

While JK's sniping of Ellen continued, he was more cautious of her given the directness of her Libyan question to Paul the night before. He still wanted to take on Ellen with every detail of the conversation. Ellen tried to pretend she was asleep at one stage but JK just talked more loudly as if he was prepared to wake her up to make his point. She gave in and took part in the discussion. It would keep her sane and distract her from all that was going on.

Paul was due to meet Arthur Scargill, and this was a major event in the life of the government. Ellen had been a key player to bring the two together. Scargill was receiving support from corners of the press and wanted to court this as much as possible.

Being seen with a member of the government was at first anathema to the NUM leader. His credibility might take a knock and he wasn't prepared to let that happen. But Ellen had been able to use her connection to Mark Turnbull to slowly persuade Scargill that he would be seen as the victor, the man to bring the government to heel if he played his cards right. He wasn't totally convinced but was willing to meet, though only on his own patch. So, the meeting was set for the county of Yorkshire and Ellen was to accompany Paul Channon and JK on the trip there. The miracle was that after yesterday's tragic killing this meeting was still going ahead.

Arriving in Grimethorpe, the three of them looked and felt for all the world like fish out of water. The rest of the people scurried about their daily business, knowing exactly why they were present and what they needed to achieve. The three of them just stood outside the hotel waiting for someone to take the lead. In the end it was Ellen who fulfilled this role. JK and Paul were content to stand and chat whilst looking like they were lost. Ellen had listened to enough of JK's scheming and wanted to find her room.

As she moved across the reception area, she heard a voice. "Excuse me, madam, do you need any help with those bags?"

Immediately she recognised the voice.

"Harry! How amazing it is to see you!" she exclaimed as she gave him a quick hug. She was sure that JK and Paul were still talking but didn't want to take too many risks.

"I know a little room by the side of the reception. A friend of Dale's Mam's, Mrs Pennard cleans here at The Star, and she said we'd be right for a few minutes. Come with me," Harry spoke with an authority different to that of the men of Westminster. Different to that of Rhys for that matter. Harry spoke with the authority of a fireman leading people to safety. Ellen followed to see where he would take her. They proceeded to a room without windows to the interior of the hotel reception. Harry gave her a proper hug there and the two of them looked into each other's eyes.

"Mrs Pennard told Mrs Edwards that the Minister for Trade was visiting. I've been trying to call you, even left a couple of messages with your brother, but you didn't get back in touch. When I heard Paul Channon was here, I guessed you would be too," Harry explained. "I'll be here tonight. In the room next to yours. Just knock when you're ready."

Ellen looked at him and smiled. She hadn't told Harry about the visit because it was prone to being cancelled and she worried she wouldn't be around long enough to spend time with him. It was just like her brother not to pass on the messages though.

"I'd love for our next meeting to be closer to home for you. How about I head down to London soon? I've always wanted to see the capital and I can't think of a better guide than you," Harry teased.

"Sure. I'm due some time off and I'm sure Paul would rather I was away than snooping around. In the next few weeks or do you think you'll still be on strike?" It was her turn to tease, before asking, "Do you have anything in particular you want to see when you are in London?"

"Just you. The rest I can take or leave," Harry shot the quickest reply he could think of.

"Any day of the week is good. Every day you can see the crowds as well as the sights. London isn't the same when it's quiet in the early morning. The tourists are out and about by 11 a.m. and the streets fill. I do love it at that time," Ellen spoke in almost a singing voice, she was that happy. Seeing Harry for the odd few minutes or hours was one thing. Spending consecutive days with him was going to be bliss. She planned to try to get her brother to disappear to a friend's house, or even book a hotel under a married pseudonym. That would give her and Harry a bit of space and time.

She had to leave and get the room prepared for the meeting. Harry beamed the biggest smile her way and Ellen was sure she reciprocated. And then she was gone. The intrigues of government and the demands of her role meant she had to get her *organised* head on. Harry watched her through the crack in the door. His smile grew even further when he saw Ellen take the lead and bring everyone into shape. He hoped she would be able to do this for him.

Chapter 13

Thursday 19th April 1984.
Doncaster, Yorkshire, heavy rain, wind and a high of 11°C.
Tarek Jibril.

The morning in Yorkshire was a contrast of the bright sun and occasional gusts of winds. At the hour of 7 a.m. this was something that happened outside of the window of the bedroom for most people. But for Tarek Jibril, this was accompanying him on the drive to his meeting place. He was due to meet with Roger Windsor and Tom Linney. And he was sure that the conversation was going to be interesting to say the least.

Tarek looked out of the window of the Jaguar he was being driven in. Not one for ostentation usually, he liked a good car. This was the kind of luxury he saved for himself every now and again. Once a year he would visit Cuba and stock up on some of the finest cigars he could lay his hands on. Most of the rest of his life was spartan in comparison. The sky filled with dark clouds and Tarek hoped this wasn't an omen for the conversations he was about to have. As the car pulled around the last few corners to his final destination, Tarek closed his eyes and hoped for the best. That was his plan in any situation, plan for the worst and hope for the best. This time he had all the plans lined up behind him. The worst was probably that he would have the rug pulled from under him. That would leave him red-faced and possibly without allies but was of no mortal danger. Tarek had friends in high places and felt safe dealing with even the most underhand people on the planet.

The driver brought the car to a halt and Tarek opened his eyes. The Danum Hotel was as sparse as he remembered. It was the perfect place to hold conversations best kept secret. The hotel was old. It had thick walls unlike the modern trend for building a frame and filling it with cheap material. Tarek liked the look of the hotel and felt safe that once inside the room he would be able to speak freely. The driver got out just as a shower started and pulled his jacket collar up to cover his neck. Still being April, the rain had no heat in it and the driver was desperate for his passenger to jump out, so he could get back to some warmth and shelter.

"Sir…" he beckoned as he opened the door. Tarek made him wait a few seconds longer to confirm who was in charge. It wasn't needed. He got out of the car without looking at the driver, let alone uttering a word to him and walked up the steps to the hotel. Once inside, he looked around the reception area to see what was going on. There didn't appear to be any guests, just staff getting ready for the day. The carpet was being hoovered and the receptionist was busy dusting the desk. The distraction of work was perfect for Tarek Jibril. All he wanted to do was get through the reception without conversation and go up the stairs to room 318. He was able to without any fuss at all.

As he reached the door, he knocked gently. The door swung open and he was faced with Tom Linney.

"Tarek, long time, no see," Tom said in the quietest voice he could muster, which was still loud enough to stir people in adjoining rooms.

"Tom. How are things with you?" Tarek responded.

"Good, good. And I'm sure you remember Roger Windsor," Tom looked over his shoulder to a man that was sitting on a chair that didn't look right to him. He was about as uncomfortable as Tarek had seen anyone. And in his line of business Tarek saw a lot of uncomfortable people. Roger got up and shook the hand of the visitor to the room. And then the three of them set to it.

"There's many things going on at the moment. We need to roll with things at times, but we also have to gain some control back in the situation and perhaps the death of this female plod is our key," Roger explained to Tarek, ignoring Tom. Tarek assumed that Tom and Roger had already had this conversation before he arrived. 7 a.m. starts were usual for him, but he knew that the English would often meet before the sun rose.

"And I think that we can do that," Tarek responded. He wanted to react rather than prompt the conversation. He had all the aces as far as he was concerned, so didn't feel the need to show his hand any time soon.

"The time has come for action. We have made some progress, but this government is all as stubborn as the woman at the top of its tree. The only way to flush her out is to start a fire at the bottom of the trunk," Tom Linney commanded the conversation in a way that made the others listen intently. The way his mouth formed the words transfixed the other occupants of the room. It was like a snake charmer teasing the snakes under his power. Even Tarek, used to dealing with diverse people all over the world and getting his own way, was fixed on the lips of Tom. He couldn't break the spell. It was only when Tom stopped speaking that he was able to think his own thoughts and gather himself to speak. By the time he had something to say, he realised that he had missed his turn.

"We need a soldier. We need someone who will help us make the most of the tension at the moment. And we have been grooming one for a short time now. He feels perfect for what we need. I'm sure you've both been made aware of Dale Edwards. He's been a leader in the strike, and we want him to take on a bigger role. Not only that, he wants to take on this role," Roger spoke, growing in confidence.

"None of this happens without financial support," Tarek said. They all knew he was right. They all knew why he was in the room. As a middleman for the Pro-Gaddafi faction, he had access to a large amount of cash that could be used for anyone who supported the Libyan leader. Gaddafi had secured funds for many years, creaming it off the top of the country and then making sure it was put to use keeping him in power. There were many that were now involved in the miner's strike that had been supporters of Gaddafi in the past. He was willing to support them if Tarek Jibril gave it the green light.

"And that's where we hoped you would come in. You know that we have been there for you. Will you be there for us, my brother?" Tom asked. The relationship between the two men had been forged over several years. They weren't friends, nobody in that community could afford to go that far but were about as close as you could get without sending each other Christmas cards and going around to each other's house for dinner.

"Let's see what you propose first."

The next half an hour consisted of the two English men explaining their plans to Tarek. He asked pertinent questions. Tom Linney was already aware that Tarek would ask ten questions for every one they put forward. He was prepared for that. Roger became agitated at times but followed the lead of his counterpart. By the end of it, Tarek Jibril was ready to give his decision.

"I've listened. I know that I have the backing of many influential people. No matter what my decision is, it will be backed up. And my decision is final. There is no appeal process here!" Tarek laughed as he spoke. He loved the power that came with his role at times. Here he had two men that were influential in their own right sat at the edge of their seats waiting for an answer.

"Tarek, let's just get on with this. Everything is in place, you've seen that," Tom Linney interjected as though the decision was still in the balance. It wasn't.

"You have our backing. I'll transfer the funds as soon as possible. This is the next step in the world battle for right and wrong. Let's make sure that our side wins, gentlemen," Tarek spoke as he rose from his seat. It was clear that this meeting was done. Tarek Jibril stood still near the door and waited for the two other men to gather their belongings.

He wondered how long it would take to pick up a few items and be ready to leave. It seemed like an age. Tom had a small suitcase. Tarek suspected he had stayed the night there. Roger Windsor had a briefcase that looked anything but brief. It looked like it weighed a tonne. If he had a heart, then Tarek would offer to help the men. But they had asked to meet there, they had brought these items with them, they would have to look after themselves when the three of them parted.

Once the three men were ready, Tarek checked the spy hole in the door (a habit he had got into when living in Libya and never felt the need to get out of) and then turned the handle. There was a noise in the corridor he didn't recognise.

*　*　*

Harry looked Ellen up and down. She'd gotten dressed and looked a million dollars as far as he was concerned. He couldn't understand how she had got this far in life and not been snapped up by someone already. He was starting to fall for her and loved every aspect of her. He'd spent very little time with women and was amused by the differences between the sexes. In the morning he ran a brush through his hair and that was that. The way Ellen brushed her hair was his particular favourite. He could watch her do that no matter how long she took doing it, Harry thought.

She was ready for whatever the day threw at her, while he was still trudging about the place. He never found it easy to get up in the morning, which was strange given the job he had. The early shifts were torture to Harry. He was rarely late but needed a full half hour to stir and get his brain in gear before he got out of bed and started to actually get ready for work; or anything else for that matter.

After their brief encounter at the Star they'd organised to meet once Ellen had checked into the Danum Hotel. The Danum was becoming her default; she felt safe there and with no resistance from either one Harry had ended up staying the night. While he showered, Ellen left the room to get the morning papers from her room next door. Annoyingly these hadn't been delivered and she stood for a moment tutting to herself. She was unaware that as she did this she had been spotted by Tarek Jibril, watching carefully from the cracked door of his room. While Tarek didn't know who Ellen was, he took a mental note of the way in which she had left the room and stopped by the door of another. It was a little unusual.

Ellen was pleased that reception was relatively quiet. She knew she was safe from both Paul and JK as they would both be taking breakfast and making phone calls in their rooms.

She went over to the receptionist who apologised for the mistake and handed Ellen a big stack of newspapers. She would sit and sift through these while Harry got ready. In her role as press secretary a grip on what was going on in the news was habitual. As well as trying to generate news themselves, politicians needed to know what was going on around them. She took the newspapers up to the room and sat on the bed reading.

As she entered, the sound of the bath water sloshing around in the bathroom greeted her. She smiled at the thought of Harry playing in the bath. She imagined him with a toy boat, moving it around and pretending to be the captain. She wasn't sure that was exactly what was going on but could see this in the playful and energetic man she was growing more and more fond of.

Reading the newspapers wasn't the most interesting of tasks. There were far too many words to try to read each of them, so she had to flick through and see if anything caught her eye. If they missed key information in a story, the press sometimes would cleverly seed a small story to see if it could become a bigger one. So, there might be a few words after a small headline on page 17. This would be a hint at something bigger. If there was no official rebuke at the story, then this would make twice the space on page 6 the next day before potentially growing into a major story a few days later. Being in front of this would ensure Ellen was in front of the impact it might have on the Minister. Ellen was expected by Paul to spot these before they became a problem. She would need more hours in the day or a team of readers to make this possible. As it was, she had to shoehorn this task into her day and hope that she caught things in time.

As he finished in the bathroom, Harry started singing. Ellen didn't much listen to popular music so had no idea what he was belting out but as he sung out "Plans for Nigel" it had a pretty good tune and his voice wasn't too bad. Her attention was easily diverted away from the newspapers. Harry had that effect on her. She could be deep in concentration on one task but a quick noise from Harry and she was back in their bubble. The world that only Harry and she occupied.

He walked out of the bathroom still singing and Ellen tried to guess what the next line might be. She got it wrong every single time but enjoyed the game, nonetheless.

"Let's get some breakfast," Harry said as he pulled on his shoes. It was clear he was ready to move. Ellen hadn't quite finished with the newspapers but didn't want to take them to the breakfast table. The two of them headed out of the room and towards the small dining room. It was a full English breakfast on offer, and both were ready to tuck in. Seeing as she had been up and ready for some time Ellen had developed quite an appetite and was ready to eat just about anything that was put in front of her.

The breakfast conversation was of something and nothing. Ellen loved talking to Harry and he loved the centre stage with her. The two of them could talk all day and all night about something and nothing much at all. Harry didn't do small talk with anyone else but found it totally natural with Ellen. It was as though she had made a change to his character without actually trying to. The night before had both been exciting and natural and a silent physical confidence permeated between them.

Ellen looked across the dining room and noticed that the two doors leading to it were wide open. She hadn't even observed the dining room before, but she was now aware that it was right next to the reception. How could she have missed it? The view out to the reception area caught her eye for a few moments at a time. As someone left, she clearly saw them go to reception and then make their way to the only entrance and exit of the hotel for public use. It fascinated her, just like sitting in the departure lounge of an airport. She would imagine back stories to all the people she saw. She would guess if they were away on holiday or travelling for work. She would decide what country they were visiting, who they were staying with and what they would get up to when they arrived. It was a little the same at the hotel. Ellen would imagine for a few seconds in between her chat with Harry what the next thing was these people would be doing.

Harry captivated her in between these brief moments of imagination. His accent was as smooth as she had remembered from the last time they met. It wasn't what she was used to, living in London, but was welcoming and calm in her ear.

As Harry started another conversation that she knew would last for minutes but feel like seconds, another group walked across her view towards reception. It was three men and they were walking in a single file like they were on a march, but without the pace. She recognised the second man in the line. It was Tom Linney. He was looking across the reception area backwards and forwards. Ellen didn't recognise the two other men that he was with. The three of them together looked like the oddest combination. It really caught her eye.

It was the first time that she'd blanked out Harry's voice and concentrated fully on something else. She knew that he had got to the point in his monologue where he closed his eyes. She had first observed this at the café in Grimethorpe when they met for the first time. It was cute to her. And it gave her the opportunity to really focus on the three men in the lobby. It didn't look right. She studied the actions and movements of the three men. They didn't look like they had anything to hide, but it wasn't totally comfortable and natural either.

"Ellen, what's wrong?" Harry asked.

"There's something not quite right over in reception. Don't turn around, but there are three men there that in all honesty shouldn't be together," she explained.

As a natural reaction, Harry's head shot around and he studied the three men before a brush of his leg from Ellen's ankle brought his attention back to the table. She had seen all she needed to see. She smelled a rat. Looking more intently might draw unwanted attention to her. In her line of work that wasn't a very clever idea.

"Well, I know one of them," remarked Harry, suddenly alert and interested in this odd trio.

"So do I."

"How'd you know Roger Windsor? He's the guy that's been leading on our Dale on the picket lines. Only after himself that one."

"No, it's the heavy-set one that I've met, he's one of Scargill's business associates, a brick manufacturer from Peterborough if I remember rightly." Ellen sighed. She knew that she couldn't really trust that many people when she was at work. Even her Boss, Paul and her co-worker, JK were people that she didn't feel totally at ease with. It wasn't that they were liars (well, not all the time, anyway) but that they might say anything to ensure that they could preserve their own careers. And she knew it in Tom Linney from the meetings they had in the past. She knew that he was a wheeler dealer and that he could do anything at any time to anyone if he felt the urge. But something disappointed her. She realised that she'd hoped that Tom Linney would be different, like an ally on the other side, but sadly not. Harry turned to her and asked who Tom was. As quickly as they got deep into discussion on who the third man might be and what they were all doing together Ellen realised that the trio had already departed.

"It seems well off, I agree," said Harry, "but what could they possibly be doing wrong and in plain sight of the visitors to the Danum?"

Ellen laid it all out to Harry; the first time she'd mapped all these thoughts in her head into one coherent narrative. The first time she'd really said it all out loud. She talked about her suspicions that the miner's strikes and how the Libyan and the Thatcher governments were all connected. How men like Tom Linney were part of the evil machinery facilitating it to the detriment of others. Working men. Persecuted Libyans. And dead WPCs. Harry listened intently, enraptured, as he had done the night they first went out to the café. He didn't totally understand what was going on, partly feeling he was watching a Hollywood Blockbuster like Clint Eastwood's Tightrope. But felt that he needed to support Ellen and help her put things right again in the world. Well, in her world at least.

Chapter 14

Saturday 12th May 1984.

Heathrow Airport, West London, windy yet sunny with a high of 12°C.

Dale.

Tom Linney sat on the plane waiting for it to take off. He wasn't the most comfortable flyer and was even worse when he was sat with someone he knew. If it was a stranger that he shared the seats to one side of the aisle or another with, then he was happy to be as rude as he liked or ignore them for the whole flight. Sat with someone he knew meant he had to be polite. Not a trait that he was known for or wanted to practice. His travelling companion on this occasion was the young and eager Dale Edwards. Dale had started to become one of the faces of the miner's strike as far as Tom and the other luminaries in the movement were concerned, so he felt the need to nurture him and keep him sweet. Rudeness and being ignored were not going to cement Dale's place as one of the soldiers that were needed on the front line of this conflict. Tom was issued with instructions from above him that Dale was to be shown a good time and be made to feel important. Surely, he could manage that for a few days.

As the engines of the plane whirred into action and filled the ears of the two men, Dale tried to make small conversation with Tom.

"Been to Tripoli before?" he asked in a voice that was almost a shout, competing with the noise from just under the wing.

"None of your business," Tom said through a grin, although it was the glint in his eye that gave away the fact that he was playing with his younger travelling mate.

"It's my first time out of the country," Dale continued. "I've never really been out of my hometown that much. It's good that I can see a bit of the world through all of this."

"Don't think that this will be a weekly event, but there are some pretty exciting perks for those that help us. You scratch our back and we will most definitely scratch yours, my friend," Tom Linney replied in a much more friendly manner. It was clear that he was warming to Dale.

The captain came over the radio and gave some instructions that sounded rushed and were muffled by a poor speaker system. Dale listened eagerly, taking in every ounce of the experience. Tom took the opportunity to push his chair back into the recline position and close his eyes. *That might keep the young pup quiet for a while,* he thought.

Dale looked up and down at every other occupant of the plane as far as he could see. It was as excited as he had been in some time. Tom only escaped the questions from Dale for a short while as the stewardess asked him to return his seat to the upright position as a matter of safety. Thankfully for him, the plane journey went in a flash and they were soon experiencing Libyan hospitality at its best.

The hotel was the finest in all Tripoli. Tom was used to spending time in such luxury and it was second nature to him to be waited on hand and foot. He didn't look in the direction of the people who brought him food and drink as though he was a superior kind of human being. Dale hadn't been in this world before and made eye contact with everyone, thanking them profusely for everything they did for him; even when he turned down what they offered he said his thanks as though his life depended on it.

"You don't have to do that," Tom scolded him.

"It's polite, isn't it?" Dale replied.

"It's not necessary. If you want me to show you some of the more interesting parts of Tripoli and the nightlife then you will have to let go of your manners," he explained. Tripoli at its worst didn't see eye to eye with the highest English etiquette. In fact, it was suspicious of it. Dale thought of home. Not seeing eye to eye was a common theme in Dale's life. His longest-lasting friend Harry didn't want to get involved with the movement at all. Dale spent a lot of time attempting to persuade him to make a difference. He didn't find the same things important as Dale and this was a constant source of frustration. It had got to the point where he didn't communicate with his dear friend much at all. In fact, he hadn't even told Harry that he was going abroad for a few days. It was a whistle-stop tour anyway. Little did Dale know that

Harry was so involved with Ellen in London that he didn't even notice his friend wasn't around anyway.

Dale resolved to put his over-the-top manners to one side and let Tom show him what Tripoli was all about. The first stop was a seedy-looking bar where Tom seemed to know everyone else in the building. From the guy on the door that looked like the smallest and angriest bouncer Dale had ever seen to the waitress who brought drinks like they were going out of fashion; Tom took a few minutes with each of them. It was in vast contrast to the way he had dealt with people in the hotel, but he could see the same level of deference from the people who served Tom as he had there. It was clear who was in charge.

Dale liked a drink, that was for sure, and was on steady ground with a pint or ten at The Plough with his friends. Drinking cocktails that sounded as exotic as they looked was another matter. It wasn't long at all before he was worse for wear and starting to show signs that he was having a great time. It was one of the tasks that Tom was given ("show the boy a good time, keep him close!")

The next day the two men woke up in their separate double bedrooms on the fifth floor of the hotel overlooking Tripoli both nursing hangovers that would take some time to get rid of. Tom was used to it. The fresh air and noise from the streets of the city were bouncing around from below and helping his senses regain their normal service. On the other hand, Dale had cocooned himself in darkness and as near to silence as he could manage to deal with the sensations of drinks that he'd tried for the first time.

There was always talk in The Plough about the perils of mixing your drinks, but he didn't think that actually happened. His experience up to that point was simply downing pints at a steady rate. His theory the night before was that if he could manage more than ten pints and get up for a shift at the mine the next day then a few cocktails and a good night's sleep would be a piece of cake. This theory wasn't standing up to much scrutiny. His head pounded, his stomach churned and the taste of the exotic ingredients from the cocktails the night before kept on reaching his mouth before disappearing again. He had to be sick.

Dale jumped out of bed and ran to the bathroom. He didn't think that his legs would be able to carry him that quickly but the movement in his abdomen forced him to run like the wind. Certainly, the carpet and bedclothes depended on his speed. He made it to the lavatory just in time. Immediately he felt better. Not well enough to venture too far from the lavatory, but well enough that he could open his eyes again and look around the lightness of the room. In contrast to the darkness he had created in the bedroom, the bathroom was strangely well lit. Dale wondered why for a few minutes, before concluding that he had left the light on in his drunken state the night before. He looked around the room, slowly feeling his torso to ensure that all the unwanted contents had been removed and he was able to get up to his feet again. This task took all of half an hour. When he was finally ready to get back on to his feet again, he decided that he would count to one hundred before rising and getting into the shower. As Dale reached the heady figure of seventy-three, there was a sharp knock at the door. He ignored it and continued counting.

74, 75, 76...

"Dale! Are you in there?" Tom shouted under the crack of the door to the room.

77, 78, 79...

"Dale, it's Tom! Are you awake?"

80, 81, 82...

"Dale, we have a meeting in an hour. I'd like to get some breakfast. Are you ready?" Tom shouted almost at the top of his voice. The doors to other rooms opened and shut as the occupants tried to work out what was going on.

83, 84, 85...

"I'll go to reception and get a key. Something must be wrong for you to not answer!" Tom bellowed. Two members of staff came around the corner, alerted by other concerned guests. Dale counted more. He had set himself a task and he would complete it. Tom would understand. If they were to trust him with bigger and better things, then something as simple as counting to one hundred should be completed fully.

86, 87, 88...

The members of staff asked Tom what all the commotion was. He could see that they were in a quandary. They wanted to deal with the noise but had to defer to the Western man who obviously had a lot more power and influence than them. Tom explained he wanted to be in. The senior member of staff saw a way to calm the situation and satisfy the English man shouting on the corridors. They let him in. Dale heard the key in the lock and counted quickly.

89, 90, 91, 92, 93, 94, 95...

"Dale what's going on? We've got things to do, places to be and you're lying here on the bathroom floor. We need soldiers, not people who buckle after a few drinks!" By now Tom was stood over him in the bathroom, trying to suppress a laugh. His travelling companion looked ridiculous but there was also the matter of their meeting. Dale finished his count out loud and rose to his feet.

"96, 97, 98, 99, 100, right! I'm ready for the day. Let me get a quick shower and I'll be down for breakfast within the next ten minutes. I won't let you down, Tom," Dale said. He then walked over to the taps and turned them on. The shower blasted away, and Tom could see that Dale was back in control of himself. He walked down to the breakfast area, satisfied that things would go well. Later that day when they were sat on the tarmac at Tripoli airport with a briefcase filled with used British bank notes to the tune of £50,000 for the NUM coffers, Tom would poke fun at Dale for his inexperience with alcoholic drinks other than beer. The meeting the two men attended was of paramount importance and secrecy. The money was there to take the miner's strike to the next level. It was put in place to bring Thatcher's government to heel. The Libyans wanted that as much as people like Tom and his peers. The time was right to step things up.

* * *

London in May brings two kinds of day. There are those days when the heat signals (falsely) that Summer has arrived. Each passing car or bus brings with it the smells and noises that overwhelm the senses. The edge of the path farthest from the road is overpopulated with people trying desperately to soak up as much sun as possible, fearful it may never return. Today, however, was more typical of Spring and freshness filled the air. Harry had arrived the night before on his first trip to the capital. Many of the people around them appeared to be passing the time of day in one of the major capital cities of the world. Others were on a mission, focused with a task in mind.

What time is the next bus if I miss this one?

Where do I have to change Tube lines?

Where is the best place to stand on the platform to avoid the crowds?

Will they have the top I want in my size?

Ellen and Harry had none of these worries today. They were on a mission of their own, but with far less stress on their minds. Ellen was looking for somewhere to live. Even at that time it was stated as one of the most stressful experiences you could face in life, to find a new home, but neither of them could see any strain in the situation. They walked along the London streets as though they were empty. There might as well have been nobody else on the planet as far as the two of them were concerned.

The day before had seen Ellen speak to several letting agents about a place close to her to work. Many were quite dismissive about a young single girl looking for a flat of her own but once they got to know who she worked for, their icy exterior melted and she was quickly able to fill the day with viewing appointments.

There were a few essential criteria that filled Ellen's mind when she was speaking to the lettings agents about somewhere to live. Practically thinking, she had explained that it needed to be near to Westminster for her to get to work. She didn't work the normal nine to five like others in the city did. The need to be able to walk to the Houses of Parliament was always going to be a major factor in her decision. There was the ministerial car that she could make use of when it was late or very early in the day, but she wanted to be self-sufficient on this front. It meant that there would be a premium to pay, needing to live in the expensive part of town, but she was prepared to do that to have that independence.

Another important factor was the proximity to the Tube system. If Harry was to make his way South, and she really hoped this would be a regular occurrence, then he needed to get to her new place without too much discomfort. For a Northern boy who was used to green fields and not many people, the hustle and bustle of London could be a real drag for him. She wanted to make that drag as painless as possible to have him with her. And the most important factor in choosing a flat was also linked inescapably to Harry. The flat just had to have a telephone. A line to Harry. These were rarer to come by than she had first thought. Needing a phone for her job as a press secretary for a minister and member of parliament, Ellen saw the phone as second nature. She used it many times a day and was always taken aback a little when she went to a friend's house and they didn't have a telephone. Speaking to the letting's agent, it was clear that she could rule out many of the available options on this criterion alone. It helped to narrow her search somewhat and Ellen could see all the flats she was considering in one day, rather than dragging this out over a week or two. Harry was becoming a greater influence in her life, and Ellen needed that link to him via the phone whenever she needed to talk. The fact that he just happened to be down for the weekend that she was looking at flats seemed like more than a coincidence. She hadn't deliberately made it happen, it didn't feel forced, and she hoped it wouldn't feel too rushed for her man.

Harry and Ellen walked to the first property on Lollard Street, a two-bedroom flat in a converted house just over Westminster Bridge. The price was the highest of the list she had in her hand, but the proximity to her work together with the beautiful park across the road made it pretty spectacular. Definitely one on the possible list, rather than being discarded straight away. But the next two were not suitable at all. Both had noise seemingly coming from all directions. She couldn't cope with that. Ellen needed her sanctuary, a place to escape all the stresses of working with Paul and JK, the dealings of government and the rest of the hullaballoo the city of London can deliver.

It wasn't until the fourth flat that Ellen started to notice all the small things that might turn an empty flat into a home for her and a place to stay for Harry when he visited. Who knows? He might even want to stay for longer.

There were architrave features in some that really made it feel like the building had been standing for centuries. Some had original fireplaces that looked and felt like they had been enjoyed by generation after generation. Others had the sneakiest view of something fascinating if you stood at a certain angle in a certain room and looked out of a certain window. She and Harry fell in love with so many of these individual elements, pointing them out to each other as they went.

As it happened, none had the impact that the first flat had, so she popped back into the lettings agent around the corner and asked to have another look, just to make sure it was the perfect place for her. Maybe one day she would live in the open space and greenery that Harry was so used to. Maybe he would fall for the city of London as much as he had fallen for her. It wasn't inconceivable that they could have a place in each and spread their time between the bright lights and the peaceful tranquillity. The flat was all she remembered when they took a second look and she negotiated a few pounds off the monthly rent with the lettings agent. Harry stood back in amazement at his girl haggling and driving down a professional lettings agent over the price of a flat that was probably in high demand. Even so, the final price agreed still made Harry feel light-headed, but he smiled at the way she handled people.

The flat was vacant, so Ellen could move in as soon as she was ready and had paid. Knowing that her new home was a place she could get to work from with relative ease, she decided she wouldn't let JK and Paul know quite yet that she was moving. She resolved to settle herself first.

The rest of the afternoon and evening was spent arm in arm with Harry taking in the sights of London that she was familiar with yet were completely new to Harry. The number of times she had seen the Tower of London and Tower Bridge beside it escaped her, but Ellen knew it was in the tens, possibly hundreds. Harry on the other hand was taking in the hundreds-of-years-old building for the very first time. His eyes widened like a child. Ellen loved watching Harry as much as she enjoyed taking in the sights with someone new. His demeanour of a tough Northern man that she had first seen had definitely made way for a softer person who just loved to see all the world had to offer. She wondered what he would make of the places she had seen in her travels with Paul Channon. But then again, Ellen wondered about a lot of things linked to the future and to her Boss.

Chapter 15

Sunday 17th and Monday 18th June 1984.

Doncaster, Yorkshire, heavy rain yet a balmy 18°C.

Roger Windsor and Tom Linney.

"This is our time!"

The two men in the room stopped talking and looked at each other. This meeting had gone on for around ten minutes prior to that exclamation. It was a simple sentence of only four words, but it had brought the proceedings to a pause. The man who had spoken had been scanning the room as he spoke. He was a suspicious man who distrusted most of the people he met. The silence between the two started comfortably. They both looked at each other as though a eureka moment had been reached. All the talk before that was irrelevant. The fact that it was now their time inspired each of them to look to a future where they were in control of their own destiny. Both felt aggrieved at the way life in Great Britain was going. They wanted to put the people back in charge of the way the country was run. Taking it away from the higher echelons of a government, especially a Tory government.

Roger Windsor looked his compatriot up and down. The meeting was one where they were discussing the strike action the following day. Neither knew exactly what would happen, but were pretty sure that it would put them back on the front foot. The killing of WPC Yvonne Fletcher had changed the mood in the nation. Libya was getting an undue amount of press and television coverage and the two men were sure that their cause would be backed by the people watching on TV the following day. The news at the end of the day would be the real test of how much progress they were going to make in the next 24 hours.

Fresh and fully recovered from his heavy drinking trip to Libya, Tom Linney was also in good mood and good form. He had found the fact that Roger had scoured the room for listening devices as they entered a little odd. He didn't care who might be listening in. There wasn't a great deal they could do about it. That was one of the things Tom found the funniest about the government. They spent so much time and money trying to discover what they already knew about their opponents. It was obvious what the NUM were trying to do, yet they still bugged Arthur Scargill wherever they could, to actually hear it from the horse's mouth. Their time and money would be far better spent dealing with the consequences as far as he was concerned. After the charade of Roger looking for bugs, the two men had started with a load of small talk that had irritated Tom. It was this kind of posturing that made their side look and feel like people who talked a lot but didn't get down to the action when it was really needed. That's when he dropped the four words that had made the men stop in their tracks. After that it was all about the action, Tom was more than pleased.

"We have all the backing we need. The money is there, I made sure of that myself, and we have some impressive soldiers organising the rest of the people we need. There's a little bit of outside help as well, if you know what I mean?" Tom spoke with a wide grin as though this was all just a game to him. That was far from the case. He believed in the right and wrong of society more than most, even with the working-class men he employed. As someone from a background of a little bit of money, his family expected him to lead a quiet life, run his business and to vote Conservative. He did nothing of the sort. Never a one to follow orders, unless he absolutely agreed with them 100%, Tom rebelled and did his own thing, moving out of the family home when he was only 17. Shortly after his father died and Tom was able to wrestle control of the family's brick business with little regard to the feelings of his wider family. He'd continued with his rebellious nature ever since.

"I'm sure you've taken care of your end, Tom. I have a few tricks up my sleeve should we need them. There will be a massive police presence, so we will need all the manpower we can get. I have arranged coaches to get as many people there as we can muster. Like you, I have a few influential people that will get the stragglers there and motivate them to help," Roger replied, still looking around the room to see if he could spot a bug.

"And we will take it to them. Remember to tell your people that the police are an extension of the oppressive government that is closing down their livelihoods. Let's not mistake them for real people, now, shall we?" Tom was warming up. He had several run-ins with the police in his early life and had never forgiven them. In his mind the Police were a barrier to progress, not a way to keep the peace.

"But the public opinion is turning towards us. The death of the policewoman has placed a whole load of attention on Libya and there are some murky links to the country through the government; not that we don't have our own murky links there, now do we Tom?" Roger loved to up the ante. Tom's comfort was a constant annoyance to Roger, so Roger did all he could to place a thorn of his own firmly in the midriff of Tom Linney. Yet it was never going to hurt or stay there for long.

"There's murkiness everywhere, my friend. We just need to focus on those pieces that will give us hope and light. We can't fixate on the ones that may bring us down. This is how we work," Tom countered in a way that made Roger Windsor sure he wasn't bothered but didn't shed any more light on the situation. Roger was easily confused when people spoke in riddles or rhymes. He was a straight thinker and straight talker. Abstraction and theory just didn't sink in. Practicality was the name of the game if you wanted to get anything out of Roger Windsor.

Tom Linney didn't. He had all he needed from the meeting and was ready to pack up and walk away. It was obvious that there was a great deal prepared and he wanted to spend the rest of the evening speaking to his trusted people just to go over the plans and ensure that everything was in place to move forward. He got up and shook the hand of the other man in the room. For all their banter and jostling Roger was pleased that the two of them could show each other proper respect. They were now under considerable pressure. This could often come out in bickering for top-dog status. Roger felt that he and Tom were too long in the tooth for that kind of game. He stepped forward and smiled at Tom. Their encounters rarely involved warmth but were always productive and left both feeling as though there was movement in the right direction. Roger was ready for the next day. He was on track with what he needed from the meeting. He too had people to speak to.

Across the United Kingdom, there were other meeting rooms being used to plot and plan the future of the country. None were quite as important as those that were happening in and around Rotherham. There was going to be a battle. There was going to be a confrontation. And neither side could see any way to avoid it.

Tom retired to his hotel before washing his face and returning to the bar to meet with Dale and a couple of other miners who had also shown promise and wiliness to help.

In London Harry had just got off the phone with Dale. Dale had pleaded with his mate to come back to Yorkshire and help the fight. Harry had agreed and was ready to speak to Ellen about it the next morning. He would tell her early and then leave, back on the first train North to help. Harry wasn't sure if his actions would help, but he couldn't just sit by and watch. Dale was his best friend and he didn't want to let him down anymore. It felt to Harry that the two of them had drifted apart a little over the previous few weeks. He was determined to set this situation right. He might even be able to persuade Dale that he should take a step back and protect himself from what might end badly. Harry had seen people rise to Union prominence and then fall rapidly in the past. He didn't want Dale to be one of those.

Harry got back to London late and what followed was a restless night's sleep. He finally gave up around 5 a.m., pulled on some clothes and walked to the newsagents to get a paper, milk and a fresh pack of No.6 cigarettes. On returning to Lollard Street 15 minutes later, he sat at the kitchen table smoking his first of the day and reading the news that Prince Andrew's former girlfriend Koo Stark was to be dropped as a leading lady in the next Doctor Who series. Putting down the asinine story, Harry looked around the kitchen. Ellen had only recently moved in, but she'd made short work of making the place comfortable. He wasn't sure how much sleep he'd mustered but knew it wasn't a great deal, but his mind was clear. He had to tell Ellen that he was going back to Yorkshire to support his friend. And he was pretty sure she wasn't going to like it. He returned to the bedroom and sat on the bed. As she stirred and turned over to face him, he decided to bite the bullet. His watch showed almost six, and he knew that she woke around this time every day before rolling back over to snooze a little while.

"Morning beautiful," Harry started. These were the first words he muttered to Ellen any day they woke together.

"Morning," Ellen mumbled through the covers.

"I've got something to tell you," Harry said, so he couldn't back out.

"What is it?" Ellen asked as she woke up even more.

"I'm heading back home today. There's some strike action and Dale really wants me there."

That was it. Ellen was wide awake, sat upright in bed and processing the information she had just been given.

"I don't want you to get yourself in trouble. And why didn't you tell me before? And how do you think that looks on me? You remember that I work for the government, don't you?" Ellen didn't mean to fire a series of questions or to sound quite so harsh, but she was shocked into a waking state by what she had just heard, and these were the questions bouncing around in her head.

"I know what it can look like. But these are our jobs. If the mines go, then the people I know are left with nothing. It might be a futile gesture going there but what else can I do? I can't be one of those that lets it happen without doing a single thing. I'm going to protect Dale from himself as much as anything else. I promise I'll stay safe," Harry threw everything he had at that answer. He desperately wanted to put her mind at ease. Harry didn't want to part on bad terms, but the clock was ticking, and he needed to get to the station.

"You had better stay away from the front, even if you are trying to protect Dale," Ellen replied in the gruffest voice she could muster, though she knew that Harry would see right through it. She knew he had to show his face. She knew he had to protect his friend. She knew he wasn't the type of man to sit back and let things happen without a fight. It was one of the reasons she had fallen for him.

As she walked Harry to the door, she was already thinking about the next telephone conversation they would have, the next time she would see him. Ellen waved him off with thoughts about his safety and her career in her mind. She worried that he might get hurt or arrested and would have loved to have gone with him, but that wasn't possible. She had work to do. Plus, it was bad enough her boyfriend being there, as a government employee, she couldn't be seen anywhere near a picketer. She worried for her career. Being linked to Harry was exciting, but this was the part of exciting that bordered dangerous.

The train got fuller and louder as it moved further North. There were more people who Harry could tell were making a similar journey to him. They were going to Orgreave to stand up for what was right.

There was a lot of talk about the free busses the government had been laying on to protect any miner who wished to pass through a picket line to work. These *Scabs*, as they were referred to, were not welcome. The mood was darkening.

Harry saw Dale stood in front of a group of people almost as soon as he arrived near the mine. Harry had shared a taxi with a group of others that got off the train and were headed to the mine. The taxi driver would take no money from the men. He said that it was his way of supporting the people. His trade had also been hit as the men in the town were not earning and subsequently were not taking a taxi anywhere. He said that the day would come when the pit reopened, and he would be back in business. Until then he would support the strikers as much as he could. Harry felt for him and left a one pound note on the front passenger seat deliberately as he got out. If only to help the family pictured on the driver's sun visor.

Dale was screaming orders at people as though he was in the army. The veins on his neck were bulging and the top half of his body was bright red. Harry had seen this before when they were kids. It meant that Dale was completely wound up and ready to explode. He stood to the side, just in the blind spot to the left of his friend and waited for him to stop shouting orders. Once Dale had sent people on their way, Harry could approach. This took longer than Harry had expected. When the first row of people moved away, Dale began shouting to the second row. With around eight rows of people there, Harry thought the day and the strike might be over before Dale had prepared his men but thankfully the remaining rows didn't need or get as much instruction as the first.

Harry approached. "Hi mate. How are you? Long time, no see."

Dale looked over and smiled. The veins on his neck returned to normal and he stepped in for a hug. The two men were not big huggers, but this seemed right to both of them. Harry didn't want to let go. But he could feel Dale wriggle and set him free.

"And where are my orders?" Harry asked without a trace of irony in his voice. This was Dale's territory and he was ready to accede to the man he called his best friend.

"Just stay close to me. I'll keep you right," Dale responded and then started to walk in the direction of the police line Harry had spied when he got out of the taxi. He matched Dale stride for stride and spent the next few hours in the company of someone he could sense had changed. Dale had found a purpose that was far beyond the way he had been when working at the pit. Harry admired that his friend believed in something so strongly and watched with a degree of pride as he got involved and organised people to move against the police and start to make a point. It wasn't until Dale started throwing missiles and encouraging others to charge that Harry felt unease at the situation. He backed off somewhat and looked for some sanctuary at the edge of the scene that was now resembling a battle.

News crews and journalists were stood at the edge too and Harry found a feeling of safety stood with these people as the place around him erupted into uninhibited violence.

Chapter 16

Wednesday 8th August 1984.

Mayfair, London, cloudy, a light wind and a high of 18°C.

David Hart.

The smoke was thick in the air around him. He laughed long and loud. David Hart wasn't going to sit in the corner and go unnoticed for anyone, even when the topic of conversation was one that should have been kept under his hat. Sat in the most central of central tables in the middle of Claridge's restaurant in the heart of London's Mayfair, Hart spoke to anyone and everyone who passed. It was his views on the world that he wanted to get out there. Others avoided his table by passing around the back and weaving in and out of other tables. It was that obvious that he wanted to verbally spar with others.

Hart was waiting for his guest to arrive. In the meantime, he was more than content to throw what he thought out there to as many people as possible. The staff waiting on the tables thought more than once about asking him to tone it down, but they knew this would be a futile gesture. In fact, it would have the opposite effect. David Hart had made Claridge's his base in London and he'd been there long enough that the people who worked there understood the kind of man they were dealing with. He was brash, rich and wouldn't think twice about loading into a member of staff with both barrels if he thought he was in danger of being publicly called out on his behaviour. A man of independent means, Hart was ready enough to go to war with anyone in the government, so a measly waiter at a hotel wasn't ever going to stand in his way. So, he continued.

Hart collared an American couple as they were heading to a quiet table in the corner for a late breakfast. They tried to shake off his attention by looking at the floor as they walked past but that tactic was never going to work with a big beast like Hart. The man told his wife to look down just as they approached.

"Did I detect an American accent there?" he asked, already knowing the answer.

"Yes," the man replied, before looking to his left to see if his wife had followed his instruction. She had her eyes firmly fixed on the expensive Axminster carpet, more evidence this hotel was one for the wealthiest in London.

"What do you guys think about what is happening over there? You must be a little embarrassed about the way your politics is headed?" Hart asked through a giant puff of an equally giant cigar.

"We're not so sure. We've been in Europe now for a few years, just visiting London for a few days, actually," The American replied, hoping that would be all the questions.

"And is that a thing? I don't think I could ever be that detached from what was happening in my own nation, especially with that actor in charge of things. How do you guys feel about that?" Hart rattled through these questions as though they were just the starters. He had eyes on the main course.

"We keep in touch on the phone with our folks, but there's so much to talk about other than politics with family you don't see very often," the American man replied. His wife was now almost completely out of view for David as she had moved behind her husband. The volume coming from the brash Englishman sat at the table wasn't what she was used to from her time in London. She wanted the conversation to end.

"I'm not sure that there is. Politics is everything my friend from over the ditch," David paused for a few seconds. He pursed his lips ready to continue but spied a member of the waiting staff next to the American couple and another waiter approaching fast.

"Sir, your guest has arrived," the first member of staff said before turning to leave.

"Sir, madam, your table awaits," the second member of staff told the American couple, who both sighed with relief.

David looked across the grand dining room of the hotel. At first, he spotted the marvellous lights that hung from the ceiling and shone in different directions depending on how he moved his head. He then looked at the tables and chairs in the room. The wood appeared as though it had been polished so many times that it picked up the lights from above and amplified it. The uniforms of the staff were as bright as a button too. He could see that the high prices he paid for the luxury of this hotel were reflected in the high standards management had in the way their team was presented. It was only the carpet that absorbed the light, otherwise David thought he might have been blinded in the vast light created by the rest of the room.

Through all the brightness, David failed to spot the figure approaching him from the right. As his guest pulled a chair up, David turned slightly to look at him. He appeared familiar, though he was sure they'd never been introduced. He rarely forgot a name. The man sitting across from him looked serious and without humour.

For his part, Mark Turnbull was well out of his comfort zone. For the last couple of months, he'd felt that fundraising for the NUM had all but come to a halt. Yes, the mine workers paid their dues, but additional funding was always required to keep the NUM operating and in the spotlight. With many miners not currently working and no additional fundraising in the plan Mark couldn't see how they were going to continue to run an effective operation. Even more frustratingly, whenever he raised this with the NUM's leader Arthur Scargill the issue was dismissed with the wave of a hand. Perhaps the media spotlight was screwing with Scargill's perspective. Mark wouldn't lie down and let that happen. So, he'd taken upon himself to meet with friends of the NUM who'd previously contributed to their cause. David Hart was first on his list.

"What do you want from me?" David Hart asked as though he was back in school, being pushed up against a fence by a bully he had no fear of. It took a lot for him to feel intimidated, but he was on the very edge of that feeling as he tried to understand this situation.

"I want to hear your opinions. Just not as loudly as usual," the man answered as the coffee was brought to the table.

"My opinion on what? World peace? The European football championships? The price of milk?"

"Don't get carried away, David. You're not that interesting. You tend to mistake being loud for having something to say that is worth listening to. If you have a truly interesting thing to tell the world, then you can say it in a whisper and they will listen. We want to know how we can put things right with the miner's situation. This is something we want to put right," the man remained sullen. David was known to be connected to the miners and the government, so had found himself in demand as the strike deepened and the relationship between the two progressively worsened.

"I think that there are some pretty big rifts to heal with the public," David started, while recalling the Battle of Orgreave six weeks earlier. It'd been particularly brutal and was beamed across the nation on the news bulletins for days. The fact that 72 police officers were injured undermined their cause massively. "Maybe we can start to get the rumours out there that the police were just as brutal as the miners? Do we have some injuries we can show? Can we make some injuries?"

"We've thought of that and it's not gaining much traction. The newspapers have their blood."

"How about we start to get the message out there of a future where we are reliant on coal from overseas? I'm thinking about one of the countries we have an in-built fear of, maybe the Soviets?"

"Now you're getting somewhere, David. It's good to hear you think like this. But there's something more practical you can do. You're in with Thatcher and the cabinet. How about putting in a word to her? How about slowing down the sea of change? Maybe she will see reason if it comes from someone she trusts, like you?" The man sitting opposite David spoke as if were already a done deal. Clearly it wasn't. Even the most optimistic of people knew that Margaret Thatcher wasn't someone who changed direction. The lady, as she said herself, definitely was not for turning.

"I'm going to continue to assume for the second that you aren't some gutter tabloid hack. But you're starting to smell that bad. You really think that I will have any effect at all? Perhaps we should all go outside and look for flying pigs?" David retorted with the ridicule the suggestion had deserved.

His table companion wasn't put off. It had been one question to lead to another and all part of a plan.

"Well, if you can't do that, then maybe a slice of your disproportionate wealth might help the cause somewhat. I was thinking of at least five figures, plus you raking around some of the other sympathetic residents of this fine hotel for some more."

It was now clear to David why he was being visited. He nodded his head in defeat. He had yet again involved himself in something he wanted to influence, but this time he might have to accept that he would be influenced himself instead.

Seeing the comprehension in David Hart's face, Mark Turnbull stood and without saying another word, turned and left the table. The sweat on his brow and shakes of nerves started before he even left the dining room. With his head down, he left Claridge's pleased with himself for getting a positive outcome for the NUM.

A full fifteen minutes later, David himself still in a state of shock, got up from the table and walked to the reception. He would spend some time there and start to work on a list of people he knew might have a few spare pounds for the cause. As he reached the lobby, he saw a familiar face. Ellen was walking across the lobby as though in some sort of hurry and almost missed David's huge hand offered out to shake.

"Hello, David." Ellen stated with a concerned smile.

"Terrible business, this miner's battle. I'd really like to make a difference if I can," the previous conversation with the unknown character bold enough to sit down with him uninvited, in his favourite restaurant no less, was still at the front of his mind.

His demeanour was so unlike what Ellen had previously seen that she found herself making him an offer. "I tell you what, why don't I set up a meeting between you and Paul Channon? That way you can see if you are able to help," she offered, already seeing that David's head was nodding furiously. That was that. She would sort this out when she was with Paul. And she too rushed off through the lobby and out into the warm morning air.

* * *

After a lonely weekend at Lollard Street, the following Monday Ellen, Paul and JK were en-route back to Yorkshire. The train journey was the usual mixture of silence and machinations from JK that Ellen detested. But the fact that they were headed to Yorkshire put her mind at rest. She had been speaking to Paul at length on being seen by others to be doing something about the miner's crisis. He had been content to let it play out, but public opinion was a major factor in all of this and opinion about Channon was becoming mixed at best. If he had greater political ambition, and he did, then it was Ellen's job to ensure his reputation didn't include apathy. As a first step, Ellen had been able to persuade Paul to meet a delegation of Union Leaders and Shop Stewards for some good PR. The fact that this was arranged by David Hart, who she had suggested should meet the minister, wasn't inconsequential.

Ellen had always believed in coincidence until she became involved in politics. After a few short weeks working in and around Westminster she could see that everything was arranged to happen. Nothing was left to chance. People outside of the parliament bubble thought that their lives were ones where they could make their own choices and develop a life of their own volition. But Ellen could see that laws were passed, and rules were made that narrowed the choices massively. People were herded into a certain way of thinking and living. She was sad sometimes to see that she had become a part of that, but at the same time she was more than capable of playing the game if she needed to. Letting David Hart know she would set up a meeting was one part of the equation. The other part was persuading Paul Channon that he needed to be visible. When these two seemingly random things were brought together by a single agent, the wheels were in motion for another event that felt random but was totally contrived.

They arrived on time at NUM headquarters on Huddersfield Road in Barnsley. Ellen was a little dismayed to see someone who was obviously a reporter out front. She didn't suspect a leak on her side and certainly wasn't expecting to keep a meeting between a Minster and NUM top-brass a secret, but she'd hoped for a little time at least to tell the story her way. Avoiding direct questioning from the reporter, the three of them walked through the doors and the necessary handshakes took place. There were many of the big players in the mining community in the room. Paul nodded his gratitude toward Ellen, this had been worth the journey.

Many of the faces that had come together at The Plough on that dark February night, the night Tom Linney had set a match to the tinder of strike action, now stood in the room facing the Minister. Weary of months of protest, without pay, they stood firm yet desperate. Fred Stokes and Lanks Armstrong from Cortonwood Colliery were there along with David Oley and Peter Dodd from the Barnburgh and Hatfield Collieries in Doncaster. From Grimethorpe and Hickleton in Barnsley were Paul Wardle and Steven Conyers along with Paul Musgrave from Manvers in Rotherham. Tom himself was conspicuously absent. Once the pleasantries were over, the group started discussions. It was plain for Ellen to see that JK was the easy target for these working men. He was brash, young and represented all that the city of London was in the eyes of those from close mining communities further up the United Kingdom.

David Hart took the leading role and was the main voice throughout, but the others chipped in. JK, trying to find his place in the discussion began by interrupting David to add something of his own. This did nothing but rile the Union reps and Shop Stewards.

"I don't think we need the opinions of a lackey."

"Minister, can you ask your boy to let the men speak."

"I can't hear him through the brightness of his tie."

It got to the point where JK had frustration and anger written all over his face. Ellen hadn't spoken much up to that point at all, for two reasons. Firstly, she didn't feel much like saying anything. It was argument and counter argument without a great deal of ground being ceded by either. It was politics at its worst as far as Ellen was concerned. It felt like neither side wanted to take a step forwards in case they were pulled completely forward and couldn't get back again to the place they'd occupied when they arrived. Secondly, she had her mind on meeting with Harry after the meeting. Being in Yorkshire brought her closer to the man she had fallen for. Her mind was on the job, even if her heart wasn't.

The meeting had been going on for some time. Ellen felt she was starting to see some cracks in the representatives of the mines, where some were for a pit closure or two, as long as it wasn't their own. She decided it was time for her to speak up. As she cleared her throat, she could see David Hart making eye contact with one or two of the other delegates. It was as though he was warning them to treat her in a better manner than they had treated JK.

"The economic situation is that we're sustaining mines that lose money to keep the jobs there. I'm sure you can see that this isn't a long-term proposition. We can't do this indefinitely. I know you're all here to represent the interest of your people, but there must be another way of resolving this. I think we need to invest in these areas and provide the next generation of jobs that people will go to when the mines have closed. There aren't endless pits of coal. If not now, then in the near future, there will be no coal left at all. What would we do then?" she spoke with an elegance that filled the room. David Hart was reminded of the words he was given when he was visited in Claridge's dining room –

"If you have a truly interesting thing to tell the world, then you can say it in a whisper, and they will listen."

The room went silent for a while. Some looked at each other with the smallest of nods. Only JK remained in the negative. The verbal beating he had taken had left a few scars and it was still raw. He would get over it, Ellen thought.

The meeting was nearly at a close, but the words of Ellen gave it a lighter note. The delegates spoke warmly to each other, but it was obvious that their minds were on the battle ahead. If they were to keep some of the mines open at least, then others would have to be closed.

As Paul, JK and Ellen left the NUM Paul turned and smiled. "That was great work team, there may be a way forward here and good old fashion pressing the flesh has got us here. Don't be too despondent JK, men like that will never respect men like us. Ellen, are you sure you won't join us for the ride home?" She had already told both Paul and JK that she wouldn't be travelling home with them, but they insisted on putting her through the embarrassment again. She had a few days off work and wanted to spend them in the wilds of Yorkshire with Harry. She politely declined.

An hour later she stood in front of Harry. They kissed gently; she could feel a tension in him that matched the electricity that was usually there. She was so excited to meet him that she could burst. She wanted to tell him all about her day but needed him to get the thing off his chest that was causing his tension. She didn't want it to consume them.

"What's up Harry? You're not your usual self."

"I've just got a few things on my mind, besides you that is!" he smiled and looked up from his feet as he spoke. Then the pause. Ellen hated the pause. She now knew this was Harry's way of delivering news that he didn't want others to hear. The pause only lasted for a few seconds, but as always with these things, it seemed to slow the world around her. People moved past as though they were wading through treacle. The speed of light slowed to a snail's pace. Harry drew breath but to Ellen it felt like he was moving in slow motion.

"I need to do something else with my life."

That sentence made it even worse. Of course, it was followed by another inordinate pause. Ellen felt like she could feel the hair grow longer on her head and her eyes grow weak with the light. What was he going to say? Was he going to break up with her? Was he going to join Dale in a futile battle for the pits? Had he found someone else?

"I want to learn a new trade. And I think that London might be the best place for me to learn it…"

Ellen blushed with excitement and anticipation. "Harry! That would be perfect. My flat is big enough for two and we could spend time together at the weekends and see all that London has to offer and go for long walks along the Thames and visit pubs in Camden and just be together." Ellen was breathless as she blurted out all of the things she could imagine the two of them experiencing together. It was a big step to let a man into her flat and her heart, but it just felt so right with Harry.

"Slow down. It's just an idea at the moment. I need to find out more about it, but I've thought of nothing else," Harry replied. As a man from Yorkshire, Harry didn't let his emotions spill out naturally in the way that Ellen did, but he was sure feeling a similar level of enthusiasm to her.

"Harry, I couldn't be happier, let's do this."

The two of them hugged tightly. The prospect of being together in London, one of the major cities of the world had Harry hooked. He would get on the telephone the next day to start finding out what trade he might learn and where that might happen. The image of being with Ellen all the time was one that filled his heart with joy. Harry had never felt this way about anyone. He wanted the moment to never end but was also aware that there were a whole host of moments ahead of them that would make him feel just as happy, if not happier.

"Ellen, I'm feeling it too!"

Chapter 17

Wednesday 12th September 1984.

Doncaster, Yorkshire, 15°C and raining heavily.

Ellen.

Ellen had been in Yorkshire for the early part of the week and was due to head back to the office. However, she decided that another day wouldn't do anyone any harm. She was only going back to catch up on some correspondence and have meetings with Paul and JK about pretty nondescript issues, so felt that she really wouldn't be missed. It was a long way out of her character to call in sick, but Ellen was feeling more and more disconnected to Westminster at that point, like she was lost, but not anxious about being lost. She knew her love of Westminster would return, she was sure of it, and decided that she should just accept that feeling like this every now and again was part and parcel of working in a high-pressure job. A good thing.

She called and spoke to Paul who was quite understanding at first but couldn't wait to get off the phone after about a minute. Ellen was sure he was nervous about listening to a woman in case she spoke about something that would embarrass him. He was a proper old-school gentleman and Ellen knew he was hard-wired to be disturbed by the fact he had a woman working for him and not at home looking after some man's children. *The world is moving on Paul,* Ellen thought.

She'd arranged a meeting with Mark Turnbull for later that day but wanted it strictly off the record. Mark was one of these people who she could trust to be discreet enough to have a meeting and not let on to anyone. She knew that the conversation could be as free as possible but would never leave the four walls of the room.

So, Ellen headed back to the Danum Hotel in Doncaster, now as familiar to her as the Palace of Westminster. She knew the people working there and that the rooms had thin walls, where conversations might be overheard and the best things to order from the menu. As she wasn't expected to stay that extra day, she headed to reception to ask about an extension. There was a copy of every daily newspaper available at reception, so Ellen had grabbed a couple of them and started to read. She might as well catch up on events that were being covered in the newspapers. Even just spending 48 hours with Harry had made her feel like she had lost some contact with what was going on. They were so preoccupied with their own world that the wider world around them didn't feel anywhere near as significant. Work meant that Ellen had to find some significance in it.

The headlines were as lurid and gory as ever but the stories behind them didn't do it justice. What looked like an interesting story from the first sentence panned out to be something padded out by a journalist who needed to fill column inches and didn't have anything interesting to write. It wasn't long before she drifted away from the words on the page in front of her and her mind took her back to the possibilities of a new life.

Ellen was normally in the position where she was booking rooms and having them billed to the minister's account. This time it was different. She used cash and went to the length of booking a different room under a different name. If it was going to be a secret meeting, then all of it should be secret, Ellen told herself.

She checked the room over and made sure the two of them could be comfortable. It wasn't going to be a long chat, but Ellen had a few things she wanted to ask Mark and she hadn't seen that much of him for a while. As he entered the room, Mark looked both left and right as though he was checking the place out for uninvited guests. It was just his way. Mark Turnbull had become one of the many people at that time who were concerned about their privacy and watched over their shoulder at least as much as they looked forward.

"Hello, Ellen, how are you?" Mark spoke softly, so softly that Ellen had to strain to hear him. It was always like this for Ellen. When she first met someone, who had a different accent or who spoke softly, she would need to concentrate fully on the words that came out of their mouth. After a little while she could acclimatise and hear much more easily.

"I'm really good, actually Mark. How are you?" she replied in a soft tone, mirroring the way he had spoken to her. The acoustics of the room allowed them both to speak in a near whisper and not be drowned out by the pipes in the walls or the people passing by in the corridor.

"It's been a pretty good time for me until recently. As you know, the miner's cause hasn't had the most favourable of media coverage. But I'm sure that will change. We have some pretty good backing and now all we need to do is turn that cash into action," Mark said. Ellen was pleased he was being that open. She had some open questions that she would like answers to.

"And would one of the places you get backing be Libya?" she asked without fear or embarrassment. Ellen meant business.

"We have friends all over the world, but yes, Libya is currently one of the most fervent backers. We have been able to help them in the past and now it's their turn to help us," Mark spoke in a warmer tone all the time. Ellen could see that he liked her.

As she thought, wherever she looked, Libya was the common thread running through it all. Libya was a word that she had heard in whispers many times in the corridors of power. Worse than the moral dilemma this presented her personally, it was clear that her Boss was involved. This in turn directly implicated her. The fact she was now openly dating a miner from one of the most prominent Collieries to the miner's strike might give the tabloids a field day. Ellen needed to think.

She'd used the meeting with Mark as the excuse but the real drive for her to remain was that Harry had invited her to dinner with Dale and his family. Ellen knew that Dale's mother, Mrs Edwards, was like a surrogate mum to Harry and wanted to meet her. Having not seen Dale since that first night at The Plough on the other hand made her rather apprehensive. Her mind fixated on a Sunday matinée movie of Caligula she and Harry had watched on ITV in Lollard Street a few weeks earlier. The last thing she wanted was any ménage-a-trois awkwardness at a key moment for them.

She needn't have worried. The evening started with light conversation. Dale's two sisters and friend Jane Stokes took Ellen under their wing and made sure she felt comfortable in the new situation. They were fascinated by London life, the clothes she wore and the job that she worked in. Ellen continued to have mixed feelings about her current working situation but talking to others reminded her of her passion. She was pleased to hear that others outside of Westminster felt it was a good way to earn a living. The doubts from earlier in the day had dissipated. It was clear that Jane Stokes had eyes for Dale, and this took the pressure off Ellen, in her mind anyway. Jane, it transpired, had always carried a torch for Dale and had got to the point where she didn't even try to hide it anymore. Spending time in Dale's company was all she desired.

"Ellen has a marvellous job, Mrs Edwards," Jane said.

"Oh, Harry has told me about it. Surely that's quite a male dominated world dear," Mrs Edwards said to Ellen as though she needed to be rescued from it.

"There is that, but it's given me the chance to learn, meet people and travel," Ellen replied

"You don't need to be in politics to travel. Look at my little boy, here. Dale has been travelling recently. Just come back from a trip to Libya, not that you'd know it. Got himself a passport and everything. Been to one of the most exotic places I've ever heard of and he doesn't want to talk about it. He didn't even want me to tell the rest of the family," Mrs Edwards spoke with her eyes closed as though delivering bad news. She avoided the faces around the room.

Dale looked sheepish and his eyes scurried around across the floor hoping that when he looked back up, he was the only one in the room. He had been told to keep his travel plans silent but couldn't help but tell his dear old mum. She would want to know where he was and where he would be day and night. Not telling her was far worse than actually telling her. At least that was what he thought. The fact that she'd just told people who had no right to know was making him think twice about that decision.

Jane eyed up Dale, ready to help console him. She was very in tune with his moods and could see that he wasn't in a great place. She wanted to hold him in her arms and tell him it was all going to be alright.

The two sisters were looking at Ellen with eyes of wonder. One worked in a local factory, the other in the new supermarket, jobs that they each wanted to escape from. The eldest had overheard Harry and Ellen talking about London earlier. That coupled with the way Ellen had described her job had got the pair of them thinking about how they could find a way to the big smoke.

Ellen and Harry were looking at each other. The usual look of love had been temporarily replaced with one of intrigue. Harry had been told many times by Ellen that she suspected Libyan involvement with her Boss and linked to the miner's situation. He hadn't believed her. Until now. Dale being seen as a pivotal player in the strike and visiting Libya was too much of a coincidence. Ellen had told him that there was no such thing as a coincidence, after all.

Ellen stored information for later. She spoke warmly to Mrs Edwards and found herself being really impressed by the strength of this tough working woman. Ellen had spent time with powerful people who commanded respect. But she realised that Mrs Edwards was in many respects even more impressive. Bringing up such fine men like Harry and Dale, her two daughters, all on her own while working well below the poverty line. Theirs was a relationship that was enhanced around a simple dinner table that night.

* * *

In another part of Yorkshire Arthur Scargill was sat waiting in his office. He saw many people come and go, pretty much a procession of those that either wanted to congratulate him or tell him that he was wrong. Neither bothered him that much. He always went with the belief in his own head that he was right. The work he had put into building his own ideas of the world were not going to be undermined by the opinions of others.

Scargill sat and looked around his office. The colours reminded him of the coal mines, all greys, dark browns with any other colour muted. The way that his office had been decorated was in keeping with the rest of his life; spartan to a point but with some hidden flourishes here and there. The colours were hidden in drawers or behind something else. The pen that was given to him as a gift from a foreign dignitary was always underneath his diary. Never on top. It was an expensive item and he would take it out only to show off to certain people, but most were not to know that he had riches from his position. That he wanted to keep a secret. It was the same with the cigars and fine cognac kept under lock and key in the drawer beside his right knee. Arthur Scargill would entertain with the best of them when he needed, but most of the time he kept up the façade of a man who was doing it for the cause and only the cause. There were a few that knew he had some side interests too.

It wasn't often he was alone. These were a few stolen moments in a day of constant chatter and chaos. His secretary told him the chaos was organised, he didn't really care one way or another. As head of the NUM, he had been catapulted to national fame. Everyone wanted a piece of his time. But Roger Windsor was late and Scargill used the time to collect his thoughts. The strike spearheaded by Roger hadn't gone quite to plan but Scargill had absolute faith that his side would win out in the end. It was a faith that he knew was shared by many others close to him. He wasn't always confident that Roger Windsor was one of them. The door creaked as Roger walked in. Scargill looked him up and down, as his friend thought he was being assessed. In fact, Arthur Scargill was looking to see where the creak was coming from, so he could fix it. Just another small job in the list of thousands that needed to be done everywhere he went. Scargill would notice the smallest details like a tile a few millimetres out of line or the smallest mark on a towel when he went to hotel rooms. He was a nightmare for any hotel owner worth their salt. The list of recommended repairs was always left. If Scargill didn't think the hotel owner was up to the task of making those repairs, then he would instruct his secretary never to book there again. In some towns he'd even run out of places to stay.

"Good afternoon, Roger. How's your day been?" Scargill asked as matter of courtesy and as a prompt for Roger to let him know why he was running late.

"Good. Yours?" he responded curtly. Roger put his hand to his mouth, he also turned his head away. Arthur Scargill was getting annoyed, but only internally. He didn't want this annoyance to show in his expressions. But it came out in his words.

"Sit yourself down, man! We've got things to do. Why are you still standing?" The words slipped out past his lips and into the air. They couldn't be put back now.

"Give me a chance. I've been talking to a few people. There's something in it for you too," Roger replied with an intrigue in his voice that immediately calmed the other man down. "And I think you'll be more than pleased with the potential outcome."

"Tell me more."

Once Roger had finished toying with has prominent friend, they got down to business. Roger could be a tease with his words. It took Scargill a few minutes to divert him back to the topic he had instigated at the very beginning.

"Now, what are you talking to me about? I'm a busy man you know," Scargill exclaimed.

"Not too busy to hear this," Roger replied and then paused. He wanted to see how long it was before his friend opened his mouth to speak. He wasn't going to let any words come out but was ready to pounce as soon as he could see Scargill had ran out of patience.

He counted to fifteen before Scargill sat forward, drew breath and went to voice his frustration. Roger was impressed he had lasted that long before jumping in and speaking.

"You know the money we have coming in from Libya?"

"Yes."

"Well, it is intended to look after us all, now, isn't it?"

"Of course."

"The mine workers are being looked after. This is the best funded strike in British history, and we have faith that we will win out. They'll get their jobs back and we will be able to sit back and look at our role in all of this. Are you with me so far?"

"Yes, I'm with you."

"So, where does that leave us? Where are we in all of this? All our hard work will help others. Who helps us?"

"I'm not sure I know what you mean," Scargill replied with an innocence that Roger wondered might be fake. It wasn't like his friend to miss a trick. He would have to fill in the blanks.

"We've secured a lot of money to come in from Libya. The miners will be more than looked after. We need to look after ourselves. Is that any clearer?" Roger spoke as though he was explaining something to a child. Scargill's eyes lit up. He wanted to know more. Without speaking this message waved its way across the room. Roger took up the instruction.

"There are some lucrative property deals that I've been discussing this morning. They'll make whoever is involved comfortable for the rest of their life. I really like the idea of being comfortable, don't you?"

He nodded. "Yes, I do. The money is well protected, there's nobody except you and I that have an idea of where it's being spent and who is making use of it. There are more requests for cash than funds we have available, so why don't we move some around here and there? That would protect our future." Arthur Scargill warmed to the idea. He knew that going into a deal with someone else carried some risks, but it also meant they both had a lot to lose. And an awful lot to gain.

"The people who you have spoken to about the deals, are they trustworthy?" Scargill asked.

"I trust them one hundred percent. The councils down in East London are so desperate to get this new business district of theirs built in their backyard, there aren't too many questions on where the cash has come from," Roger replied with a sincerity in his voice that eased any slight concerns that his friend had. "I can't see any problems. Our solicitors will be able to tie this up in enough red tape that it would take decades to unravel. By then I suspect we'll be on with our lives."

"Canary Wharf, yes, I've heard about this development. This is the one for us to go for then, let's get it done."

"I'm looking forward to doing business with you, Arthur. We have to make sure we look after everyone involved and that does mean you and me. There's nothing in providing a long-term protection for the miners if we don't have a long-term protection plan for ourselves. I know that's what most people would do in this situation."

They then went back to small talk. It was a common thought that if there were bugs in the room then they would listen to the start of a conversation and then dip back in at a later time. Both men were vaguely aware of this and tried to keep discussions about sensitive issues to a minimum before returning to bland conversation that wouldn't excite. Scargill wasn't afraid of the bugs. He felt comfortable in the thought that whoever obtained information about him couldn't really use it as it was gained in an illegal fashion. Roger was more circumspect but still didn't lose any sleep over it. This was just part and parcel of the war they were fighting. It was time to add a little personal fortune for their efforts and risks.

The two men concluded their meeting. After all, as Roger said, the money was provided to look after the movement. If the head wasn't looked after, then there was no hope for the body.

Chapter 18

Thursday 13th September 1984.

Lambeth, London, cloudy, windy with a high of 19°C.

Ellen and Harry.

"Morning chuck," Harry said before opening his eyes. He was laid on the right-hand side of the bed, close to the window. He wasn't fully awake , but he knew Ellen was there. She wasn't moving or touching him and didn't make a sound, but Harry just knew she was there.

"Morning Harry," Ellen said as she yawned. It was a large yawn that distorted the two words into something that might have been indecipherable without context, but Harry knew what she was saying. While still new to him, it just wouldn't have been the right start to the day in London for him without this small routine of theirs.

Harry had been staying with Ellen for the last few weeks and they had settled into a bit of a routine, which neither minded. Harry was enjoying being a Yorkshire man in the heart of London. He quite fancied that there weren't too many of them around, none that he had met so far anyway. The time he'd spent in

London before moving in was quite like a day tripper might experience. He was there, saw the sights, spent time with his girl and was gone again. Even when he spent a few nights there, Harry might as well have stayed in a hotel. But living in Lollard Street was very different. He thought about the contrast as he got out of bed to make a cup of tea for the pair of them. Ellen had rarely drunk tea before she met Harry, but it was now part of her morning ritual.

Harry moved across the bedroom and thought forward to his commute that morning and back to the commute he used to have when going to the pit. It was like a series of changes.

He changed the loneliness of waking up alone for the companionship of waking up with Ellen. He really liked Ellen and could see them being together for the rest of their lives. She had made a massive impact on him. Before he was gruff with strangers and would have struggled in a place like London. Now he was starting to feel more at ease with himself, even if he received very little from the other Londoners around him.

He changed the greenery of his hometown for the concrete jungle of London. Where he was used to seeing the fields wherever he looked, the view from the window was now one of buildings. No more or less interesting, just different, he kept telling himself. The fact that he'd rarely left his hometown before meant that this was a fascinating world of contrast.

His over-ground commute to an underground world had had its roles reversed and he'd swapped the walk to the pit surrounded by people he knew for an underground journey surrounded by far more people; all of them strangers. London in the early Nineteen Eighties was still London, busy yet isolated. Not many people spoke to each other; the carriages may well have been empty for all the conversation he got. Back at home when the pits were open, he talked all the way to work. He had to make up for it when he got to college.

He changed earning a living in the coal mine to studying most of the day at the Polytechnic of North London on the Holloway Road in Islington. It was an old building that was showing signs of major stress. Harry often thought that he was safer underground in the pits than sitting in a building that looked as though it might fall around him at any moment. If he was nervous about a collapse, the teaching staff certainly didn't share his concern. Having been used to a life where his fellow workers thrashed around and made a lot of noise, Harry thought it odd that people walked slowly and softly all day. He put his mind at ease, telling himself it was just a different type of movement of people.

Harry heard the click of the kettle and proceeded to make a pot of tea. The tea brewed, he poured a couple of mugs and took them back to the bedroom. Ellen moved her head from under the blankets and tried her best to raise a smile. She was more than happy but tiredness was still present from the day before and she wanted to do nothing but stay in bed all day. Work however meant that wasn't possible.

"Thank you, Harry," she said with all the energy she could muster. It wasn't a lot. Harry was accepting of the way she was with him in the morning. The mines had forced him to develop into someone who could function in the small hours of the day. The mines had previously been his only real option of working. Leaving school with very little in the way of grades meant that he would follow in the footsteps of so many other people from his hometown. Into the pit. It was an honest way to make a living and Harry wasn't afraid of hard work at all.

"It's almost half seven," Harry stated, hoping that Ellen was still awake enough to receive the information. She was but wanted to mull it over in her head before she responded. Harry pushed himself back into the corner of the bed he'd vacated earlier, but which was now populated by his girlfriend. Momentarily he began to worry that this was Ellen's house, her bed, her place and he shouldn't encroach. He nudged her over and reclaimed his place. Ellen relented, smiling. As Harry settled back into their bed his mind wondered to the other thing that was worrying him. The one that was not so easy to resolve.

They'd been there together on and off for some time. The last few weeks had been as if they lived together. They'd been out for drinks, had a meal out and even visited the cinema. But, in all this time, she hadn't introduced Harry to any of her friends. Not one. When he had mentioned it in passing Ellen changed the subject. It was like she didn't want to even contemplate Harry meeting people that she knew. It unnerved him and every now and again he had to remind himself that she wasn't ashamed of him. It felt like Ellen's life with Harry was something she wanted to keep a secret from her life with everyone else. It puzzled him from time to time. He hadn't lost any sleep over it, but when he stopped to think about it, Harry wondered if he might ever meet them.

For now, he forced it from his mind. He had to get across London to college with his first assignment to hand in. He was studying for a Diploma in Electrical Installations and had been asked to put together a drawing of the way he would install a fuse box. This was a task that Harry didn't enjoy much at all to begin with. Starting something new always filled him with self-doubt. He hadn't done any homework in his life, not even at school. So, when his tutor asked for something to be completed at home, Harry immediately felt anxious. But then the practical side of him took over. He would complete it as soon as he got in then he could put his mind at rest. This was the day that he was due to take it back and for the tutor to see how well he'd performed. Harry wanted to pass the course. He'd resolved to change his life. He wanted to earn a proper living again. Getting the diploma was his way of stepping away from the mines and being what he considered a useful member of society again now that mining was a lost option.

Harry leant over and kissed Ellen on the cheek. Then he snuggled up alongside her and started to pretend to snore. Ellen laughed under her breath and the two of them made snoring noises, getting louder and louder all the time before they were both laughing out loud together. They kissed passionately in the doorstep before leaving the property and going about their days. Harry longed for the time he would get back home again and have Ellen in his arms. Ellen felt exactly the same way.

Another world away, less than two hundred miles up the country, discussions were going on with Harry's best friend Dale about his next trip to Libya. This time he was to be accompanied by Roger Windsor and Tom Linney as the fervour to make contacts with the Libyans grew within the realms of the NUM and their wider family. Dale wanted to be involved with things but had some reservations about these foreign trips. They always felt as though they were tinged with a little danger. The last trip with Tom Linney was a real eye-opener for Dale; he hadn't seen the rest of the world and really hadn't expected the kind of welcome he got in Tripoli, the Libyan capital.

As much as Dale had mixed feelings about going to Libya, he was glad for the guidance that Tom had given him before, even if he hated the way the man treated people. Now that Roger Windsor was on board as a fellow traveller, Dale wondered how his presence would affect the behaviour of Tom. Although Dale had been welcomed into the upper echelons of the struggle against the closure of the mines with open arms, he was painfully aware that he was a newcomer to this world. The reception he got could just as quickly be taken away if he ever put a foot wrong.

"Dale, we're going back," Tom Linney said. He could see that Tom was already picturing exotic bars and being waited on hand and foot.

"I know Tom. I'm looking forward to it." Dale tried to convince himself that he would have a good time. He wasn't sure if the doubt came across in his words.

"And this time, we're taking dear Roger here with us," Tom bellowed as he patted Roger Windsor on the back. Roger was taken aback by this welcome. The two men had continued an uneasy truce throughout the years. Roger distrusted Tom and the feelings ran both ways. Nobody seemed to be able to trust anyone in the climate of sabotage and spying. It wasn't just one side pitted against the other, things were far more complicated than that.

"Have you been to Libya before?" Dale asked as a matter of courtesy. He wasn't interested in the answer but was more interested in the man.

"You can't ask a question like that, my dear boy!" Tom shot straight back at him. It was the first time Dale had detected any real anger in his voice.

"I'm sorry. I didn't mean anything by it," Dale countered with an innocence that was immediately understood in the room.

"I know you didn't, but you'll understand I can't answer that question directly, Dale," Roger replied, softer this time. The fact was that Roger had been to Libya more than once. He was as familiar with the place as Tom, and that much would be obvious when he arrived in the place with the other two men and was greeted like an old friend.

The three men talked travel plans together like they were young boys going on their first school trip.

"I've always wanted to swim in the Mediterranean Sea with no clothes on," Tom Linney said, conjuring up a less-than-pleasant image in the minds of the other two.

"Can you do that before we get out of bed for the day?" Roger said coldly.

"We're only there for a couple of days. I'm not sure there will be much time for sightseeing," Dale spoke for the first time in the discussion about what they would do. In truth he wanted to get in and out and back home like he'd never left. The plans of the other two men made him feel nervous and he didn't want to end up drinking as much as he did the time before. The more he had to drink, the more he felt uneasy in the company of these men who were shaping the future of the United Kingdom as much as the government.

"Give it a rest, Dale. You sound like my mother," Tom replied with a voice that stopped all other noise in the room. It was like he had created a vacuum and sucked all the atmosphere from the place. Roger again felt the need to stick up for the younger man.

"He's right, Tom. We're there on business and this is an important trip. Don't forget that this money does more than it did the last time. Don't forget that we're doing this for ourselves as well."

Dale's instincts were to ask a lot of questions about that last statement. He was concerned before that the money which was supposedly helping the miners had been lower than expected. He wasn't involved in politics enough to see where that might have ended up, but this talk from Roger sparked his intrigue again. He decided that questions would shut the conversation down again, so he shut up and listened.

Tom spoke, "Dale, this is the most important trip I've made to Libya. So, it goes without saying that it's by far the most important one of your life. We're securing the future here. This money is earmarked to help everyone involved in the fight to keep the mines open. When we have secured victory, which I'm sure we will, you and your people will be back with a living again. We must think about all of those who don't have a job in the mines to go back to. Our future ends when the pits reopen. We have to take care of ourselves, if you know what I mean."

Dale was stunned for two reasons. Firstly, he didn't think that Tom would speak this freely in front of him. It was the first time that Dale truly felt like he was in their inner circle and close to the leaders of the NUM. Secondly, he was completely shocked at the behaviour of the two men. It was clear that they were looking after themselves and not putting all the investment they could into the cause. Dale saw for a few brief moments the inner circle of the NUM and realised an unpleasant truth. Yet keeping his mouth closed had worked so far in the conversation and it was a tactic he wasn't going to abandon right there and then.

"I understand."

That was it. Those were the only words that came out of Dale's mouth from that moment until it was time for the three of them to part ways. The rest of the conversation was filled with idle chat about the struggle and how they were the right people to bring it to an end. All Dale could see was two men posturing about the good they were doing when in fact they had poor intentions in them. He was less than impressed.

As they parted ways with an agreement to meet each other at the airport the following week, Dale shook both men warmly by the hand. What he was about to do didn't fill him with any satisfaction. He was becoming more aware that he could play a pivotal role in the situation. He had to decide which direction he would steer things in.

Later that night, Dale sat at home wondering what he would do. His mum and sisters all went out at various stages of the night, leaving him and his thoughts alone for a few hours. He needed to speak to someone. He needed a voice that would bring him calm and that he could trust. He grabbed his jacket, keys and some change and headed out himself to the payphone down the street.

He picked up the receiver and dialled a number that he hadn't used before. Harry had jotted it down for him the last time the two friends had been together. Dale wondered why he had bothered, and it had remained in the back pocket of his jeans. He began to dial.

"Hi mate, how's things?" Dale spoke as soon as the receiver was picked up at the other end.

"Hi. Is that Dale?" a female voice replied. It was Ellen. "Dale, are you OK? It's been a little while since I saw you. You calling after your friend the London-based big Yorkshireman? How are things with you?"

"I'm good, Ellen. It's actually really good to hear your voice," Dale replied.

"I'm sure it always is!" Ellen came back with mock confidence. "Do you want to speak to Harry?"

"That would be grand, Ellen. Thank you." Despite everything, Dale still felt a twinge of awkwardness each time he spoke to Ellen. When on that first night, full of bravado, he had approached her in The Plough he had no idea that she would become a constant part of his life. Albeit a distant one as the girlfriend of his best mate who now, it seemed, had moved permanently south. With that, Ellen came off the line and Harry sounded almost instantly.

"Hi matey, how are you?"

"I need someone to talk to, Harry. There's a lot going on here and I'm not sure I want to be involved in it," Dale spoke in a hushed voice that gave over the message to Harry that this was to be kept a secret.

"Involved in what?" Harry responded.

"I'm not sure where to begin."

Chapter 19

Saturday 6th October 1984.

Grantham, Lincolnshire, sunny, a light wind and a high of 9°C.

Ellen.

On a Saturday morning, the dark corner of the hotel lobby in the sleepy town of Grantham wasn't dark enough for Ellen. She felt that she had the most to lose of the three people meeting there. It was quite fitting that the town where Margaret Thatcher was born was to be the meeting place of three very different people. People who were meeting to talk about an issue that was threatening the government Thatcher was leading.

"Harry are you sure that this is the place we're supposed to meet Dale," Ellen said in a whisper. She'd gone through the meeting arrangements time and again with Harry. At first, she wanted to change the meeting time, then the venue and then maybe not meet at all. Harry could tell she was nervous from all the questions, so took control of the situation. Ellen was told when and where she would meet, Harry even booked the train tickets. It was a neutral venue, far away from the Westminster machinations of government and the intense scrutiny of the

National Union of Miners and all their hangers-on. It was as close to perfect as they could manage in the country.

"This is the place. I've known Dale all my life and he's never been one for timekeeping, especially when it's somewhere he doesn't know. He won't have left himself any wriggle room for getting lost," Harry replied with a clam control that took away the fears of his companion and lover.

Ellen gave him a new purpose, a drive. However, this interest in what her Boss was up to in Libya gave Harry cause for concern. He understood that she could lose her job along with her reputation if she was seen meeting with someone in the militant part of the NUM such as Dale. But the people who had eyes in many places couldn't have eyes everywhere. A sleepy lobby of an even more sleepy hotel in Grantham wasn't going to be anywhere near the top of the list of potential meeting places on anyone's list. The press, the government, the NUM and the rest simply wouldn't pick this as a place where some of their own would come together to discuss delicate issues with the other side.

"He's here," Harry said without even moving his head. The connection between the two was strong. He didn't need to see Dale to feel that he was there.

"He's walked through the doors, past the receptionist and walking along that wall," Harry pointed as he traced where he thought Dale might be. "His head will pop out from behind that wall in five, four, there, two, one…" And like a magic trick Dale appeared at the gap at the end of the wall. He glanced both ways as though he were an incompetent spy in a cheap movie. For the minute Dale revelled at being part of this plan. He didn't walk directly from the train station to the hotel. Dale thought that taking a few detours would put people off the scent, even though he only saw one person the whole journey; an old woman who was out to get the newspaper for her husband.

"Morning," Dale spoke as he neared the two of them, shaking Harry warmly by one hand with two of his before giving Ellen a hug that bordered being uncomfortable.

"Morning Dale," the other two said in unison.

"Wow, couldn't you have chosen anywhere livelier Harry!" Dale said in a quiet voice that told volumes about the way he was feeling. Rarely did he speak under his breath, but this was one of those occasions.

"Discretion, you know me my friend," Harry replied with a smirk, trying to keep the mood light. "Let's take a seat, I'll get the teas in and we can talk from there."

Dale sat in silence with Ellen while Harry went over to the reception area and ordered teas for the three of them. Order made, Harry turned to see Dale and Ellen each individually staring into space. It was clear that the enormity of the situation was putting a massive strain on both their shoulders. He evidently had the least to lose.

Shortly after Harry retook his seat the teas arrived.

"Harry, we need to get up to speed first," Ellen said. She wanted to hear things directly from Dale, rather than second hand from Harry. It wasn't that she distrusted the words Harry had relayed but he did tend to leave out details and gloss over cracks if he didn't fully understand what was going on.

Dale took the next ten minutes to explain to Ellen the conversation he had been part of. And in the meantime, he had been party to similar conversations that made it clear Roger Windsor and Tom Linney were not the only ones lining their pockets with cash that had been promised to the miner's cause. This was a scandal that went all the way to the top.

"We need to be extremely careful with this information. I'm not sure about many of the people in government from my experience, especially where Libya is concerned," Ellen explained. It was refreshing for her to speak after a full ten minutes of listening to Dale. He was an engaging talker, but Ellen felt that she should have been asking more questions of him. But none came.

"This could be across people from the top to the bottom," Harry interjected, "and my worry is that the people at the bottom end up being blamed and dumped with all the problems."

The three of them sat in silence for a few moments. Harry just reflected the behaviour of the other two. He was there to support the pair of them and wasn't sure if he could be of any practical help. He wanted both to be safe most of all.

"The best way to get to the bottom of this is to create a media storm. Without much in the way of evidence, we must get the story out there and allow it to take its course. There is a long way to go with this; from my experience it'll only grow legs if we give it the light of day," Ellen used her expertise to explain to the other two how she felt the truth should develop.

Dale listened and then replied, "Is that the way things work? I wanted something a little more concrete."

"Without any evidence, we're really going to struggle to do anything else. Besides, I don't see this as a weak option. There's a lot of benefit to giving this to the press. They'll do their own investigation and the people near the top will have to answer some pretty difficult questions. There is a lot to be said about the press keeping the political classes in check." She was determined that some action come out of this meeting. She knew the press better than the others and was in awe of the power it yielded at times.

"Right, I understand," Dale responded. He would bow to the greater knowledge of Ellen on this. She explained things well and he was more than happy to follow her lead. The way in which she took the time to explain impressed Dale. He felt that he had been left in the dark with much of the dealings with the NUM and their connections in recent times. To have someone talk him through a decision was like a breath of fresh air.

"Is that all agreed, then?" Harry asked, looking between them both. Nods all around.

"We need to make sure we get this story to the right people. We need a newspaper that is sympathetic to the truth and sensitive to our own involvement," Ellen explained.

"We have a lot to lose here," Dale added.

"But they have more to lose," Harry replied. This comment changed the mood. A determination to make things happen overcame the three of them. Their fear for what might happen was overtaken by a feeling that right was right and wrong was wrong.

"So, Ellen, you have all of the connections in that world. Do you have someone in mind?" Dale asked.

"Now you mention it, I do. Dale, it's critical that you start to very carefully document everything. Don't get caught doing it, but keep a record, a mental one if you can, of anything said or agreed on. The devil will be in the detail here and fuelling a media storm requires detail."

*   *   *

Early the following week Ellen was sat in the parliamentary office with her Boss, Paul Channon and JK. The three of them were discussing future plans for the department. This was always the way that Paul spoke about the future. It was really his plan to further his career, but it was dressed up as plans for the department. Ellen and JK had listened to it so many times before that they just played along with it. The first time Ellen was in the room when Paul spoke of 'the way the department would become more important in the eyes of the Prime Minister,' or 'how the department could gain promotion,' she was unnerved. It went against all the things she got into politics for. Plus, it just sounded weird for a young woman to hear. After time, it became part of the background noise that accompanied every day working in and around Westminster. That's why Harry was such a revelation in her life. He was intelligent, but he didn't play games, didn't lie and especially didn't try to get one over on everyone else.

"Ellen, what's the most pressing thing on your mind right now?" JK asked as a full invitation to the conversation. Ellen could see that the testosterone levels had subsided and was willing to commit full-time to it.

"I think we need to get the success stories out there. In a situation like this, the press battle is more than half of the war. We've been on the winning and losing sides at times over the last few months. It's time we brought out something positive," Ellen said in a way that she felt was turning the conversation in her direction. She didn't want to be persuaded to do anything that went against her principles, and with the way things were after talking to Dale, the last thing Ellen wanted was to be exposed in any way. Under the radar was the order of the day, perhaps even the year as far as Ellen was concerned.

"And I think from what I hear, you have one of the success stories living in your home with you. Without the closure of the pit, Harry would be still working in those dirty conditions, getting up at the crack of dawn every day and face a future that is as bleak as the landscape up there," Paul interjected with his usual tact. Ellen knew there was a Southern bias in the government but was always taken aback when she actually heard it out loud.

"He's having a good time of things here, that's for sure. Harry started college and is even enjoying London life. But, enough about my private life, there's other people we could find that have benefitted from the closure of the mines without getting so close to home..."

"Yeah, that's not gonna happen," said JK excitedly like he'd just found the last piece to his jigsaw. "Let's get you out to one of my favourite journalists, maybe your boyfriend can tag along with you too. It's time for us to call in a favour with The Times. I'm really keen for you to meet with Timothy Philpot to talk about the positive impacts the closing of the mines is having. Are you ready?"

"Yes, JK," Ellen spoke. She could see that Paul was looking over JK's shoulder for a response too. "Yes, Paul," she repeated.

"Then it's set. I'll give Tim a call and we'll put it in your diary," JK spoke with all the confidence in the world. Ellen wasn't sure whether she liked him when he was like this, or even if he remembered that she already knew Tim. It was as though this had all been agreed by Paul and JK before she even set foot in the room. But Ellen didn't care. Timothy Philpott was exactly the person she had in mind to break her own story; that of Dale. She just wasn't sure how to approach him. The fact that JK had set up a meeting between the pair of them meant she didn't have to come up with a reason or excuse to meet. She would see how things went in the meeting before deciding if he was the right man.

The following day, Ellen walked into Tim's office in the Times' building with a mixture of nervousness and excitement. She had toyed with the idea of taking Harry along as part of the main story but decided against it. If Tim wanted to meet Harry, then that would be for another day. She had bigger fish to fry and wanted Tim to feel like he was the only other person in on it. Taking along her boyfriend might make the journalist feel he was hearing something that was part of a grudge or just gossip. Hearing it directly and exclusively from a trusted source like Ellen would give the story more credibility.

"Hi, Ellen. Long time, no see," said Tim.

"Hi, Tim. It's good to see you. Thanks for making the time," Ellen replied as though he was doing her a favour. She hoped if he was receptive to her point of view that they would be doing each other a favour by the end of the meeting.

The two of them chatted for a while before talking about the story JK had pitched to Tim. It featured far more of Harry than Ellen was comfortable with, but the human element was always a great part of any story. She was closer to that human than anyone else on the planet and knew his story inside out, as did Tim by the sounds of things.

As they spoke, there were the odd things that Tim threw into the chat that gave Ellen heart when it came to mention what she, Dale and Harry had discussed in Grantham. Every now and again he confided a mistrust in the NUM leadership or wondered about the links between Libya and the miners' strike. After a good chat about the upside to closing the mines and the story she was supposed to be there for, Ellen decided it was time to speak up.

"Tim, I've got another story that I wanted to run by you. It's probably far more interesting than this one..." She let those words hang in the air to see if they landed. And they did.

"What is it about? You've been somewhere else for large parts of our chat today and I thought it might have been something to do with a man… is there another story? Tell me more…" It was Tim's turn to practice the art of silence.

"This is well outside of my Westminster remit and I need to tread carefully. You're the closest thing I have to a trusted member of the media. The fact I work in government is unrelated to this." Tim raised his eyes. "There's something going on at the top level of the NUM. I've been given information by someone who is connected to that world and has heard this with his own ears. They're syphoning off money for their own end. Some of the leaders are buying property with money brought into the country illegally from Libya. This is a story that needs to be out there in the public domain. I'm just not in the right position to do this," Ellen explained with a look of terror in her eyes. She wanted to offer this story exclusively to Philpott and wanted The Times to lead the fight for truth, but she was concerned that he would just laugh her out of the place.

Her concerns were unfounded. "I knew there must be something going on there. Too many hangers-on, too many people for that small sphere of influence. The NUM have had their detractors over the years but have never been brought to book. It might be time to change all of that," Tim spoke with a clarity of vision that matched the purpose she, Dale and Harry had found when discussing things in that Grantham hotel.

"I want The Times to have this story exclusively. I won't discuss with anyone else, as long as you protect me as the source. I've got dates, times and places that these discussions took place as well as the people who were involved. Please run with this, as I want justice to prevail, but I can't be clearer, I need to be protected," Ellen explained.

"Wait there, while I get a fresh notebook. I don't want this one to be left around the office," Tim spoke as he looked around the drawers behind Ellen for a new pad. It didn't take long for him to re-emerge with a fresh notebook in one hand and a pen in the other.

"Now tell me all about it..."

Chapter 20

Thursday 11th October 1984.

Brampton Bierlow, South Yorkshire, 11°C, heavy rain and wind.

Dale.

Dale put all thoughts of the discussions he'd been in with Ellen at the back of his mind as he jumped into a car with Tom Linney and Roger Windsor to take him to Heathrow Airport. He was soaked within just 25 meters getting to the car through the rain. Acknowledging the other two, he ran his hands through his wet hair to straighten it as the windows in the car began to steam up as they pulled away. Dale and Harry had spoken on the phone a few times but there had been little for the two of them to discuss in terms of the story. Dale had to assume that Ellen was doing her thing. He'd been around enough people in the NUM that were suspicious of everything and everyone the he found himself becoming increasingly suspicious of everything too. The calls he made with Harry were from a different public telephone each time. He figured that if someone was watching him then they wouldn't be able to tap all the phones in Yorkshire. Some nights he walked over an hour to reach a different public telephone than the ones he had used before. The sight of the familiar red box with their panes of glass typically broken or defaced provided Dale a calmness he hadn't realised he needed.

Dale sat in silence for most of the journey. He was the last one in and the other two seemed already engulfed in a conversation that Dale had no wish to join. Instead he sat back, closed his eyes and pretended to sleep. The ride to the airport felt like it took forever to Dale, but in reality, was just over three hours as the car sped down the M1. He wasn't the best traveller by road but sucked up all the negativity he was feeling and just went along with the flow. The traffic coming into London was always a pain and he couldn't do anything about it. He had seen Judith Hann on *Tomorrow's World* a few weeks before presenting significant progress on flying cars to put an end to all the traffic congestion in the major cities of the world. He didn't care about the congestion. For Dale the car ride reflected his situation, slowly progressing toward a place he now didn't much want to be in.

In the last few miles to the airport the others ended their conversation and clearly wanted to start a new one with Dale included this time. They wanted to plan the drinks in anticipation of arrival at their final destination. Tom was happy to stay in the hotel and get stuck into the drink there without having to travel any more. Roger was looking forward to spending time in as many bars and clubs as possible. They were both looking for Dale to land on one side or the other to settle the argument. Dale wasn't bothered either way and felt that staying in the hotel was going to be best for him, but his dislike of Tom had grown to a point where he was prepared to oppose him for his own end. Roger won. The three agreed to spend time in the city under the stewardship of Roger Windsor. He knew the city about as well as any Englishman and had a few drinking spots lined up for them all to enjoy. Not that enjoy was the word Dale would associate with the trip. He felt an unease with the other two men since they had hinted to him about the plans to syphon money off that was supposed to help the miners. Spending hours of time around them caused him to feel sick, with them as well as with himself. He resolved to try and make good his mistake.

The flight was much better than the car journey as far as Dale was concerned. The part where he was up in the air allowed his mind freedom under the cover of his closed eyes. His sleep was long and filled with dreams. Dale could see an end to the miner's strike in the next few months and one way or another he would ensure at least some of the money he was about to collect would help his fellow workers. His part in the struggle would probably go unnoticed by most but he would be able to sit back at the end of it all and know he had made a significant difference to the world, his world.

Once in the Libyan capital of Tripoli and with their belongings safely in their hotel rooms, the three men were out in a taxi, heading to the first night spot Roger had arranged. At first Dale thought it was familiar but soon realised that it wasn't the place he'd visited before. This place was much quieter, not at all like the kind of spot Roger had discussed in the car previously. Roger was far more deferential than before to the people in the bar as they showed the three of them their table. He passed money over to the man who had seated them. The man spilt the notes into three piles, one for his pocket, one behind the bar and the third to someone sat two tables away.

This place was small, with only a handful of people in and all of them looked official in one way or another. There was something about the faces and demeanour of the people in the bar. Dale couldn't quite put his finger on it but there was something in the air.

As Roger ordered drinks, he spoke a few words of Arabic. It was the first time Dale had witnessed either he or Tom speaking in the local language. Usually they barked orders in English and expected whomever they were speaking to simply understand. Dale was intrigued.

"I didn't know you could speak the local language, Roger," Dale said.

"There's a whole lot you don't know about me, sonny," Roger replied with a tone that gave Dale the clear message to leave well alone. He took this in and let Roger get on with his performance. That was the word Dale attached to it. This wasn't quite like the Roger he knew; this one was clearly playing a role.

While the waiter was getting the drinks, Roger excused himself and went across to talk to someone on the table behind Dale. After the rebuke about asking the question, he didn't dare turn around to see what he was doing but Dale became very aware while Roger was behind him. The air in the bar was thick with tension. Dale looked at Tom to see if he was feeling it too. He didn't need to ask. It was written all over Tom's face.

As Dale prepared to start a conversation with Tom to see if idle chat would make them both feel more at ease, raised voices sounded from behind. Dale and Tom turned around at the same time. It was the table next to where Roger was stood and there were two local men shouting at each other. It was as if they had to do something but neither of them wanted to be the first one to move. Dale was fascinated by the spectacle, as were the other scantly placed members of the bar's clientele.

Then it all died down. Roger glanced in the direction of the table and the two men stopped shouting. He looked to where Tom and Dale were sat, sending both men spinning back round on their chairs to face the way they were before the commotion.

The drinks arrived. Dale dived into his as soon as it hit the table. His nerves were getting to him.

The room darkened. It was as though a light bulb had blown but turning around again, they could both see that it was the presence of three other men that were blocking the lights from behind.

The first man said something quietly in Arabic.

The second man said what sounded like the same thing but in a much louder voice.

The third man was Roger Windsor. As Dale and Tom looked at Roger for some clarification, he smiled.

"Roger, what's going on? What did they say?" Tom asked

"I'm afraid they said that you two are under arrest. I'll have to leave you here," Roger explained. And with that he calmly walked out of the dingy bar he had contrived to take his travelling companions too.

Roger went straight back to the hotel and checked himself out. He ordered a taxi and headed back to the airport. It was a short trip. Even shorter than he'd explained to Dale and Tom. And while Dale and Tom were taken to a local police station, Roger boarded the plane with a suitcase that he'd picked up from a safety deposit box in Tripoli airport. Inside were bank notes again. This time to the tune of £150,000, non-sequential numbers, unable to be traced. With official focus on the other two, Roger slipped out of Libya and was back in the UK less than 24 hours after he left. The money intended for the miners was now certainly to be used for a different purpose. Roger and his high-ranking friends were set on bank-rolling a small block of upmarket apartments that had just received planning permission in the newly developed Canary Wharf financial district in London. There was always money to be made in bad times, Roger thought as he stepped through customs.

"Anything to declare?" the customs officer asked.

"Nothing. Nothing at all," he replied smoothly.

*   *   *

The following day, Ellen was lying in bed at home with Harry. She was awake a few times during the night as if something was making her restless. She looked at the ceiling and tried to guess the time. This was one of the ways she hoped to get back to sleep.

While others counted sheep, she thought about what time it was. She also went through the people who lived in her street when she was just a girl. She remembered the people either side of her parents' home for six houses in a row each side. Then the people on the other side of the road and then some of the odd ones farther down the street where they had other kids she used to play with. The rest she struggled with. These strategies were tried and tested to get her back to sleep and ready for the next day. But something that night stopped Ellen from getting back to sleep. She couldn't quite put her finger on it but there was a quiet ticking in the back of her head that put any plan for sleep on hold. Ellen guessed the time at 3 a.m. but had overestimated her sleep by an hour. It was only two. She cursed. Looking at the clock meant she was now annoyed as well as awake. Not a great combination.

The seconds ticked by one by one. Ellen was sure she could feel each one of them pass by slowly. It was the most excruciating night she'd ever endured. She tried thinking about the people on her street, but her mind wandered, and she didn't get anywhere. She decided to look at the clock again. Not even three. What was happening? Ellen did this several times hoping that the clock would speed up and she could get the night over with. The last time she looked at her alarm clock that night was at six minutes to three.

As well as dealing with the closure of the mines, the government of the day had a long-running encounter with the Irish Republican Army over the governance of Northern Ireland.

The IRA believed that it should be brought under Irish rule and independent of the UK government, while others in the country wanted to remain as part of the United Kingdom. This saw people killed, beaten and persecuted in a series of incidents known from the other side of it as 'The Troubles.'

The IRA were heavily involved in activity within the borders of Northern Ireland but were also aggrieved at the way the UK government had stationed troops in the country and were trying several ways to bring about change. The militant arm of this organisation, the Provisional IRA, had moved to bombing places on the British mainland to attempt to scare the government into changing policy or scare the people into pressurising the government to do something different.

At six minutes to three, while Ellen was struggling for sleep, the Provisional IRA detonated a bomb in the Grand Hotel in Brighton. Their past bombs had gone off in public houses, so a hotel wasn't a massive leap from this. But the fact that the hotel contained the government, including the Prime Minister Margaret Thatcher meant that this marked a direct threat to the people in charge of the UK and its policy towards Northern Ireland rather than something that aimed at the general public.

Ellen's phone rang at around twenty past three. Still awake, she walked across the home to the living room to answer it. The fact that she'd decided to travel to Brighton by train on the days she was needed rather than stay in the hotel with JK and Paul was not lost on her. She was thankful for that. As she listened to JK, talking to her from the street from the nearest phone box he could find, she heard Harry stir behind her.

"It's chaos, Ellen," JK spoke. She could detect real upset in him that she had never witnessed before. "Paul is OK, and I've seen the Prime Minister leave but there must be people dead or seriously injured in that building. There are bits of rooms scattered all over the ground outside. I'm worried for some of the other people we know and work with. I think you should get yourself here."

"JK, I'll be there soon, and we can check how people are. Where are you going to be? I don't want to wander the streets," Ellen replied. She felt for JK. Although he got on her nerves more often than she could remember, she was concerned for him. The long hours in the close confines of Westminster meant it was a friendship of sorts, a little more than a work relationship.

"I'll be in the café in front of me. It's called Café Ponderosa. Sounds much better than it looks but the place is warm, light and serves a decent cuppa. I had one there when I gathered myself some fresh air yesterday and the owner has kindly opened the doors now for people who have had to move away from the Grand. I'll see you later in the day," JK replied, longing for a friendly face. Paul had been whisked away with other members of the cabinet and wider government infrastructure. JK had no idea where this was but fully understood the need to protect the government in the face of whatever had just gone on.

Hours later and much further up the country, Arthur Scargill ate his breakfast while watching the morning news. The coverage of the Brighton bombing was all they were running with. As Ellen and Harry dashed frantically across London to get her on the earliest train out to Brighton, Scargill listened with some glee to the story unfolding in front of his eyes. The coverage here only meant one thing. That there was no coverage of the miner's strike. It meant that their problems of recent months were kept off the front pages. It meant that they could go under the radar for a short while. There is a phrase in government circles known as 'a good day to bury bad news.' The fact that no news about the NUM was appearing on either the pages of the newspapers or the TV screens meant there were no reporters sniffing about. Scargill enjoyed this reflection. He was joined at home by Roger Windsor. The two of them were due to go to a rally together later that day and Scargill had invited Roger over for breakfast to discuss what they were going to say. Many public speakers had their speeches written for them days or even weeks in advance. Scargill didn't operate in that way. There was so much going on every single day that a speech written a week before would be out of date before he was able to deliver it. Plus, he wanted the words to be his own. His usual method of working a speech was to discuss the current events with someone and then weave that into his words later in the day. Every now and again he would write a few notes and stuff them in his pocket but the most common way of remembering this was just to rely on his prodigious memory.

"Roger, this is a happy day. We've got ourselves a distraction that can help take the focus away from us. There's been a lot of discussion about our links to Libya recently and the more that spotlight was shone, the less comfortable I felt. This puts the government back under the spotlight. Questions will be asked about their role in Ireland and they will be under the cosh when all the fuss about the damage and injury dies down. We need to make the most of this situation. Now is the time to act," Arthur Scargill said firmly.

"With that in mind, I think it's about time to make the deal with those flats in London over the next few days. This is the perfect time to make our plans for our futures. The press will be all over Ireland for the next few weeks at least. I agree that we use this time wisely and get as much done as we can," Roger replied.

"We need to make sure we can profit from this situation," Arthur Scargill said, and the message came across loud and clear to Roger Windsor, *conversation over, time for action*.

"Now, about this speech."

"Don't worry, Roger. The IRA have already written it for me."

Chapter 21

Thursday 8th November 1984.

Tripoli, Libya, overcast with a high of 26°C.

Dale.

"How did I get here?"

Dale had asked himself that question a thousand times or more over the previous few weeks. Weeks where he had barely seen another soul, let alone had anyone to talk to. This gave him all the time in the word to think about his life, the situation he was in and that all important question again. "How did I get here?"

He thought back to the life he'd led over the last few months. The situation with the miner's strike had consumed him. He was a miner, as was his father, his grandfather and as far back as he could tell. Closing the pits was like a dagger through his being. It meant the loss of a livelihood to him and all his friends. A loss of a life and lives. More than that, it ripped the heart out of the community he belonged to. People's lives centred around that mine. That's where the men worked. That's what paid for the food on the table, clothes for the kids and a few pints at The Plough when the working day was done. This was all disappearing and the void that replaced it was what was most frightening. If they closed the mines and replaced them with another form of employment, then he could look to the future with some hope. But unemployment and the dole were the only promises Dale felt he had been given by the government. He felt sold out. Betrayed.

These feelings multiplied by the way he had been treated by the NUM. His trusted ally, the NUM, had turned out to be just as quick to sell him out too. At first, he had thought that he was accepted. Dale knew that they needed soldiers on the ground to help organise the strikes, motivate people to carry on and keep boots on the picket-line. And with the movement stuttering in places, Dale thought that he would be needed more than ever. The miners didn't have all the successes that they were initially promised. They needed more momentum, more soldiers and of course they needed more cash. Dale's visits to Libya made him feel like royalty in the NUM. Others weren't given the same privileges as him. A boy from a small town in Yorkshire was at the cutting edge of the struggle and was travelling the world to make deals that were shaping the future of the United Kingdom. If only he could talk about them. His friends wouldn't believe him and there was nobody he trusted enough to share the secrets and adventures with. All apart from Harry and Ellen.

He knew that he wasn't totally respected by the likes of Roger Windsor and Tom Linney, but he felt that they accepted him for the role he had in the hierarchy. He was a vital cog in the machine, at least that was the way he saw himself.

Dale was distraught. The past few weeks had him only seeing two people who spoke any form of English. He didn't know a great deal about UK law let alone about what law meant in Libya. He hadn't been given the right to a phone call. He hadn't been given access to a lawyer. He was pretty sure that his family, or the British Consulate, or whatever hadn't been contacted. His mother would be worried sick about him. He hadn't been away from home for more than a few nights before this, even on his last trip to Tripoli.

Dale kicked himself and then the door in front of him. He kicked again, then again and one more time. The pain at least made him feel alive. Without any contact with the outside world he was losing the concept of time. Even after such a short period it was clear that his brain was failing him in many ways. Deprived of light, surviving on very little in the way of food and water and with constant diarrhoea, he feared for the loo. He was in a bad way. Only his thoughts were there to accompany him on this journey.

The irony that Sunday was Remembrance Day was lost on Dale as he'd lost all track of what day it was, let alone what date. The NUM hadn't done anything to save him, as far as he was aware. Tom looked like he was being arrested at the same time, but it happened so quickly that Dale couldn't be totally sure of that fact. He hadn't left his cell for more than a couple of minutes at a time when officials checked him over. In all these times he had never seen Tom Linney; or even Roger Windsor for that matter. He was sure that Roger had high-tailed it back to the UK at the first sign of trouble. Thinking about it, Dale grew more and more suspicious of Roger's role in all of this. He was speaking in the local language to more than one person during the short time they were in the country. Dale hadn't seen any sign before of Roger even bothering to speak to people in their local tongue, let alone knowing any words of Arabic. The conversations between Roger and the Libyans were strange. The superior actions that had been written all over Roger's face, into his words and body language on previous trips had vanished. He was respectful, even treating them as equals.

Could it be that Dale had been used as a fall-guy to allow for deniability for both sides? Dale sat and thought, straining to keep his mind focused. His role was managed and orchestrated from start to finish by someone higher than him. It just had to be Roger. There was nobody else that could have put him in that position and then let him drop so far. Dale's anger turned to despair. He was out of options, reliant on someone else to sort things out for him. Unable to converse with people and having no idea if help was on the way. In rare moments of positive thought, he was able to replace the question "How did I get here?" with a promise to himself. "When I get out of here!"

Within the time he'd already served he was able to build on these thoughts and was able to focus on physical exercise. If he couldn't keep his mind fit, at least his body wouldn't suffer. He started doing exercises, as much as the cell allowed. Obviously, there was no room to run but sit ups, press ups and jumps were possible. He practiced these several times a day and asked the guards for more water and food every time they brought him something. Usually this was greeted with laughter (maybe because they couldn't understand a word this English boy was saying) but every now and again he got a little more. His mind however remained filled with terror. He had no idea what might happen to him. Dale had lost his strong Yorkshireman resolve and found himself crying frequently. All the forced positive thinking and exercise in the world couldn't dampen the dread of what might happen to him. Little did he know that Christmas and New Year would come and go without him even realising it.

* * *

In Barnsley, Roger Windsor sat a happy man. The ink was still wet on the deal for the flats in Canary Wharf that he had identified a few months before. He could see a future for himself that was filled with comfort. And all he had to do was drop two other people in it. He didn't have any respect for the young boy who was riding on his coattails through the trips to Libya. Dale wasn't ever going to make it; Roger knew that from the first time he met the lad. He was the scapegoat when needed. There was no point in those at the top sharing their new-found wealth with people like this from the bottom rung. Dale would have to get what he was given. Jail in Libya was a place where he could do Roger no harm at all. There was little chance of him coming out of there soon.

But the added bonus in all of this was that Tom Linney went in the same direction. Go straight to jail. Do not pass go. Do not collect your share of one hundred and fifty thousand pounds. And hopefully, stay there for some time too.

Tom had always felt like a thorn in the side for Roger. He was always there in the way when Roger wanted to get something done. Tom felt like he was just there to get on the nerves of others. The fact that he was now locked tightly away in Libya, probably in the same place as Dale, made Roger happier than ever. It was probably more satisfying than the property deal in many ways. Roger sipped his whisky and laughed out loud. Nobody else in the room knew what he was laughing about. But they were definitely in no doubt that this was a very happy man indeed.

"What the hell were they thinking?"

The room fell silent. Arthur Scargill's face was turning redder and redder. He reached out and turned up the volume on the television. The News at Ten was just beginning. From his demeanour it was clear to all assembled that this was looking like being a long night for all of them.

"In Airedale, Castleford where most miners were on strike, a working miner, Michael Fletcher, was savagely beaten earlier this evening. A masked gang waving baseball bats invaded his house and beat him for five minutes, whilst his pregnant wife and children hid upstairs. Fletcher suffered a broken shoulder blade, dislocated elbow and two broken ribs."

Scargill was surrounded by some of his trusted lieutenants and demanded to know how his men might have been involved bringing the miner's cause so quickly back into the public eye.

Realising that this was nothing to do with what had happened in Libya, Roger Windsor, the most prominent face around the table, scrambled his mind. For once he had no idea whether an action like this had been sanctioned by anyone involved at the top of the NUM. He squirmed inwardly. He suspected not, but as Scargill's right hand the spotlight would be quick to shine on him. The others looked at each other for answers. None were forthcoming.

Scargill looked around. He loved controlling everything about the NUM machine and was always incredibly disappointed when someone stepped out from under his shadow and did their own thing. Even more so when that action was going to cause him, the NUM and miners in general some pain. And this was going to deliver a whole lot of pain.

Roger sat forward in his seat. He looked in the eyes of each of the men sat in front of them. Among them were people he respected and others that he wished were rotting in a Libyan prison cell alongside Dale and Tom. If he was honest, the silence meant that he had lost a little respect for every one of them. As he sat in a room set aside for the higher echelons of the miner's movement in the back of a working men's club, Roger breathed in the cigarette smoke coming from his colleagues. It was as though each of them were producing their own personal flume of carcinogens while sitting. A dozen chimneys couldn't do this much damage, Roger Windsor thought to himself. As he looked for inspiration, aware that Scargill would explode with rage if he wasn't satisfied, Roger decided to speak.

"If any of you know anything about this, then we need to know now. All we're looking for are answers, not recriminations. The more we understand about this, the better we can deal with it," he started, hoping that his calm manner might hide the anger that was stewing beneath the surface. "It's about time, so we will listen to the news. While it's on, think very carefully about what you might know. Once the news is over, I will ask you the same question again. Anyone with the merest hint of an idea had better speak up."

Across the country, people were tuning in to news that was going to transform the way the nation looked at the miners and their behaviour. The news that was breaking suggested this was the action of a few miners who had decided to take the fight into their own hands. As the divide between those who supported militant and aggressive action and those who saw a different way of moving forward grew, each side became more entrenched in their way of thinking. There was a section of the NUM that wanted more and more action that made the news, created headlines and kept the cause in the mind of the public. Injuries were commonplace on the picket lines. The Battle of Orgreave was testament to that. But entering the home of someone who was exercising his right to work was stepping way over the line in the sand that Scargill and the other leaders believed existed. Sure, they were ready to bend as many rules as it took, even to advance their own personal situations, but this even to them felt like a step too far.

In London, Ellen had just arrived home and was discussing with Harry why there had been no word from Dale when they were interrupted as the News at Ten bulletin came on. Ellen sat at the edge of the settee. She was completely engrossed with what was happening, feeling that she was a massive part of the story that was playing out across the country, yet momentarily unsure what her role in it was.

The news bulletin didn't have a great deal of detail. It was still breaking quickly. But after the first run through of that story, the phone went. Ellen had learned that the only person who would call her after ten was JK. He didn't sleep much at the best of times. The bombing of the Grand Hotel in Brighton had sent the government into a period of quiet chaos and he didn't know where Paul Channon might end up. It was stick or twist time for JK. If he stayed with Channon, then he could be on the gravy train to a much higher government department. If he jumped ship to another minister, JK felt he was a massive asset to anyone in government, then he could affect that promotion without needing his Boss to do the same. It was the same JK but in overdrive as far as Ellen was concerned.

"Are you watching this?" he asked before she had even been given the chance to say hello.

"Of course I'm watching this. It's part of my job description, isn't it?" Ellen asked half-jokingly, half sarcastically. JK had chastised Ellen in the early days that she didn't consume nearly enough current affairs. She'd responded at the time that she had better things to do, while secretly acknowledging that he was probably partly right.

"This is a game changer. The Union men are now on the back foot. This might be the crack in their armoury that we've been looking for. If we play our cards right then we can change public opinion for good with this one," JK plotted.

Ellen actually smiled at his plotting this time. She'd been so close to it in the past that JK's constant machinations irritated her. But the distance between them made it funny. She knew that JK felt he was part of the wider government. He always referred to the government as 'we' as though it was them and us against the people. Ellen had been annoyed by this in the past. But now it just sounded plain daft.

"JK, this is some not very nice men doing a not very nice thing. It doesn't represent all miners, that's for sure," she replied with some disdain. Harry chuckled loud enough for JK to hear at the other end of the phone.

"I'm sorry, I forgot that you had a miner for a lover. I'm sure he's different, but far too many of them are militant and intent on causing disruption rather than accepting their time is up," JK replied in double quick time.

But Ellen was having none of it. "And you don't think that they might be trying to protect their livelihood, their families? What if the government decided to close the Civil Service? Would you just accept it or fight for your job?" she countered. Moving the subject on she continued, "my immediate concern is for Paul. He's on Good Morning Britain tomorrow, I'm going to see if I can join him in the car at 5 a.m. to brief him on how to respond to this". The new morning news show, similar to formats from America was proving popular. A quicker way for a Minister like Paul Channon to be seen as more accessible and gain popularity.

"One step ahead of you Ellen, I've already organised the car, it's picking you up at 4.30a.m." JK wasn't going to miss out on this one either. "I've already spoken to the hospital looking after the beaten Michael Fletcher. He's under police guard the poor sod. Well, see you bright and early."

And with as much compassion as Ellen expected, JK rang off.

Chapter 22

Friday 4th January 1985.

Southwark, London, 2°C, snow with a cold wind.

Timothy Philpott.

"I'm sick of all this," Tim said to his reflection in the mirror. He looked terrible. He had never worked so hard on a story. That wasn't to say that he didn't usually cross all the t's and dot all the i's but this time it felt different. The story that had been given to him by Ellen Minor was one that he felt could make a huge difference to his career. It was that thought that kept him going whenever he hit a brick wall, reached a dead end or found that people were not willing to talk to him. It got that way with some stories that he tried to evolve but this one was just unlike anything before. It felt like the story had a mind of its own, twisting and turning away from him every time he felt he got close.

The snow falling outside maintained the Christmas spirit for many Londoners. Not so for Tim. When he was at university, he worked in retail to make ends meet during the holidays. It was the same then. People wanted more and more out of Christmas, from the presents to the Christmas dinner. He worked in a supermarket and found that it was three times busier than normal in Christmas week and three times busier again on Christmas Eve. And he remembered being sat at the Christmas table feeling exhausted and sick to the sight of carrots and potatoes. He didn't want to feel like that again, so had planned to work tirelessly before the big day and find a couple of days rest and was ready for Christmas with his family. Unfortunately, it didn't turn out that way.

Tim turned away from the mirror and remembered how he felt at the Christmas dinner table a little over a week ago. It wasn't the exhaustion he had felt in his university days; more like a depression. The hard work he'd done felt like it had frittered away to absolutely nothing at all.

It had all felt so different in December. He was making progress. The corruption in the NUM was linked all the way to the top. As he spoke to more and more people, it was obvious that there were shady dealings from start to finish. Those in the lower ranks were shipping people backwards and forwards to make the strikes look bigger than they actually were. He had statements from the coach drivers. People were being paid to turn up to picket lines rather than being there due to the depth of their feelings. Others were sent to make as much of a commotion as possible to 'look good for the news.' But this was all low-level stuff. The real corruption grew bigger the closer he got to the top. Even with all the 'no comment' answers he got; Tim was able to uncover enough people willing to talk about each other that he could piece together a really good account of what was happening in the higher echelons of the organisation.

And the links to Libya were as plain as day. At first, Tim struggled to find out how the money was making its way from Libya to the UK. Bank transfers were so cumbersome that they would have stood out a mile. The sums involved got Tim thinking that they couldn't have possibly been delivered in bank notes. That's where he was steered back in the right direction by talking through things again with Ellen. She'd explained that Dale had been to Libya and brought money back with others in suitcases. Dale hadn't mentioned that fact when they spoke before, only that money had made its way from Libya and that he had been part of a party sent to secure it. Tim first thought that meant the negotiation. After doing further research, it became clear that the negotiation was already complete. It was the money run that needed to happen.

And then the real bombshells came to light, sending Tim into a frenzy of excitement and activity. The money made its way to the leadership of the NUM. From there it should have been distributed to the members, potentially left without a job as they closed the mines. But it was clearly being syphoned off and used to buy flats in the new Canary Wharf development in the heart of London of all places. There was plenty of anecdotal evidence about this being the case, but it wasn't until Tim had a few drinks with a loose-lipped estate agent on the Isle of Dogs that he was able to hear it from someone directly involved in the transaction. The offer of a few drinks and a few hundred pounds was enough to persuade the estate agent to turn up to the same pub a few nights later with a copy of the agreement, signatures and all. Clearly the desire of the council officials was to pump money into their area for development and asking questions on where this money came from was lower down the list of priorities.

Tim was piecing together all the remaining obscure parts that made the picture complete. There were so many other elements to all of this. He had no idea that his questions would shine an unfavourable light on the government too. The links to seedy MOD middlemen and undermining the NUM to the press were prevalent themes wherever he went. There were links to Libya on this side of the debate too, but Tim was focused on the story with the NUM as there was clear corruption and obvious wrongdoing. He had promised his editor a career-making story and this was the one that he had fact-checked rigorously.

Tim strolled into the office of his Boss with all the confidence in the world. The Times was renowned globally as a newspaper with high morals and an eye for uncovering corruption wherever it lay. He'd pieced together an incredible story, the truth stranger than a fiction. He could demonstrate that his facts were correct and was ready to stand and fight if the questions came.

"Sit down Tim," his Boss, Robert Brim said levelling his eyes at him. A rotund and beady-eyed man, Robert was well respected, both by the journalists who worked for him and the paper's owner, Rupert Murdock.

"Thanks. I'm ready for you to look at this story now. It will shake a few trees, that's for sure," Tim said with an excitement that he couldn't hide. He loved being the bearer of this story and wanted to see a smile on the face of his Boss in anticipation. Tim imagined the two of them taking this a long way. Promotions, pay rises, and congratulations were all on the horizon as far as Tim was concerned. He was also eyeing an award or two for his investigations.

"I'm ready to take a look at it too," Robert replied, but without the expected smile on his face or eagerness in his voice. Tim's anticipation turned to concern. And rightly so.

"It's time you dropped this, my friend," Robert went on.

"Dropped what?" Tim replied, narrowing his eyebrows in confusion.

"All of it."

The colour drained from Tim's face. He felt sick.

"All of the story? You want me to drop the whole story? All the work? The time? The questions? Is that what you want me to drop?" Tim asked by way of clarification, but also because he wasn't sure he believed his ears.

"That's absolutely right. Pretend you never spoke to anyone about this; that's my advice anyway," Robert spoke with a clarity that cut through all of the questions. Clearly this wasn't for debate.

"And can I ask the reason for all of this?" he pressed on.

"We can't run the story. That's all there is to it. The decision has been made," Robert replied, his eye contact from before no longer there. Robert looked for someone who was going to make this conversation easier. That person didn't exist. It was early for a newspaper. The reason he'd asked Tim in at that time was so they could talk alone. This now felt like a poor choice, there was only a cleaner at the far end of the floor present. Tim drew a short, sharp breath.

"And who has made this decision?" Tim demanded.

Robert sighed, then re-focused on Tim, deciding to credit one of his stars some respect with a little information as to why his story wouldn't make print.

"I've had a call from Tim Bell."

"Thatcher's ad guy?" Tim knew the name. The Saatchi and Saatchi advertising exec was credited with Margret Thatcher's powerful image. A slick operator, he was often referred to as the *Silver Fox*. But rumours abounded that he was wired into a network of Moles being run by Mi5 and GCHQ to infiltrate the NUM to destabilize the miner's cause, while maintaining The Iron Lady's *image*.

"Well, he's someone way over our pay grade or sphere of influence. The story is dead. End of conversation." And with that Tim walked out of the room as dejected as he had ever been in his life. He had no clue what to do with his career at that point. The dreams of uncovering the corruption and finding his name in shining lights had been taken away from him in a short meeting with his Boss. If The Times wasn't ready for the story, then at that moment Tim felt perhaps nobody was. Perhaps it was as much of a fantasy as it read. He now couldn't unscramble his mind.

* * *

"I want my son back."

They were the last words spoken on a long telephone conversation between Mrs Edwards and a Foreign Office receptionist about the plight of her son.

Dale's mother had gone to the expense of having a telephone connected to her home. The man from BT had been helpful, walking her through the contract and now she worried about the bill. Yet her son had been in prison in Libya for months and she was reaching the end of her tether. The rest of the conversation wasn't quite as direct as the final exchanges but nevertheless, Mrs Edwards came off the phone with a banging headache and could feel herself falling into another bout of depression, the kind she had been suffering recently with her Dale in his perilous situation.

She had asked time and time again for the Foreign Office to get her son out of jail. In the past, the replies had been vague.

"We'll look into it."

"The Foreign Office has the best interest of all British nationals at heart."

"Diplomacy is taking place."

Mrs Edwards felt like she had heard every excuse in the book.

But the latest conversation wasn't anywhere near as vague. This one told her in no uncertain terms that Dale wasn't going to be released via their help. She would have to try to go it alone. What was a thankless task for the Foreign Office now looked like an impossible task for a cleaner from Brampton Bierlow.

They told her that they were of the belief that Dale was a criminal and was banged up rightfully. They would not challenge the Libyan courts or authorities in a case where they believed they had no chance of making any difference. Although they hadn't been shown evidence, the connection in Libya indicated to the Foreign Office that this man would stay in prison for a long period of time and that there was no chance of release. They also told Mrs Edwards that their time was short, their resources finite and they had much more deserving cases to focus on. The last sentence was the one that cut the deepest.

"The only way to have saved your son from prison was to have brought him up with better morals."

Plainly not true, only words that could be delivered on the phone rather than face to face, but they still hurt Mrs Edwards. She sobbed. Her daughters tried their best to console her that evening but all she wanted to do was climb into bed. They were happy to let her do that but the unspoken concern among them was that she would never want to get back up again.

Dale, for his part, was suffering at least as much as his mother. The food was poor and there was very little of it. Every now and again he would get a plate of something that was neither nutritious nor hot but that had to suffice. It was probably something he would have turned his nose up at when he was back home, being a fussy eater and all. But in prison, when he had no idea when the next plate would arrive, he ate it all. One might expect that he would gobble up every last morsel in a matter of seconds, but it didn't feel right for Dale to consume his measly portions in that way. The willpower he was able to muster allowed him to slowly eat the food. It meant the gap between that meal and the next was shorter, if only by a few minutes. That made a difference.

He still hadn't seen a friendly face in all the time he'd been there. Tom wasn't anywhere near him as far as he could tell. The times when a guard walked past the front of his cell with another prisoner in tow, Dale could tell that they weren't English by the noises and smells that were coming off them. Dale still had the keenest sense of smell and swore blind that he could tell the nationality of a person by their aroma alone. At least it gave him something to do while he was locked in almost darkness. And that was the part that got to him the most. If he could have a few minutes of sunlight every day, then he would have been able to feel like he was on the right path through this ordeal. The fact that he was sheltered from natural light impacted his mind as well as his body.

As far as his mind was concerned, the darkness mirrored his plight. His dark state of mind was exaggerated by the dark state of everything he could see. The floor was dark, the walls and ceiling too. The door was dark. This meant his mind was dark. He lived in terror, his future potentially one of being locked away in a Libyan cell for the rest of his life, or even worse. Dying without seeing one last time those important to him, his sisters, Harry, Ellen even and most of all, his mum, one last time.

His body suffered from the light too. He had contracted rickets, although he didn't know it and it was undiagnosed, he struggled to walk around his cell as a result. The lack of Vitamin D was affecting the strength of his bones. Dale felt brittle and wondered if he had a chance to escape whether his aching body would be up to taking the opportunity. Not that he had seen even the slightest laxity in the security in his part of the prison.

Dale hadn't been told what he was charged with, let alone been given access to a lawyer. He was sure that the people back home would be trying to see him and free him. But he didn't see any activity on this front. At least if he saw a lawyer, they would be able to keep his spirits up. Maybe that's why the Libyan authorities didn't want him to have access to legal redress. The last thing they want when they have flimsy evidence and a kangaroo court is a defendant with spirit, Dale told himself.

He hoped that his family and friends would be able to make things happen. Wrongly accused, alone in a foreign place, his situation was desperate.

Harry asked Ellen what she could do to help. She'd tried to discretely ask around in Westminster to see if there was any influence she could muster.

She had been on the telephone many times to Dale's mother and explained that she was putting the case forward wherever she could. Harry still didn't have a full grasp of the way things worked in the Westminster bubble but thought Ellen could do more. Dale was his best friend and he had put a lot on the line to let he and Ellen know about the misdealing's in the NUM. And now Dale was stuck.

"How can you help my friend?" Harry asked Ellen with an air of desperation in his voice. It wasn't typical Harry, but the situation wasn't typical either.

"I've spoken to as many people involved in that part of the government as possible. If I push any further that could well be the end of my career in politics and I'm not sure it would have any greater impact than what I've already done. Westminster is a funny beast. When there's no appetite to get something done it just doesn't happen," Ellen explained.

"It's the Foreign Office, isn't it?" Harry guessed. He'd overheard Ellen and Dale's mum talking about it and heard the words Foreign Office used a few times. He put two and two together and hoped he had four.

"Yes, and I've spoken to my counterpart there. He's asked the question of his superior. They believe that Dale is a criminal and don't want to sour relations in what is already a delicate relationship. They don't want to push forward a case that they don't believe in. Ill-informed as they are, I understand their stance. But that doesn't help Dale one bit," Ellen spoke again with a frustration at the machinery of government.

"I know you'll throw everything you have at this," Harry replied as a marker that he wanted the conversation to end. Ellen wasn't going to fight him on that. She was as frustrated as he and would rather focus on something else altogether. Ellen felt a large chunk of responsibility for the turn Dale's life had taken. She wasn't one hundred percent sure but believed that him telling her all the juicy details he had gathered from his time in the NUM certainly wouldn't have helped. Ellen was worried that this was the reason he was now sat in prison halfway across the world. She wasn't to know that he was always intended to be the sacrificial lamb.

Ellen had spread herself thinly over the last few months. She had started out as a Press Secretary and pretty much nothing else. Now she had a boyfriend that she was looking to spend her life with, was involved in a major story and carried a massive amount of guilt for the situation Dale was in. This all took its toll and Ellen often found herself staring out into nothingness when she was supposed to be working or spending time with Harry. She had lost her way a bit and wasn't sure how to find it again.

Chapter 23

Wednesday 23rd January 1985.

Lambeth, London, sunny yet windy with a high of 5°C.

Ellen.

Ellen woke early. The thoughts crashing through her head the night before had all hit at once. She was feeling sick. At first the sick feeling got her worried. She herself was a day late and wondered initially if she and Harry might be now expecting a baby. There was more than enough complication swirling around her life at that moment in time. Getting pregnant would just make things a hundred times more complicated. Though she'd have been lying to herself if she denied the rush of excitement that had just gone through her.

Harry lay next to her fast asleep, sleeping deeply as always. His calm sleep didn't reflect his waking mind. Harry was desperately worried about the situation his friend Dale was in, as well as the pressure the whole saga was putting on his girlfriend. But he didn't deal with stress in the same way Ellen did. He was a man of action. If his actions didn't make a difference, then he wasn't going to lose sleep over it. He would just get a good night's rest and think about it again the next day with a fresh mind and a fresh pair of eyes.

Ellen laid still and looked at the ceiling hoping for inspiration. It was during the next few moments that she began to realise the feeling she had in her stomach wasn't pregnancy but was actually a nagging realisation of the action she had no choice but to take. She couldn't put it off any longer. Protecting her career from the likes of JK and others was one thing. She felt at that point in time that she was protecting it at the expense of Dale. And who knew what condition he was in while in the prison. She hadn't had much word about Dale but the people who had been imprisoned in Libya in the past had all come to sticky ends. The official word from the Libyan authorities all went along the same lines, hunger strike, starved themselves, suicide. But these were men who just disappeared. No form of justice, no trial, no embassy visits, just gone.

Ellen tried to force herself back to sleep. She closed her eyes, but this was even worse for her conscience. It was telling her to act. As a reference point for her mind she could see the face of Dale's mother, Mrs Edwards. The face and eyes of Mrs Edwards were pleading with Ellen to make a difference. She could take no more.

Ellen thought she knew what had to be done. She got out of bed and walked around the home she now shared with Harry. There wasn't a great deal of room, but she wanted to expend some of the nervous energy that was building up inside. The flat becoming her makeshift athletics track Ellen walked backwards and forwards as many times as she could. The energy built up at first to uncontrollable levels. Ellen shook her arms as she walked, nodded her head and walked in zigzag patterns. This seemed to sate her need to expend energy and she soon settled into a more normal rhythm of movement.

When Harry arose to find her pacing up and down the living room, he simply watched Ellen's movement. It proved mesmeric to him and the rhythm she had established caught his attention for some time. He just stood in the doorway, with his first morning No.6 cigarette in his mouth ready to light . Ellen hadn't noticed Harry enter the room, as she was now walking backwards and forwards with her eyes closed; the number of steps she had to pace had already been memorised having walked them so many times.

One.

Ellen had a look on her face that couldn't quite be described. Some might have seen it as akin to the enigmatic smile on the face of the Mona Lisa. But not Harry. He had never had the time nor interest for art and wouldn't know his Mona Lisa from his Guernica.

Two.

She expertly kept to a straight line across the middle of the room. Harry wondered if she would be this good at the test the police asked you to do if they suspected you were driving after having a few too many pints.

Three.

Harry broke into a gentle smile at the way his beautiful girl was working her way across the room. He could see all the features on her face that possibly he had taken for granted over the prior few weeks. Chastising himself he resolved to look at her face at least once a day and take it all in.

Four.

Ellen looked as though each step was measured precisely. They didn't deviate from right to left or from one end of the small living room to the other. Left and right she was metronomic in her movement.

Five.

Harry suppressed a laugh. His natural reaction was to guffaw, but of course, this might break the concentration and spoil the moment.

Six.

Ellen was counting the steps herself silently. Harry could see the movement of her lips and noticed that she was saying "six." The amused him even more and the laugh came closer and closer to his lips.

Seven.

By now Ellen was nearing the end of the room. Harry guessed that it would be one more step before she would turn around and head in the direction away from him. He was looking forward to watching her walk the other way just as much as toward him.

Eight.

He was right. This stopped her around fifty centimetres from the end of the room, swivelled on one leg and about-faced to walk the other way.

And off she went.

Harry watched this a few times before his laugh finally came. Ellen opened her eyes in a serene manner when she heard the laugh, as though she wasn't surprised at all to find Harry in the room. She looked him in the eye and said, "Harry, I know what to do."

Harry smiled and knew from deep inside that whatever it was she had decided, his girl was going to get things sorted out.

Within an hour Ellen was sat at work waiting for Paul to enter the room. She had been there only fifteen minutes when the door swung open and Paul Channon MP, her Boss, walked in. Ellen didn't want to wait another minute. She had been ready for this for a few hours and would rather have had the conversation without the ears of JK in the vicinity.

"Paul, can I talk to you?"

"You already are Ellen."

"I have something to confess," Ellen said as an opener.

"We have put someone in a perilous situation, and I need your help to get them out. The NUM have screwed someone who was helping me find a way forward for you. Harry's friend Dale is now rotting in a Libyan prison and I can't help but feel responsible," she tried to maintain Paul's eye.

"Fuck!" he said almost as a relief. "I had a feeling. This of course puts us both in a sticky situation. Ellen. I need you to tell me the whole story," Paul replied, his calm manner returning. Ellen had feared that Paul would react negatively to having been undermined severely by one of his team. This could blow up in both of their faces and cost him his political career. But he wanted to learn as much of the facts as he possibly could before planning any course of action.

Ellen detailed the situation without reservation to Paul. The way that Dale had become involved at the top of the NUM, the underhand things he saw and brought to her attention. Paul listened very carefully as she told of the goings on in Libya. Ellen had long suspected Paul had some dealings himself with the North African nation and his eyes widened when she told him the stories Dale had recounted from his trips there. Ellen told of the connection she had made with Timothy Philpott of The Times and how the story hadn't gone anywhere.

She finished the story to find herself exhausted. All that was left was for her to ask for help.

"Paul, is there anything you can do? I don't want a man, a friend, to die in a jail cell halfway across the world because of my actions. I wouldn't be able to deal with the consequences of that."

"I know Ellen. You really wouldn't."

Paul trusted everything Ellen told him but some of the facts presented were from third parties that he didn't know, particularly Dale. He needed to do some digging for himself. Although he had no desire at all to see a British citizen die in a prison cell in Libya, he also didn't want to break the ties he had already made. He wanted to forge a career in politics and part of this was being to call in influence whenever he needed it. The big picture as far as he was concerned was mounting a leadership challenge in the Conservative Party when the time was right. Building up these contacts and influences over several years would put him in the best position to make that happen. Approval ratings at an all-time high for Margaret Thatcher meant these aspirations of leadership were several years away. Paul decided that, on this occasion, he could risk using some of his influence to help Ellen without causing significant detriment to his own network of power.

Paul picked up the phone, dialled a number that he had memorised and waited for an answer at the other end. He didn't have to wait long.

"Dusty. We need to talk. Usual place? Half an hour?"

And that was that. Paul was now alone in the office, so didn't have to make up an excuse of where he was going or who he wanted to see. He gave Ellen the day off when he could see that she was far too upset to work. After telling all to him, he could see that she was shaking. She was normally a rock he greatly relied on, he needed her that way, so told her to go home and get to bed. As Paul readied himself to leave JK arrived in a foul mood. Paul knew that the best thing for him when he was like that was to send him on some errand or other. He decided that rattling a few cages in other parts of Westminster would satisfy the need JK had brought with him for destruction, so he asked his Permanent

Secretary to enquire with other departments what they were willing to add to the conversation about the miners' strike.

Alone again, Paul could get his coat on and walk to the destination he had arranged to meet his contact. The weather was sunny and not particularly cold for a January day. There was a gentler breeze that brought some chill off the Thames but not enough to stop him from opening his coat nearer to the location, a dingy café in a nondescript part of London. The person he was there to meet wanted it to be as ordinary as possible. They had met there a few times before and Paul liked the fact that it wasn't that far from the centre of government in the UK yet wouldn't be recognised by a soul. Not that there were many of those around. The early-setting sun had driven all those that didn't need to be out and about back indoors. Paul walked into the empty café. He asked for a cup of tea and decided that a biscuit or two would help the sugar levels and prepare him for a conversation that had the capacity to turn nasty. He sat with his back to the door to show his counterpart that he was confident enough to not have full view of passers-by. A small gesture but one that he knew wouldn't go un-noticed. The door creaked as it opened. A figure walked past Paul and up to the counter. It asked for a few items by the sound of the tone but spoke so quietly that Paul couldn't hear a word of it. As the figure turned towards Paul and sat at the table opposite, he wore a frown that indicated he had much better things to do.

"Good afternoon Minister. How are you?"

"Pretty good Dusty. Yourself?"

"Yes. I'm doing well. Really well in fact."

Dusty Miller was a contact that Paul wanted to keep deep in his pocket in case he needed something significant one day. But the amount of times the two of them had worked with each other meant he had lost the score of who helped who and who owed the other. They were implicated in enough deals that neither one could untangle themselves from if they tried.

"I would like to talk to you about a British citizen who is currently being innocently held in another country and is receiving far from the best treatment," Paul began with a calm demeanour that he hoped would stay with him for the whole conversation.

"I have no idea what you're talking about, my friend. I don't get involved in that kind of stuff," Dusty replied.

"This country is a place where we both have links of one kind or another. I know that you can help me here," Paul said firmly.

"I'm not sure you heard me the first time," Miller replied one notch firmer than Channon.

"I know that you've deceived me. I know that your dealings in this are linked to your friends in high places. I have made a few enquiries already today and there is a lot of muck to start flinging around. I suggest you come clean before you and several members of the government get dirty," Paul lost a degree of the calmness he brought with him. The conversation lulled for a few seconds while Miller's food and drink were brought to the table. A hungry man, and one aware that Channon would foot the bill, he ordered a pot of tea, a bacon sandwich, two cheese rolls and a bag of crisps,. The café owner took her time bringing all the items over on a tray, so the silence between the two men was prolonged. Eventually she stepped away far enough to be out of earshot and the two men picked up where they left off.

"You have a great deal to lose with this as well," Dusty explained.

"Yes, but I'm certainly not linked to the death of WPC Fletcher. But you, however, can be quite easily linked to that. This goes from something murky to something downright criminal. They'll string you up alive if they get to see what you've been up to. Do you think a politician will protect you?" Paul countered Dusty in language that he would understand. Miller had a well-known mistrust of the political classes. He was happy dealing with low lives but was always watching his back when working with a politician.

"Checkmate."

It was the only word Miller could muster at that time. He sat forward in his chair and took the first bite of his bacon sandwich. His face curled up in terror before he picked up the tomato sauce bottle and squeezed what would have been a month's supply for most people across the bacon and bread combination. Miller looked at the white, brown and red concoction in his hand before biting in again, mixing the second bite with the first as to redress the missing red sauce issue. Channon watched his counterpart eat through the sandwich, washing down each mouthful with a swig of scolding hot tea.

"Let me know who it is. I'll see what I can do," Dusty restarted the conversation hoping to regain a little of the authority and control he had entered with.

"Not good enough, my friend. This man is in dire straits. We need a resolution by midday tomorrow or I go to the press. Don't worry, you'll get some form of recognition for your efforts here," Paul countered, trying to help Miller save some face.

"Sir Dusty Miller; I like the sound of that!" Miller joked, "or at least a little football pools win coming my way. I know you guys can make that happen." Channon told him about Dale and added Tom Linney in for good measure. He was someone else that Ellen had mentioned. Paul figured it was just as easy to get two out at once, so gave that task to Dusty Miller as well.

Paul smiled and the two of them resumed normal progress. They were compatriots in many ways and Channon felt it was a shame to have to push the man into a corner at any time but that was the way of the world at times. As Dusty chewed on the rest of his food, shouting up at the counter for a refill on his tea pot, the pair of them spoke at length about all their worries for the future of the United Kingdom. Miller's were inextricably linked to his role in the MOD, where he feared being in a world where he couldn't do his job properly; greasing the wheels of progress as he called it. Channon's were more connected to the troubles facing the country at that time, the coal situation, unemployment and regional disbalance. The two men put the world to rights and then went their separate ways. Channon was sure that he had made himself clear. Miller went straight to work. He had the resources to resolve the situation. And for the luck of Ellen and Paul he could do it quickly.

Chapter 24

Saturday 16th March 1985.

Barnsley, South Yorkshire, 2°C with a light dusting of snow.

Roger Windsor.

"I think we can safely say that was a success."

Roger Windsor was feeling pleased with himself again and it showed on his face. Sat deep in the tea rooms at Betty's in Harrogate, he could still see out to the white winterscape facing him. It was a windy day but the blustery spring showers that had accompanied most of the month had been replaced with snow. He'd ordered a pot of tea and a cream scone. Not for any reason other than that was what he wanted. His companion looked across the table clearly equally content with his own situation.

"Roger, I think we've come out of this well my friend," Arthur Scargill replied. They had both been on the news the day before, Scargill in the foreground and Roger in the shadows (as always) when the miners strikes were officially called off. Of course, as was the way with modern politics, both sides claimed victory. The government, particularly Prime Minister Margaret Thatcher said that she had stood strong and resisted the "militant NUM". For their part, Scargill felt that he spoke for all the NUM members when he said that he had delivered a "bloody nose" to the government. Either way, Scargill and Roger had walked away with heightened reputations with the public and a very private, though very lucrative, property investment. The fact that many men had lost their jobs, with little prospect of finding another, had less impact on the pair as might have been expected from all the rhetoric during the strikes. It hadn't really had any impact on the players from the other side either. The world had changed, they had all done well out of it. Only the everyday people had suffered.

"I like the investments you've made for us, Roger. I think they're something in the way of reward for all the hard work we have put into this. The long hours, the public speaking out in the cold and all the attacks from the government need some form of redress. Property will comfort me when I look back at all that pain," Arthur Scargill spoke in something little more than a whisper. He wasn't sure who was around to hear, even though the tearoom was quiet. The cold start overcoming the clear sky to keep many indoors. Fear and distrust now their normal, they had sat in a corner where nobody else could hear their conversation without even thinking about it. The previous few years had taught the two of them to be careful with their conversations. If their private rooms could be bugged, a back corner of Betty's certainly wasn't secure.

"I think we made some good choices there," Roger replied. He always spoke of the 'we' rather than in the first person. It helped him to spread the blame and influence in his own mind. He wasn't going to be the scapegoat like Dale or Tom Linney at any cost. Attaching Arthur Scargill to his actions made him feel far more secure. There was no way that Scargill was going to take a fall as easily as the other two. Plus having something to call the NUM leader's bluff with at a given point in the future was always a handy thing to keep up his sleeve.

"We certainly did."

*   *   *

In London, Paul Channon sat at his desk staring at the wall. His first thoughts were on why someone would arrange an office where the main view from the desk was plasterboard. It wasn't a particularly nice shade of off-white that the wall had been covered with either. But those thoughts were just a distraction from what was really on his mind. The world had moved a fair bit over the past few years and Paul Channon had been close to the epicenter of a shift in politics that would go down in history. He was excited that he himself would be recorded in this history as a key man in reforming industrial politics. It was a major addition to his political CV. The man still harboured dreams of one day leading the party and the country as Prime Minister. Coming through this tricky time not only unscathed but with his reputation significantly enhanced, Channon smiled. There was little in the way of his outward appearance that suggested he was anything other than delighted for his role in ending the strikes and furthering his position in the cabinet.

Inwardly he was more than comforted by the fact that he'd secured the release of Dale. He'd done the right thing when the call came. He could have quite easily walked away from the situation and kept his powder dry with Dusty Miller, a contact that he was sure he would need in the future for his own ends. But seeing two British citizens rotting in a Libyan prison when they were, for the most part, innocent would have played on his conscience for a long time. Doing the right thing wasn't always easy for a politician, but Channon was sure this was the only thing he could have done in the circumstances. He had looked after them in the only way he knew how. It might seem underhand to some, but they didn't understand the way that politics worked. The ends always justify the means as far as Paul Channon was concerned.

But the one thing above all else he wished he could have changed was losing Ellen. The conversation with her was painful for him, and it felt like it was more painful than it was for Ellen. She approached it in a philosophical manner, taking in all the information and accepting there were far worse fates. The fact that her boyfriend's mate had come close to death in a prison halfway around the world probably changed her view on what a disaster was versus something she could just manage and get on with. Sure, she felt some degree of bitterness for the situation but would get on with her life. She had Harry out of all of this and couldn't complain about the way the rest of it had panned out.

Paul looked deeper into the wall as if to see clearer answers on why he felt like this. He couldn't afford to suffer any political fallout from the events of the previous few years, especially the events leading up to the release of Dale. His Press Secretary had gone behind his back with a story that could cause damage to the government and was quite easily linked to him. Although she had come clean in the end, the damage was done as far as Channon was concerned. She had to go. And that made Channon feel relaxed about his position in the world, if not about his relationship with Ellen. He consoled himself with thoughts that she was a smart girl and would find herself back on her feet again in no time.

The way she had left was as though there was nothing untoward going on. They all went out for a drink, he, JK and Ellen accompanied by a few other contacts from the civil service that Ellen had got to know over the years she worked there. It was a jolly affair and the topic of conversation was about exciting new times rather than asking why she was leaving. Neither she nor Paul would talk to anyone else about the why. In fact, it was those two and Harry standing as the only three people on the planet that knew the exact nature of the circumstances surrounding Ellen's departure from the office of the Department for Trade. And that was the way they were all happy with the situation. Paul watched Ellen talk to others as he listened to JK's latest round of scheming and climbing. Paul contrasted the two of them. There was Ellen who wanted justice and fought for the good. Her misdemeanour was that she wanted to help someone else and uncover the truth. By contrast, JK was only out for himself and the power that servicing government could provide. He didn't see the good in others or even see them in another light to his own. In many ways Paul was aware that he was getting rid of the wrong member of his team. JK would sell him down the river if he thought there was a promotion in it. But Ellen had to go, there was no two ways about it. At the end of the night he hugged her gently and wished her the best. He truly meant it.

As she walked off into the night, Paul felt a tear well up in the corner of his eye. He would survive, he would thrive. It was always those in lower positions that took the fall. Especially those who dared stick their head above the parapet. It left a bitter taste in his mouth.

Dale's plane landed back down on the tarmac at Heathrow Airport with a bump. It had been that kind of flight. The flight was no smoother than the potholed road he had travelled on from the prison to Tripoli Airport. As least the roads back in England would run a lot smoother, Dale thought to himself. Not that he would be experiencing much in the way of roads for the next four years. That was the sentence he was given as part of the extradition agreement. The Libyan authorities bowed a little under pressure from the UK but still stood form on certain parts to save face.

They insisted Dale was guilty.

They insisted on a cash settlement as part of the deal.

They insisted on Dale having a custodial sentence when he returned to the United Kingdom.

They insisted he not return to Libya.

Of course, the last point was the last thing on his mind. He looked out of the window at Britain for the first time in a long time. Sitting in a prison cell without access to people or regular daylight had left him disoriented. He wasn't sure at all how long he'd been away. It could have been anywhere between three weeks to three years. He had asked the police officer sent to accompany him back how long it had been but as a member of the criminal classes now, Dale wasn't deemed worthy of an answer.

He was seen as a potential flight risk. The British authorities wanted to keep relations with Libya as cordial as they possibly could. This would have been soured if Dale ended up missing on his return home. Dale was offended. He had worked everything by the book as far as he was concerned. He followed orders, took people on good faith and never questioned what he was asked to do by respectful people in positions of authority. And this was how his life had turned out. At least he now had a fighting chance of getting his health back.

The weather was atypical as far as he could remember. Dale remembered Spring as a time where there were blustery showers and intermittent sunshine. It was an early landing, but he could see a beautiful dusting of white snow, seemingly cleansing the entire landscape. It was beautiful. Maybe the country had changed in his absence. Maybe things would be cleaner and clearer now.

The police officer couldn't bear to talk to Dale and gave him a sharp jab in the ribs to state that it was time to get up and out of the seat. A police van was waiting on the tarmac near to the front of the plane. It was ready to whisk Dale and his guard away to Wandsworth Prison where he would be detained at Her Majesty's pleasure for some time. Over the last few days, better food led

Dale to feel some fat returning to his weak frame. A jab like that in the ribs a week before might have broken one or two of them. Since an unknown agent secured his release, he had been afforded a hotel room back in the same place he stayed when he first visited Tripoli. He was paraded around in Libyan prison clothing and guarded around the clock, but at least he had access to daylight and proper food. If he had been forced to guess, then Dale would say that he had put on the best part of a stone over those few days. The reality was far less than that, but it was enough for him to start on the road to recovery.

The way that he had been treated left a sour taste in his mouth. Dale could feel it every time he swallowed. In fact, he felt that he had swallowed a lot. He had swallowed the sneers and looks he got from other higher-up members of the NUM. They didn't feel he was worthy of the attention and respect he was getting particularly from the leadership. He had swallowed the way that Roger and Tom treated the people over in Libya when they visited. He saw them as fellow human beings; the others saw them as slaves to be ordered around and used. He had swallowed the fact that his best friend hadn't seen the closure of their mine, their place of work, their livelihood as something to really stand up for. Harry had just accepted what was thrown his way and started training to work somewhere else. His friend Harry however was a beacon of positivity for Dale. He smiled when he realised that his new home would be close to Harry and Ellen. And then who knew what? Dale had swallowed his arrest, not that he had any other choice. He was a foreign man in a foreign land and was surrounded by the sound, smells, sights and touch of desolation. And he tasted it too. He had swallowed all that the prison guards were throwing at him in terms of neglect and anger. He swallowed the notion that he could make a difference because he actually felt helpless from start to finish.

And every time he swallowed; he tasted the bitterness. It tasted like a thousand lemons straight off the tree before the sun had got to them. Before even a dose of sweetness had been added.

The police van started up and he was on his way to the place he would have to call home for the next few years. Dale closed his eyes and decided to get some sleep. He might need his wits about him in prison and didn't have the strength to fight back. He would have to stay sharp. Sleep would be his passport.

The prison lived up to the ideas Dale had about it. While an improvement on the Libyan hole he'd been in, Wandsworth was grotty and hostile. In truth, it was all he had expected. He'd only been there a fortnight when one of the guards told him there was a visitor for him. It was a Wednesday afternoon, visiting time, and Dale had experienced two of these times while incarcerated and had sat in his cell, feeling like he was the only man on the block. It had been an experience that reminded him of Libyan prison at first but as he got used to it Dale quietly enjoyed the momentary solitude. It was an oasis of calm in an otherwise busy, noisy and regimented life. He was looking forward to another peaceful hour or so on his own when a guard stuck his head around the cell door.

"Edwards, Tate, visiting time."

Brian Tate, Dale's cell mate was ready to up and go. He had talked endlessly to Dale about his lovely wife who would travel across from Essex every week to see him. Dale had images of this blonde, leggy beauty as described by the young man on the top bunk who was serving two years for burglary. As he had also been called to the visiting room, he would get the chance to see her in the flesh.

"A visitor for me?" Dale asked.

"Are you deaf? Get down there now. You haven't got all afternoon," came the curt reply.

As he walked into the visiting room, packed with family and sad faces he saw Harry sitting in the back corner like he hadn't a care in the world. Dale remembered the faces Harry pulled and over the years had accepted that it was just his way. Harry would have been concerned about his friend's plight but didn't want it to show. Dale predicted that the first words coming out of his friend's mouth would be 'nice place you got 'ere,' and wasn't disappointed when he sat down. It broke the ice and the two of them started chatting.

"How's things with you? They said that you weren't in a good way. The diet has done wonders for your cheekbones. I can see them now," Harry said with a gleam of companionship in his eyes. As far as he was concerned, they were back on the playground messing around like they did every day in school; well, every day Harry bothered to turn up.

"I'm feeling a lot stronger now. One day I'll be back out and I'd love to have a word with the people who led me here," Dale replied with a sense of purpose which Harry liked.

"I'm sure we can do that together. What's the food like in here? Ellen's cooking isn't that great, and I was wondering if I could pop over for dinner a few nights a week, it's not that far on the tube." Harry continued the banter, but Dale was running out of patience and out of visiting time.

"Harry, how are things with you? How's Ellen?" he asked.

"She's lost her job. Kind of sacrificed it to get you out of that hell hole. But it's what she wanted. The things she uncovered about the government, with your help by the way, have turned her head. She can't work for a system that does that to the people it's meant to help. Ellen is looking for something that opposes the government rather than supports it. I hear her say that phrase several times a day. I have it memorised now. Impressed? Of course, sounds like someone else I know. Let's hope it doesn't get her in as much trouble eh?" Harry laughed the last sentence out. He was deeply in love with Ellen but persisted on talking about others. Dale had already picked up on that.

"Ellen did that for me? I thought as much, I can't begin to thank you both. Be sure to thank her for me. She saved my life, I'm sure of that. Ask her to come and visit me, I'd love to see here again. And what about you? What's going on with you Harry Turner?"

"I've finished my training and I'm all over London fixing fuse boxes," Harry replied. "It's the kind of thing that I could get used to. It's lighter than the pit and the air is fresher that's for sure. Listen Dale, I'm so happy you're back home and in a better state. Your Mam's been a wreck."

Sitting for a moment in silence Dale considered he and Harry's situation. The two boys who'd grown up together, and for a while walked the same path, were now men on two very different ones. Dale had thought all along that Harry had chosen wrongly. He thought that his was the path of justice and what was right, in a life they had been born into. As he looked at the four walls in the visiting room, painted in grey and in need of a fresh coat, his certainty that he had chosen wisely evaporated. Still the closest of friends, they looked and smiled at one another.

"I'm OK now," Dale said partly to convince himself. "Could you do me a favour? I'd love to see me Mam. But coming all this way on her own is too much for her. Might you and Ellen be able to accompany her here one day?"

"Course mate, we can make that happen."

The Ellen Minor Series

Ellen Minor will return in Walls of a Minor as a freelance political advisor helping the British and American governments through a key part of the Cold War. Bridging time from the disaster in Chernobyl to the fall of the Berlin Wall, Ellen finds herself as a key player in the tension between East and West. Wrongly implicated in a Russian deal done in London she fights to keep her reputation, her influence and her relationship with the one man she can trust.

Search "The Ellen Minor Books" on Facebook to find out more.

Acknowledgement

With thanks to the friends who gave their time to support me to bring this book to life. To Steven Thompson for assisting me in my writing. To my editor, Paige Lawson for all the work and late nights. To my English teacher, Mrs North, who taught me how to manage my dyslexia all those years ago. To Tony the Policeman on sharing his experience of policing through 80's Britain. To my kids for putting up with me being sat at my desk lost in the words. And mostly to my beautiful Lyndal for everything in my world. Thank you all.

If you liked this book, please provide a positive review on Amazon. Thank you.

Printed in Poland
by Amazon Fulfillment
Poland Sp. z o.o., Wrocław

59351783R00171